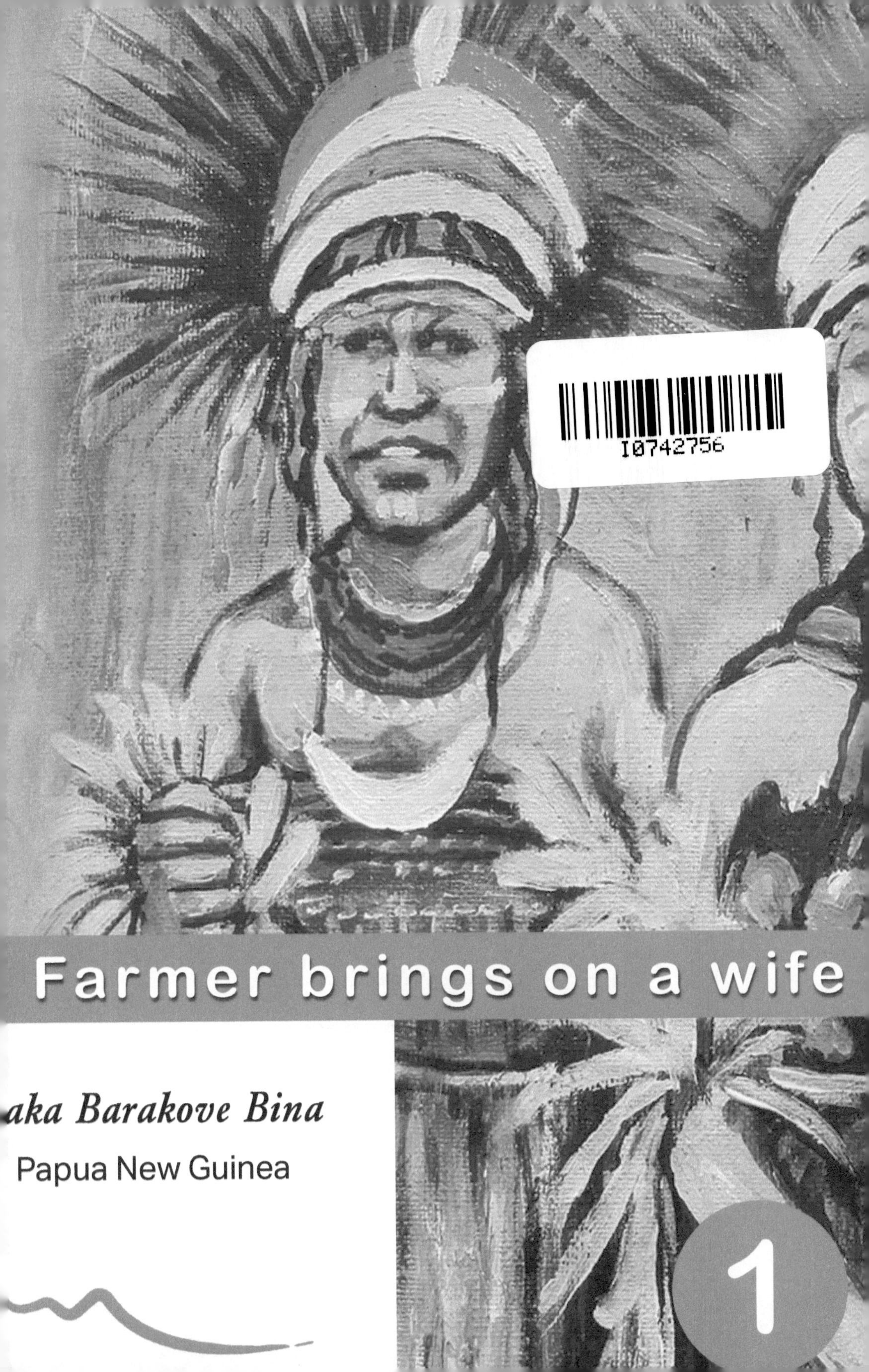

Farmer brings on a wife

aka Barakove Bina

Papua New Guinea

Paperback ISBN: 978-0-6459322-9-4

First Published in 2025 by

First Nations Writers Festival International Limited T/as First Nations Publishers

A Registered Charity (ABN 79 655 932 979) 2/53 Junction St, Nowra NSW 2540, Australia
Phone: +61 491 851 353 Email: firstnationswritersfestival@gmail.com

Web: www.firstnationswritersfestival.org

FB: www.facebook.com/firstnationswritersfestival.com

Cover Design: Busybird Publishing

Cover Painting: Laben Sakale John

Typeset: Busybird Publishing

Line Edited: Anna Borzi AM 2025

Printed and bound in Australia by IngramSpark

Special thanks to:

Nihuvo Isoi (late) of Nagamiufa Village, Goroka, EHP.

Aishi Nokovano (late) of Kotiyufa village, Iufi-Iufa, Goroka, EHP.

Mrs Taki Relaro Gumove of Kabiufa Village, Goroka, EHP.

For contributing titbits of traditional knowledge

And to:

Emily Sakepe Bina for her ever-enduring patience – no, ours was a shotgun affair.

Editorial assistance kindly provided by **Ed Brumby**

And To: **First Nations Writers Festival**

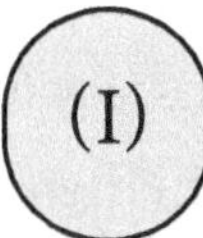

MEMO TO THE READER

Dear Reader,

Sigkaut Long Puk'im Moni - is Part One to the trilogy: **A Farmer Brings On A Wife**. It is a play on words with the type of Tok Pisin spoken by the pioneering Goroka Tok Pisin speakers.

The narration of events in one highlands village in Goroka Eastern Highlands Province of Papua New Guinea. It is but one of the many - as many as 860 marriage practises in a country with as many as 860 different peoples with very distinct and different languages, cultures, and yes – ways of living.

This was and had been the Goroka Apo way.

In the novel, **Sweet Garaiina Apo**, the highlands parents of Rudolf-Urrdong, the main character in that story decided it was time for Rudolf to have a wife. Following their traditional 'Highland' practises and customs, they decided and made *'a walk'* with their bride wealth down the Papuan Coast to look for a wife for him.

Where they come from, especially around the Goroka valley cultures and customs, it is tradition for the parents of a son to pool together resources as their bride wealth – which includes money, pigs, plumes of the Bird of Paradises and other items of value and take that collected bride wealth for *'a walk'* to a prospective bride's house.

The parents of Rudolf are now resident in the metropolitan city of Port Moresby. True to their tradition, they tried to do *'a walk'* with the bride wealth down the coast to a Papuan village. They laid out their bride wealth in front of a prospective bride's house waiting for a response. The dumbfounded 'Papuan' parents of the prospective bride when told of the intent of the display, were taken aback. That form of bride selection did not happen in their village and culture. They asked in jest if their 'visitors' were *'trying to hook a fish'*.

The cultural practises down on the Papuan coasts who also practise bride price payments for their women, are not the same as the *many-mountains-away* practises of their countrymen.

This small mention in the book *Sweet Garaiina Apo* had led to this narration and book.

Papua New Guinea is a country of more than eight hundred and sixty (860) different languages and cultural practises. Each language group has its own cultures that dictate amongst other practises, how they bring women into their tribes, as brides and wives for their sons.

It is hoped that this story will bring the reader into one such tribal group and rural village near Goroka in the Eastern Highlands Province. It is intended the reader will walk with the parents and the leaders of the village as they go about each day, each week, and the few months to find a young girl, make her a bride and finally install her as a married woman in this new village.

The reader will also walk through the intrigues that fester in and around village life with all their everyday activities during the entire process.

In part one of the trilogy, the difficulties in a village gathering to pool their resources as bride wealth is told. These are items #1 and #2 of the process.

Items #3 and #4 will be in Part Two of the trilogy and Items #5, 6 and 7 in Part Three.

THE VARIOUS STAGES IN THE PROCESS:

#1. A need is created by a son becoming a man.

Traditionally when a boy comes of marriageable age, i.e., when the beard on the face becomes strong, he is now deemed to have become a man, and so comes the time to start thinking about bringing a wife for the boy.

A boy could be courting girls earlier like when his voice starts to change but it is the beard that decides the boy should settled down as a man with a wife.

A girl however can be deemed to be at a marriageable at an earlier time and this has been the case in some child betrothals. For most though, it is when *menarche* sets in. The appropriate term in the Tokano language is equivalent to a girl having *'something pricking her leg.'* This is followed by her *'going into a house'* and the later ceremony to *'take her out of the house'*.

Immediately after this ceremony, the girl can decide if she wants to start courting boys. She is also game for drawing attention to herself for bride wealth to be brought to her house as a bride price irrespective of her being a minor.

The author is aware of one girl for whom bride price was accepted and whilst living with her new in laws did have her *menarche*. The appropriate *coming out* ceremony was held at her marital village.

It is to be noted in this case that *the coming together* ceremony for the bride and groom had not happened yet. The parents of the groom makes a judgement call, and the ceremony takes place when they think is the appropriate time.

#2. The process is initiated by the pooling together of the bride wealth.

The first is a collection of shells of various denominations (this is now replaced by cash money), Bird of Paradise feathers and several pigs with tusks growing through on the part of the parents of the boy or groom.

The second is the pooling of pigs by close inner family and relatives and the rest of the village.

Pooling together resources is based on debts created within the village. This contribution is either a debt paid back or a new one paid forward by the party contributing to the pooling together of bride wealth.

Apart from the pooling of bride wealth by the immediate family, all other activities are activities for the village as a community collectively. It is expected that everyone will contribute meaningfully and actively be involved both *'in cash and in kind'* throughout the whole of the program.

All of these are done with good will.

#3. When enough is pooled together, one part of the bride wealth, the cash component, is taken out for *'a walk'*.
It can be taken out for one or more *'walks'* and to several villages until it finds favour with a prospective bride's people.

#4. When that part of the bride wealth is accepted; the second part is to deliver on the pledged pigs from the groom's village.
This completes the first stage of the process, and the bride wealth is now converted to a bride price.

The agreement to accept the bride wealth as the bride price is reached by the uncles of the prospective bride. The prospective bride would have very little say over it. When the uncles agree with the bride wealth and accept it; it is a done deal.

#5. The bride is delivered.
The girl can be married off as a bride, never mind her not knowing the groom ever. If she were to have been involved in any courting activities that would have happened, then the bride would have seen the many that the groom would have courted and vice versa – always with a chaperone present all through the night of courting.

#6. The bride is settled in at her new home.
As part of the delivery, the bride's people are required to make a new garden for the bride in her new village. In the meantime, other villagers, especially a relative who may have sort of adopted the groom, may show her parts of their ready-to-harvest section of their garden where the bride takes over and keeps until her own garden is ready. If she has a house to build for herself, her people are supposed to help build this for her though this may not be necessary as again a relative may take her in and became a *was papa and was mama* to her until the bride and the groom are brought together as a married couple.

#7. After living in the village as a bride, there is no contact between the bride and groom.
It is taboo for the groom to be seen near to the bride and to be around places the bride will frequent. The length of this time usually is between a 'season' or two. **They are finally *brought together* as man and wife.**

The getting together of the bride and groom as man and wife is another story. In the author's village the last time this happened, the bride had been living in the village for two years without ever seeing the groom and gave up, returning to her village. That marriage was annulled.

Not all the above process are strictly observed in format and form. There are variations and degradation of each of the set steps.

There are many small and varied *public ceremonies* and *mumus* during each phase of the attempt to get a bride; starting from the pooling of bride wealth to when it becomes a bride price, the delivery of the groom, and finally to bring the bride and the groom together.

The whole event starting from the time to start pooling to the installation of the bride in the groom's village may take up to three months or more. This will include the time to make the garden and house perhaps for the bride. Sometimes it may take a bit longer.

However, the delivery of the bride is usually done within a month from when the bride wealth was laid out in front of the bride's house.

The reader should note that the narration in this novel is intended to capture and tell how this one act of marriage is arranged from start to finish.

The narration will try to bring you through the process as it happens. It will through the narrations try to help you understand the progress with dialogues that characters speak to explain situations as they go through them.

It will also showcase village scenarios as these events play out.

There will also be reflections, as those who participated in earlier such events state how these earlier events were staged and what experiences can be learned and used especially in the bride's village.

These will be the many things done to bring on the bride and then after the bride is installed in her marital village.

Please note that the whole process is termed *'buying a wife'* in the local vernacular and in Tok Pisin also. In this trilogy, the title is changed to 'bring on a wife'.

NON-ENGLISH WORDS

A lot of non-English words are used.

The reader may be compelled to break constantly to consult a glossary, or to read what is written without understanding parts of the sentence.

To ease the readers mind, the meanings are written into the sentence and paragraphs or in the next and is contextualised so that the meaning is captured in the sentence. It is also repeatedly used in innovative ways so that the repetition is not too obvious. There will be a few instances where the repetition may be glaring.

Some of the non-English words used are from the *Tokano Tok Ples* and *Tok Pisin*. They are used and the meanings are imbedded with usage.

Tok Pisin is fluid and growing. New words are constantly being added. Words from the other local languages by popular usage are being accepted as mainstream. For example, in the last few years, *kob'le* - stone or money in the Sinasina and a South Simbu *Tok Ples* has been accepted as the hush word to use when talking money. It is used as a slang around with words like *wan lus* and *wasa*. *Wasa-buai* is a hawkers hark when peddling their product - *buai* or betel nut and with mustard, at most city bus stops.

Local Goroka words like *ghetto* - any lady past the marriageable age that has no partner; is now getting used and is being normalised in the vocabulary around the Goroka Town area.

By popular usage, *Apo* has universal acceptance in Papua New Guinea, and it is accepted that an Eastern Highlander always is an *Apo* but to the local person, the original intended meaning remains.

These new words have now taken root through repetition and usage in the local lingua franca.

There are a host of other new words that are used that are from here, there, and everywhere, given the richness of our more than eight hundred and sixty (860) distinct languages in Papua New Guinean. It must be borne in mind that the definitions may not be correct as usage in other settings may distort the meanings.

GLOSSARY

A glossary provided tries as best to explain the word as it is set in this story.

Before the glossary page, there is a table of the Tokano counting system and another table that mentions the names of traditional trade items used as bride wealth.

SETTING

The story is centred on a typical Goroka village in the Eastern Highlands Province. The people in this area speak the *Tokano Tok Ples* and are called *Iufi-Iufa or Yuhu-yuho* people. *Iufi-Iufa* is twelve kilometres west of Goroka town and the Okuk Highway runs through it. The language group starts from just past Kabiufa SDA Secondary school and stops before the Asaro Community School and includes speakers from Wantrifu, including the Kempeni hamlets on the Wesan side.

DISCLAIMER

All the characters in this novel are fictional. All the personal names and positional terms have been conjured from the author's mind.

The author offers his unreserved apologies if any character in the novel resembles a real person.

The names mentioned in the story don't depict any known living persons but are names that are given to people and were selected randomly to use in this story to provide authenticity and to reflect the setting in a rural *Tokano* speaking village in *Iufi-Iufa*.

The currency of the country is called Kina and toea, like Dollars and cents.

CONTENTS

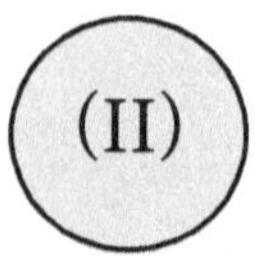

WHO'S WHO? IN THE STORY

Mr. **Hoveyau** and
Mrs. **La'ano** Hoveyau Solepano aka *Big Mama*

Te'enike Liivelave - (also Teeé and Tela) - Daughter 1
Ghitume Monopoliso - (also Ghihumo) - Daughter 2
Josiah Mamu - (also Josh) - Son and Groom

Mr. **Pilipo** and
Mrs. **Sisipulime** Solepano *aka Sisi-Vena*
Robin Solepano - Their son

Mr. **Goi Siyoli** and
Mrs. **Ambaii Urr** Solepano *aka Meri Simbu*

Mr. **(Papa) Ave** and
Mrs. **(Mama) Heloiseh** Solepano

Uncle Mr. Tota and
Aunty Mrs. **Avise Nuhenahe**

Shahilime *aka Shalili* - (Bride's maiden names).
Milikine *aka Millie* - (Bride's marital names).

Kelekele - Garden owner

Pheeiie - Whistler

Greenie - Village caller

Aishi - Ballad

Holoe - Village banker

PROLOGUE

A mid-morning shout from across the gardens echoed loud and long across the valley gulleys and ravines shattering the day's peace in the village.

'Lukautim pik bilong raun long garden olgeta taim ya, skin gras pulap pik ya!'

Ambo's mother Kelekele was mad. Her loud hoarse and angry voice carried over to the men and women in and around the village.

A pig may have gone into her garden and dug up something she had planted. She was shouting out stinging words swearing at and berating the owner of the pig. Sure, enough the words came.

'Always raising pigs that goes into another person's garden, and a pig covered in hairs!'

A pig had again breached the fence to go into her garden and destroyed her seven rows of *sweet potato kaukaus.*

'Bai yu kilim bilong ol mahn o long toktok o long baim meri!'

Kelekele repeated loud and long. She knew whose pig it was but refrained from calling out the owner's names. Instead, she was throwing insinuating and barbed disparaging words that would be demeaning to them.

'Is this a pig for slaughtering to present to a person when there is a situation or are you going to use it to buy a bride to come along as a wife.'

Kelekele's torrent of words belied the fact that she spent considerable time to work the *kaukau* garden plot during a very hot time of the dry season.

Now the first rains had made the garden a very appetising green. Her disappointment was put in the words and tone of her screams.

And all the while she knew that the owner of the pig would be at the *kandis* all day long.

'*Gutpela pik we! Meri ting em lukautim pik! Pehe-peheva ya, samting bilong kas ya.*

'How can you be caring for pigs when you stand erect as the fence posts at the *kandis?* The woman thinks she is a good pig farmer when the pigs are as bad as herself!'

'*Traim lukautim pik wantaim gaten!*'

'*Your* grassy gardens and bush lands are like your pigs, full of strong hairs and grass. *Sanap pehe-peheva*, attending and wasting your days at the *kandis* means empty stomachs and hungry pigs have stomachs if you don't know.'

'*Kas ol mekim b'long yu oh! Meri b'long pilai kas tasol ya. Sanap-sanap long kandis ya, inap ya!* Did they make the *kandis* for you, oh? Get your darned bones away from the *kandis.*'

'Why cannot the woman have the pig on a rope? She is caring for pigs like she has gardens. One who walks the roads all the time like she has nothing? *Meri bilong raun nating-nating long rot ya*, like she wants to do something with the pig.'

'*Egghe, kasparr ya! Hii! Ulo – ulo! Egghe, egghe*, the gambler! Why don't you have your pig on the rope?'

'I sweated in the scorching hot sun to get this garden up and in a matter of days your stupid pig has destroyed my best efforts. *U-u-u!*'

The angry loud voice echoed and traversed the ravine over to the village and down the ravine past *Iye-numuko*. The angry tone with its sarcasm did not get lost to the winds.

Hoveyau cocked his ear to the angry voice and his hairs stood on their ends.

He was at the *hauspik* at *Iye-numuko* on one of the very rarest occasions when he was troubled by his wife to do something about the pig's house. He was trying to fix the pen for a pregnant sow so that if she had the litter of piglets, the bigger pigs could not get at them or trample the little piglets.

The now pregnant sow was a new pig that La'ano had recently moved from the village house to the *hauspik*, and she would be attacked by all the other pigs because she was a stranger.

La'ano had weaned this pig at the *hauslain* and since it was having litters, they had wanted her to be at the *hauspik*, but they could lose all the litter if she did not have separate quarters and at this stage she was not accepted by the other pigs.

Hoveyau's rare visit to the *hauspik* was because La'ano had set her foot down. The young sow would remain in the village with them if he did not make their separate quarters at the *hauspik*. The sow was already a nuisance and was making as much annoying whinnying noises as best as she can. Hoveyau could not accept additional and more noises from the additional impending little piglets.

He therefore begrudgingly moved to visiting the *hauspik* this once in a blue moon visit and worked to erect a separate pen for the new introductions.

It was hard and dirty work. He was cleaning the dried grass that another pig used as a bed. Pigs being pigs had used the enclosure as their toiletry area. It was stinky and nauseating. It should be and was a woman's work.

The angry words were screaming thick and fast. While he heard no names being called out, he could deduce from the disparaging words and innuendos that he and La'ano were the subject of the *vitriols* echoing down the ravine. The reference to the *kandis* and *yomba post* inferred him. The *bilum* at the *kandis* referenced La'ano.

It was La'ano this and La'ano that with the *bilum* and spade with her *yomba post*. The woman was screaming torrents of words that would make the ears bleed. That woman really had something against La'ano and him.

The screaming words were irritating and here he was, doing her work. And where would she be. La'ano would certainly be at the *kandis,* either watching or joined in the game of gambling herself. She was hoping that she would have heard all that racket and would try to get here to get the pig on a leash.

Kelekele's loud voice traversed with enough explicit swear clauses that were never mentioned but it was there in the tone and choices of words.

Hoveyau heard the name shaming and imputed swear words with unmentionable meanings and his anger started rising.

Her continued reference imputing him to a *Yomba fence post* at the *kandis'* riled him further.

It was the stupid woman's fault for trying to raise a pig she could not feed. The stupid La'ano.

And now amidst all these shouting, where would she be? What was wrong with the woman? She should now be looking for the pig. She surely must be hearing all the shouting around impuning them both.

'La'ano!!! *Uu-u!!!*'

There, she called out the name of the pig owner at last.

Hoveyau looked up the ravine to the ridge. Through the shade of the *Yar trees,* he could see the angry woman standing and throwing all her aspersions towards the *hauspik* and at them.

He quickly put out the fire he had lit to burn off trash. The smoke would have indicated someone at the *hauspik.*

Kelekele must have seen the whiff of smoke. She had moved to the edge of the garden so that she was shouting her wrath into the gulley and the echoes rang out menacingly loud. Her rumbling screech bumped of the walls of the gully down to where Hoveyau stood.

He could hear each word now more clearly. He cringed.

'Like she wants to do something with the pigs! *Raun na sanap nating-nating olsem hap sting yomba diwai long rot ya, maski ya!'*

The *Tok Pisin* reference again to the *Yomba tree* and the words *'hap sting yomba diwai long rot' - the rotting away 'yomba' on the roads* were an onslaught on him and his character. He swallowed up more of his own bile in anger. He angrily kicked the sod of earth in front of him.

The stupid woman was not stopping. She rambled on.

This time the echoes resounded from the ridge to the other ridge and echoed down so that it sounded like there were more than one angry woman. Hoveyau poised, his ears already hot, to listen further but the voice now had moved away from the edge and the echoes came on as more noises. He could not discern the words thereafter.

Hoveyau waited for the voice to die down and then returned to his maintenance work on the pen. He tested his handiwork. It would hold for a couple of weeks, and he can come back to fix it when the baby piglets were born.

He quickly flushed into place the wooden hand-hewn slates. At the bottom rung, he moved three of them halfway along, leaving a hole for the pigs to squeeze in and out of the house. He pulled the *mehe* - a screen of banana leaves folded over a stick, together. He firmly secured the door with *pitpit sticks* crisscrossed into place to lock and hold back these *mehe* leaves. He stood up looking at his handiwork. This was one thing he was doing right.

Making sure that the fresh *kaukau* bag was placed up on the kunai roof, he picked up his blunt *sopolo* bush knife and his small *bilum*. He looked inside his *bilum* to make sure he did not leave behind the match box.

He started up the incline for the village. He took a glance up the ridge on the other side. He was relieved there was nobody looking in or over to his side of the ridge. The garden owner had stopped her yelling and there was quiet in the air. This did not stop the anger burning in his stomach.

The *Ya yomba* and *kandis* rebukes had really got to him. *Pehe-peheva*, his mind raced and tried estimating his hours standing around at these *kandises.*

'Bah! ... ...' That should be of no business to her. What has my *pehe-pehe* standing business around at the *kandis ples* be the reason for rebuke by this woman, Kelekele.

Hoveyau blew hot air through his nostrils as the thoughts raced angrily through his head. He could feel the heat in his anger.

Damn, it was that skinny one with polka dots all over. It was called the *Lupiye-Tapiye* because of these spots. He didn't like that pig and now it was causing all this angst.

Wasn't it only yesterday that Nokowano, their neighbour had passed on the message the same *Lupiye-Tapiye* was seen in Kelekele's garden. Hoveyau had mentioned what their neighbour said, and he suggested to La'ano to tie this *Lupiye-Tapiye* pig on a leash and keep it on leash. He had even given her the new rope that he saw in the house which she could fashion up a leash with.

He had also told her that this pig had long limbs and was not a good breed.

The long legs meant it could stretch out from its back legs and reach over fences into gardens from impossible places. It spelt a troublesome pig that would bring them more trouble than they deserved. He had even suggested they slaughter the pig when there was an occasion to hold a feast for one of the girls.

La'ano heard but the pig was a gift from her uncle, and she dismissed it citing Hoveyau was jealous that her relatives still maintained an interest in her.

The second issue was that the nipples of the pig were spaced a bit far from each other and that indicated a far better breed to their local ones. She was going to keep this pig as a stock breeder in her *hauspik*.

Hoveyau thought it was too much interest and as interest goes, that means a lot of money to do the traditional customary obligation of *thank you to the relatives* - to be given when it came to giving *Het Pei* for herself and her children. He truly deemed the piglet had been an unnecessary gift.

He cut an angry figure walking up to the village, the veins on his arms pulsating hotly over the grip to the bush knife, a *sopolo* that hardly sees any work.

Under the shade of the gum tree and three houses away, there were two 'kandis.' The *hauslain* leaders had decreed that card game gambling can start from Friday night through to Sunday evening, but the people had disregard for it. They gambled every day and all night long. Hoveyau took part in these gatherings at the *kandis* but today that realisation was moved to the back of his mind, and everything was just red. The humiliation from the calling out was his and his alone. The sweat running down his spine infuriated him further.

Seeing her sitting squat with her back to him made the bile in his mouth bitterer. He swallowed hard as he tightened the grip on his *sopolo bush knife*. His anger was going to burst through the sinews of his veins.

'Stupid *pipia* woman', he hissed under his breath. 'Like she always does, and with no shame at all, she darn displays that useless old *ghotoloheya bilum bag* and her useless spade always lying idle besides her.'

It raised his blood level to boiling point. The veins on his fisted hands ballooned up. He stormed up on her.

La'ano was oblivious to the angry man walking up behind her. She was so engrossed with the cards in her hand.

Those who had a direct eye view of her husband shifted their positions uncomfortably.

Hoveyau face was burning fever. The villagers knew from the skirmishes in the village between men and drunks, Hoveyau was a very vicious fighter. It was better to be careful.

The approaching stern face made several of the gamblers shift positions with unease.

La'ano turned to see behind her what was causing her fellow gamblers to be agitated.

She instantly froze. The fisted knuckles loomed very, very big in *her face*. She blanked out.

1

MIKU IYE − GARDEN DESTROYING PIG

She woke up in her house all dizzy and wondering what happened to her.

She groaned to the aches in her body and probing headache. She slowly got back her thinking and it was the start to her troubles with her husband and the world.

She felt a large throbbing pain on her nose and at the back of her head. She was stinking badly of urine and wondered where it was from until she realised, she had wet clothes that included water that was poured over to revive her. She realised in shame that she had peed on herself.

She was more embarrassed that she may have wet herself in the presence of other people - especially among men, women who let their mouths run in gossip and before children who will make sneering comments and ridicule in the future. The shame of facing these ridicules in the future made her choke and the tears started falling.

Hoveyau was sitting on the edge of the *pitpit* bed talking to himself trying to justify his action.

She did not hear the berating that her husband was pushing her way to shift the blame from himself for his action.

'Gosh, did you ever think of leaving this … this idea of sitting at the card games. Didn't you ever hear all the disparaging words said about you? Didn't you ever hear the screaming woman about your pig? The naming of the pig as a *miku iye* is the worst shaming name to have. An owner of a pig that breaks into people's gardens. That, for your pig to be named a 'garden going pig' is very, very shameful. I told you to keep that *Lupiye-Tapiye* on a leash and what happens now. You are as bad as that *miku iye* pig.'

She groaned as the words 'bad as the *miku iye* pig' hit her.

There was a pot of water on the fire. La'ano got off the bed and gingerly tended the burning woods. Horrible thoughts passed through her head. She felt the piece of dry timber wood beside the fireplace. She put her hands on the hot pot. She thought of a thousand nasty things she could do to take revenge against him.

'Oh, and that is nothing to your *pehe-pehe* time wasting stand around doing nothing.' She silently minced her tearful retort back to herself.

He was not showing any remorse but shifting blame to her.

She yearned vengeance and wanted to clobber the useless man sitting there feeling stupid about what he had done but she just could not find the strength. She was sapped of all energy.

She instead broke into a teary whispering murmur.

'You blame me for the action of the pig. You class me a pig and bash me for the pig. You think that I don't look after the pigs well.'

Her voice broke.

'My good man, pigs, I have looked after them for you but where is your garden? Where will I get the *kaukau* from to feed these pigs?' It was a voice that surprised even herself.

La'ano had got back her wind.

'You don't have any strength to make a garden. All your land is all bush. You have plenty of bush land but no proper garden. A fenced portion of bushes is not a garden. You expect me to make a garden in all these bushes. I needed a man to dig up the soil and you carry your man strength around for nothing. You want to make fences at the *kandis* all day and you expect me to swallow my shame and to go looking for *kaukaus* for the pigs in my peers … my … my … *poromeri's* garden.'

'No, you are not going to let me do that and I will not allow myself to grovel that low – forget the thinking that I will beg for *kaukau* to feed the pigs from my peer's gardens.'

'You know, I must buy *kaukau* from the markets to feed the pigs and you think that I have money every day. Where do I get the money from to buy *kaukau*? Your strength is for walking around the village and like a dog, smell out where all the *kandis* groups are and to spend your darned day there just doing your *pehe-pehe* thing.'

'You don't ask where I will get the food to feed you and the darned pigs. You expect me to do all of that from the one old garden. And that garden is as old as me in this village. I am the only one in this village who has this one old garden. That garden is exhausted. It cannot feed you and allow me to also look after the pigs.'

'You think it is right for you to come and knock me on the head and kick me around like your football because one of the pigs goes and digs up somebody's garden. You find it okay that you football me to make me *pispis* and *pekpek* in the eyes of the village where every man, woman, and child with his or her dog can see me spilling it or even better, may have seen my bare backside.'

'I am and will be the joke of the village from here on. – *meri bilong kapsaitim nating-nating* – a lady who let's go - and you think that jeer behind my back is going to be no joke.'

'You tell me what that whack did to me. I am sure I would have been sent sprawling into the middle of the *kandis*. I am sure you would have whacked me good the second time – to bolster your ego that you are a man.'

'You tell me about those - my friends at the *kandis*. You tell me how they would retell their skitter-skeeter scampering too … and with glee too.'

'I sure I would have been wetting myself over and over at your footballing and punching bag that I must have become. You tell me that my friends were jeering when they tried to pry the helpless comatose and bleeding me from my every pore. You tell me what you think they were thinking when they cleaned me of my own urine and excreta. I could go off on a monologue here for me, but it be a waste of my breath and air.'

'Okay, I appreciate what the woman Kelekele was screaming about. On the first day the *Lupiye-Tapiye* went into the garden, I immediately leashed her up and she was tied up for three days. As the leash was eating into her legs, I removed the rope around her front legs last night. She was inside the pen and inside the locked *hauspik*. She breached the pen and somehow got out of the shut house. The stupid pig could not have done all the damage to the garden in one night.'

'I am always looking for *kaukau* and you come and give me a *ghalise* knock. You could have given me a small knock, but you wanted to prove your wasted man muscles and man strength to the village.'

'Well, if I was a man, you ... you watch out. You can count your blessings that I am a woman.'

'You carry your man strength and walk around in the village like a bird, moving from tree to tree looking for food or a perch to sit. That is what you do all day and for a change, I asked you to do something for me and you hear a screaming woman, and you must give me your best *ghalise* knock and football kicks and to rub it in, you must do it - in public and with all eyes watching.'

'The shouting references about the *Yomba tree* were all about you and those rebukes eat into you, and you unleash your wasteful fury on me.'

'Those words were all truths and I feel so shamed by them. You could have felt big time ashamed of yourself but no – you have a *plastic skin*; words would just wash over you. I have been saying the very same things but in a good way and you don't want to listen. Now when another woman screams out the same to the whole village and you... you *see red and humiliation* and you think me as your punching bag and football.'

'My shame has gone from the house down into the pit toilets. That stupid *Lupiye-Tapiye pig* is supposed to be used for the work to get your son's bride price ready and you shame me by giving me pain in public over it.'

La'ano applied the hot water press to her head. The bulge was painful, and the throbbing pain was easing off.

But the humiliation of being knuckled on the head was a shock that she had been least expecting, and that act galvanised itself into the recess of her inner being.

La'ano could only feel the hot tears weaving down her tender cheek.

'You wait, only tomorrow and you will see your true colours. If a man cannot make a garden, he should not have got married. I came to you in marriage, but it is all wasted. When will you make me a new garden? You boast your lineage as being the *itehetus*, the original villagers here. You boast to own most of the land here but what good is the land if you don't make a garden with it. You count off your eleven portions of land proudly and snort at your neighbours over their lack of land.'

'Only yesterday, you placed leaves as a taboo – a *hahn tambu* over at Laheko. You do not want your cousin twice removed to make a garden on your land. That portion of land has not been gardened since your great grandmother passed on. But you are happy that I have this one old garden at Sogopex, and you are as cocky as a cockatoo bird to carry your strength around doing nothing and placing *hahn tambus* over unused and wasting lands. You could have built me a new garden over there for me to feed the pigs. Instead, you find grace in aimless strolling around *kandis* places.'

'*Whaa, lusim ya,* - stop this wasteful life of walking around *pehe-pehe* and *nating-nating* on the roads!'

Hoveyau let La'ano ramble on. He remained still, daring himself not to make even the slightness of noise. It beat and ate into him, all these references about him walking the road doing nothing and they were true in every sense.

He hung his head down low, taking it all in as La'ano rambled on.

'You fault my sitting at the *kandis*. You don't want me to do that, but you think it is your duty as a man to be the fence post, a *yomba* wasting it at the roads and the *kandis* places. You cannot be bothered to be thinking how a pig should eat. You think that grazing them off worms and grass is going to be okay. That type of thinking will either make you *long-long* or your pigs will always go into somebody's garden. You can be sure that there will always be one or two irate mothers of a garden. You like it that I can have no complaint against that.'

'You don't think about these at all. Ha! And you think it is your mandated duty to be a man and your right as a man to be the *kandis* post.'

'Ha, because you have balls, you fault me as a woman.'

'You think it is all my fault. It is a woman's fault that the pigs must go into somebody's garden. It is a woman's fault that the pigs are so hungry and do that, ha! – to dig up someone's garden.'

'Now since when was the last time you came along and helped me with making the garden. If you did, I'd feel comfortable working the land to grow their food. And you think it is your fettered right to lord it over me.'

'You dare fight a woman when you cannot make a garden yourself. All these years I have been caring for the pigs, where do you think I got the *kaukaus* to feed you all from.'

'Since I don't have a proper garden and pigs that need to eat, where do you think I get the money to buy *kaukau* for their feed from? Do you think that I go around selling myself for the money to buy these pig's feed?'

'Your eyes must be in your backside and shut closed.'

'I gamble at these *kandis*' to buy the *kaukau* from the markets. Lucky for you that I gamble just enough to make a few kinas, enough to buy the three or four piles of *kaukau* at the afternoon markets, then I move off.'

'I even swallowed my humiliation and indignity and went over to see the garden and screaming woman early on today to see the damage done by the stupid pig. I was sitting down to my second game. It was unfortunate that earlier in the morning I had an unlucky streak and was stuck at the *kandis* longer than what I normally do. I wanted to see if I could win a bit more to buy *kaukau* and yet it was worth your while to knuckle knock and shame me in public.'

'Now in this day and age, even if I had a garden, all the women are terrified of working in the gardens all alone with all these crazy marijuana junked boys who wander aimlessly around and take opportunities with women.'

'I was not going alone late in the afternoon to try digging for *kaukau* in the garden. You are crazy to think that your *itehetu* title will save me from being raped in my own garden.'

'Let me repeat myself here for you. You make me *pispis* and I wet myself badly in front of my peers. I just cannot join them tomorrow even to sit around and make *bilums* or prattle in gossips with them.'

'They are gossiping about me and laughing over my misfortune. They will jeer at me behind my back saying that I am a woman who will let run. You think that is a good thing they will say about me?'

'I could leave you now with these horrible bruises. I could return to my village and break up this useless marriage. But it is my son that I've got to stay back for.'

'You are just a *pipia mahn*, nobody is going to think much of you.'

'*Negi nhagii tukai'iq, long-long*, crazy, gosh, do I have to tell you all these! It is only a crazy man who would have his wife leave him and go away. It is only a *long-long* that is left behind to care for all the children and pigs.'

'For that boy, I will swallow my pride and live with this indignation you have inflicted on me for a few more months. I will bring him a wife and then I will leave you.'

'You're a lucky man that all the children are big and married and you will only have to worry about the pigs. I am sure you are thinking that you are going to feed them on air, *long-long*, ha, you are a *negi tukai'iq* big time.'

'I am not going to let you worry over them because if I leave, all these pigs in the *hauspik* will to go waste. Instead, I am going to use all of them to look for a bride to bring on for your son. For that, you will count your blessings that you don't have to exert unnecessary worry over feeds for the pigs and you can just laze your normal *pehe-pehe* standing around – yeah – *sanap-sanap long kandis ya.*'

La'ano wanted to be as brutal as she could in her sarcasm but pulled up short. There would be plenty of times later for that. There were going to be more talks and opportunities where she will rub that in. And she needed a big audience for that and to include the family while she was at it.

La'ano wanted to force Hoveyau to go looking for Papa Ave. He would know what to do and to organise the work for making sure that what she wanted was done. Instead, she continued in disgust hoping that Hoveyau would at least retort back. She would like to think that he would be man enough to think big like her - and say something about the idea to bring on a wife for their son Mamu.

Hoveyau remained mute, stuck with his head down on the bended knees watching the flames flicker and dance on the timber on the fire hearth next to the centre posts. Either he was sorry for his action or that he didn't care.

La'ano paused and waited. The silence was heavy.

After a while, she continued.

'I will start talking about bringing on a girl as a wife for my son and you will facilitate that. It should not be a big issue for you. You let your brothers know of that.'

Hoveyau leaned back into the centre *yakise* post – a woman, that meant bride wealth gathering and bride prices – something that in his head was not registered at all.

He let her ramble go past his head. He was thinking of other things she said earlier that bit into his ego. He knew the sentiments expressed about him were mostly right.

Negi nhagii tukai'iq, long-long, that was an appropriate double worded appropriation of two languages into a handle to call him. He ruefully reflected on it. He knew he was a darned crazy ala a *long-long* person. This fight: in the spur of the moment, he wasn't thinking straight then and perhaps never had. Darn - *negi tukai'iq!* He wanted to smash his hands into the *yakise* posts.

He was born an *itehetu,* into the original family that had plenty of land. He needed to fence these in so that his family can have better and bigger gardens. The one garden they had, was his wife's bridal garden and La'ano shared it with his mother and two of his cousins who had small plots themselves. His father had asked them into the garden a long time ago. Even with these cousins having small parts, there was a big part inside the fenced-in-garden that was still bushland that were not made into gardens.

How this happened was something his father never explained. So much for their *itehetu* land holding title. Their father had a lazy streak and he acquired it full on. His brothers however had in contrast to him, seemed to like working their allotted portions and gardens.

It was fair enough when he grew up as they had another garden at *Seveti Nosa,* and the mother divided her time between the two and didn't have the ability to maintain the two gardens. As a result, his mother never had a good garden and was never good at rearing pigs.

It was the days of plenty when he was growing up and people shared their garden excesses. Now with the introduced money economy it meant excesses are given away in exchange for money. It was no longer the days of plenty though plenty were grown. This money economy was destroying their way of life.

Nowadays, people forgot how to share their excess production, instead, they put their surpluses up for sale to the villagers at the makeshift markets around the *kandis* areas or they lined them up in front of their houses indicating that they were selling them.

And the villagers grew items for the markets. You had to buy all things, even the small pieces of *kaukau.*

He could recall his childhood days when a person walked through a garden, and you took one item here and there, nobody complained. Now you do that, and the world will fall on you with the mother of the garden screaming 'robber'.

Now those who had no gardens, lived by stealing from their own villagers. People lived during the day an idle life around the *kandis* area and by night stealing to live another idle day.

La'ano had her own garden that was built for her by her people when she came as a young bride. She maintained this and the other older garden her mother-in-law owned.

His younger brother got the *Seveti Nosa* garden. It constituted a problem. It meant that he could not go to that area and the spare lands around this garden were to be inherited by his brothers. He had no reason to complain that he had only one son but what if this son had more sons. That idea that there would be more male sons in the future was kept at the far recesses of his mind, but he need not worry over it now. That was for a future this son had to worry about.

It was land however that was not used and was the envy of the other villagers.

'I know that, that stupid *Lupiye-Tapiye* is a pig for going into the gardens, but it does so because it is always hungry? I do suspect it has worms. However, I did say before it was because it has a long stomach.'

'It is a man's business to know bushcraft about raising pigs and I did ask you some time ago that you ask the old man Hoho about the stomach-ache grass for the pigs. I know you don't like to talk about pig husbandry, and you have not asked the old man yet.'

Hoveyau looked up into the rafters of the house.

La'ano was talking loudly to herself.

'I think the pig is infested with worms so that it is always hungry and is trying to get a quick feed from the gardens.'

'Kelekele's fence on this side of the garden is all made of strong *pitpit* cane. A *pitpit* cane fence is good when it is new but when it is old, even the rats can make a hole in it. That fence, on this side of the ravine, is very old. Where the *kunai* grass has been overgrowing that part of the fence, so rotten.'

'My Hoveyau man, please don't ask me to fix up the fence to Kelekele's garden. That is a man's job and since when did you last do a man's job. Your *poromahn* laughs at you for being the laziest man in the village. A normal man would hold his head in shame. A normal man would readily accept responsibility for the actions of his pigs and would have gone and replaced that fence the very first instance the pig went into the garden. Instead, here I am nursing a wetted and bruised ego and bruised face.'

Hoveyau cringed at her sarcasm. The bruises would heal and be forgotten in time but her wetting herself was good gossip conversation and she would again and again keep repeating it for his shame. It would be worse reminder than, he mused - rebuilding fences. Fencing was hard physical work, work that he had no appetite for.

La'ano prepared her bed. She moved it the furthest place possible on their *pitpit* bed in the dilapidated round house. She already slept on her own but for some reason, she wanted to make it dramatic.

'You hear me. I said I am leaving you. You sleep on it and tomorrow you will speak to me and all about your viciousness in fighting me. But you decide for yourself. It must stand you in good deed after I am gone.'

She was always the *yakise* of the family, the centre post to them all, both within and out of the family circles here in the village. The thought of her pulling herself out and going - this house was going to collapse.

Hoveyau stared intensely into the red embers. He could smell his own vomit as bile in his throat threatened to burst out. He knew that he had done something utterly wrong. He made it worse by letting her speak her mind and he had let them all just wash over him.

La'ano gritted her teeth. She was going to prepare for her taking an exit in the life of this useless man.

She gingerly brought her hands over her bruised face and gently wiped off the tears that had streamed down. She was resolute as she sniffled her teary thoughts.

Her children were all grown up. The two girls had moved to their husband's village and their son was somewhere in the village, she suspected, all stoned and becoming useless like his father, another nut case. He was indulging in smoke, and she knew he would graduate to using marijuana which was now an easy thing to do. *Maunten Mahn* had a huge tree of it up on the side of Mitega Mountain going towards

Goposalo. The young ones congregated up on the side of the mountain all the time.

She suspected it as recently as Josiah Mamu had taken a liking to smashing the only good speciality saucepan they had in the house if there was no food for him. She had no more good pot to cook with. It was a shame that her best pot looked like a beat-up van. It was a fourth-handed down donation from a friend who had received it from another friend who had received it from yet another friend. And as always, the pot would be knocked back into shape after it was kicked around a bit.

The onslaught of the current anger had stemmed from a pig that she was raising to make a feast out of and with that to start talking about bride price payment for a bride. The father was a useless comic, and the very stoned and useless son was not going to contribute meaningfully to the whole idea of marriage for him including the rearing of pigs.

She gingerly wiped the tears that stung her eyes. The throbbing had gratefully receded, but the head was very sore from the knock.

She grabbed her old towel with a half piece of a soap and went out into the dark of the night. She took her thinking along with her as she tried to work the track to the creek.

She felt the tender aches and wondered why she was still married to a useless man. She felt a sliver of thought – what could life had been like if she had not been married off to this man. What if, what if she was married to this other one or that other one? Could her life be any different? She let the cold stream wash over her in the dead of the night.

She shivered from the cold night air, but she knew the shivers were deep within her - from her ego that had the most lashings.

2

GHEHENE TOLUMO – POOLING MONEY

She had come as a young normal bride. After four miscarriages early on, she had been blessed by two girls and the last, a boy. She was the first in the village to undergo tubal ligation when that last pregnancy was difficult, and doctors advised that her next pregnancy was going to kill her.

Now thirty years on in the village, though they were *itehetu* people with more land than the average villager, they were still as poor as the next household.

Hoveyau and his family had a habit of at every opportune time reminding everyone else in the village that the family was the first to arrive in the village. The villagers responded by calling them the biblical *Atamu* and their wives - *Evako* as the *itehetu* word became more normalised. With it came certain privileges but it never meant you were not to be abused if your pigs raided a recent arrival's garden.

La'ano however did not like the word *itehetu* and tried to keep it out of her vocabulary. The idea that they were *itehetu* families had no meaning and bearing in her life.

La'ano returned and kept a mute night but tossed and turned all night long. She could hardly sleep.

Her thoughts returned to her young days back in her own village. She grew up in a house where her parents kept three big gardens. Her father even had his own yam and taro garden where no women were allowed to wander in or around near to it.

Her parents raised the very tamest pigs in the whole village who never went into another person's garden. Even the wildest of these tame pigs when Ma called, they came quickly and would remain quietly around her. They never were heard to make raucous noises. In fact, her parents sort of talked to the pigs and the pigs obeyed them.

She remembered one time, there was a lot of pig stealing happening and her mother told her pigs not to go far. The pigs remained around the house digging up the bushes that soon after, dad quickly fenced it and made a garden. When the garden was ready, dad did the craziest of things; he let in his pigs to dig up the new garden and eat all the *kaukau* mother had planted. Her parents were fun loving crazy.

She did not have it, this fun-loving crazy thing. The finesse in pig rearing was not passed to her and she struggled to rear her pigs. This was the beginning of her problems – the struggle to rear pigs to make a name for him and his family.

The whispers about the jeers of Kelekele's throwing barbed comments about why she was keeping a pig from going into gardens somehow got embedded as a jeering voice in her head. It repeated like a broken record, over and over in her head.

'Bai yu kilim bilong ol mahn o long tok-tok o long baim meri!'

Why had she bothered? Her peer had thrown down a challenge. Was she rearing the pig to contribute to a family or village feast or to bring on a wife? She tried to remind herself, to find some reason – initially, raising pigs was a chore and role for a married woman. She used it to establish herself and cement her standing in the village. However now it was her duty towards her son following traditional norms to ensure she brought on a wife for him. Their son Josiah Mamu was more than ready for a partner, and she was raising pigs for the inevitable.

She tried to recollect if her son had a girlfriend. Normally the boys keep that a secret from their parents but the small children in the village knew who was courting who and from what village. She would have to ask the other village ladies to make the appropriate enquiries for her with the children.

Kelekele had thrown down the challenge about using the pig to get a bride wealth ready for bringing on a bride for a son.

She bridled at the thought that she was challenged by a non-body in the village.

The last thing she could remember before falling asleep was she was leaving the man. She woke with a resolve that first she was going to rise to that challenge and bring on a girl as a bride and wife for his son.

'Are there people sleeping in the house or what.'

A voice from outside broke into her slumber and she gingerly turned in her bed. There were body aches all over her. The throbbing around her face had intensified and she could feel the skins around her eyes puffed up swollen. She guessed they would be turning blue. The aches were at their greatest now as she struggled to get off the bed.

'*Seliné ne*, why, open the door!' Tota brushed past his wife who had pushed open the closed door.

'We hear that you people were trying to kill each other.'

Avise rekindled the fire from a small piece of log stuck in the hearth. She added some more pieces of timber and looked for a saucepan and water. She found a half full jerry can which she poured into the pot and placed it on the fire before turning to La'ano who was struggling to sit up on her bed. Avise moved to the bed to hug her but stood up short. She was shocked to see the extent of La'ano trying to extract herself off the bed. Her injuries were extreme. Avise was afraid to touch her, to hug her, instead she let her tears do the commiseration for them. La'ano was black and blue all over and hurting from head to toe.

Avise begrudgingly returned to the fire and tended it to speed up the heating. The poor woman will need to wash and apply hot presses to her wounds.

La'ano groggily remembered - she sent word for them – Hoveyau's younger brother – Papa Ave and his wife to come in the morning but it seems her request had been passed on further. It was Hoveyau's uncle and aunt instead who are first of the relatives to come.

She flinched at the pains as she tried yarning and slowly threw off the blankets. The stretching muscles sent screaming pains through her body at which she sucked in air.

She had visitors. She sat on the edge of the *pitpit* bed and threw her legs over it. She attempted to stand upright but then buckled back immediately onto the bed. The pain and stars erupted with new intensity all over her. She cringed through the pulsating pains and sat down, her head bowed and the first tears for the day streamed down her cheek.

'Aunty, the man caught me unawares at the *kandis* yesterday.' She whispered a matter-of-fact statement to them.

'The man fought me very badly. Something was up his backside.'

'Yeah, we heard that he was very vicious.'

Uncle Tota sat by the *yakise* posts and murmured his nothing angers towards his nephew for the horrific actions. It was becoming a norm in the village for the men to beat up their wives sometimes over nothing or something very irrelevant. He felt this was one such fight - over-nothing even if there was a valid reason for Hoveyau's aggression.

'*Apo, Seghané,* we feel sorry for you, he should have been easy on you. What was the fight about?'

'I think our pig went into a garden. He heard Ambo's mother, Kelekele colour his name badly over the pig destroying her garden and that must have bitten his heart because when he landed his hand on me; it was a madman and not the useless man of a husband that I normally have.'

Avise went to her side and tried to touch her body. La'ano flinched as Avise tried to massage these bruised spots.

Tota stretched back to see behind him on the bed if Hoveyau was still asleep but found his mattress empty.

'The man must have left early for either the *kandis* or the *hauspik.*'

'Ha, if he did leave for the *hauspik*, that was good for him, for once he can do something right by the family. I doubt it though, his instinct for the *kandis* is as good as the pig's instinct on where it can get a good feed of *kaukau* from somebody's garden.' La'ano could hardly utter the words.

Aunty Avise looked up from her ministration of the fire. 'You two, stop rubbishing a man. He has done something dastardly here and has gone somewhere to pay penance for it. He may be sorry for his yesterday actions.'

'Mama Avise, ha, you too want to support this man. That nephew of ours spends most of his young manly strength up at the *kandis* place.'

'I know. Now he has done some dastardly thing to make his wife not leave the house. He must know that she also keeps another household - a *hauspik*. I hope he realises that there must be some very hungry pigs. I don't support him, and I agree with you that he wastes his young manly strength hanging it up as useless as it is on his body when he stands around all day. Do you know if he ever realises the wastage that he does to his strength?

La'ano groaned at the prospect of going down to the *hauspik*. The pigs needed to be let out of the house. She was not counting too much that Hoveyau could realise his blunder and go down to tend to the pigs. She was thinking that all the rebukes and the talks about bringing on a wife for his wayward son would give him some purpose at least for a couple of days to tend to the pigs.

Otherwise, the pigs would still be in the house. After these visitations she may have to drag her bruised body down to see to them.

If Hoveyau has gone to the *hauspik* instead of the *kandis* place that would be good for him, as La'ano was not going to see to the pigs for a couple of days.

There would be no *kaukau* for the pigs either and whether she was bruised or not, La'ano rued she was obligated to go to look for *kaukau* for the pigs for the day. The thought of going bruised blue and black to the village market intensified her body aches.

This morning though, the *Lupiye-Tapiye* was Hoveyau's problem, and it should be from now on. She racalled these thoughts again painfully.

She needed to send word out to one of her daughters, perhaps Te'enike Liivelave to come assist her for a few days with the pigs. The poor girl. I hope her marriage pans out well for her. It would be shattering and more devastating if her husband bashes her up too. She had seen a lot of young people bash each other up.

∿

Hoveyau had slept badly, all guilty and listening to his wife exhale whiny moans as she tossed and turned. The night noises inside the house took on an eerie form and these scared him. He rued his own feelings knowing well the blows that he exacted on his wife were not their normal play fights early on in their marriage.

He remembered the raw anger that he had felt then and the power he had mustered into each punch that he had inflicted on her. At one glimpse of time in that anger he was sure that he had knocked the head off her neck with his hands.

He was scared now of the anger in him. Where that came from, he had no idea but boy, he had been vicious.

Then he remembered the pigs. They would be still on the leashes where he had tied them up outside of the house. He had left them there when he came in. The pigs would be in a bad way, all tangled up on their leashes and the *Lupiye-Tapiye* pig that got into the garden may do so again today.

The knock to La'ano's head was bad. He was going to amend his ways. He left the house at the crack of dawn to go to the *hauspik*.

She was restless and sleep-talking to herself, asking for Papa Ave and his wife Mama Heloiseh, uncle Tota and his wife Avise. She repeatedly called for her son.

His first thoughts were that she was trying to die and wanted her son to be near. It gave him the shivers thinking she was going to die on him there and then. Her call-out to his brothers and uncle was a bit intimidating but he was not sure what she wanted from Uncle Tota and Avise. She may have just wanted them to be involved in their affairs. It was village life – everybody is involved in one or other's life in one way or another.

What Hoveyau failed to understand was that La'ano had been lamenting that she had unfinished business in her life. She wanted to attend to these businesses first and there were also secondary reasons for her.

Hoveyau failed to see these, nor did he hear her lament over her marriage. Her marriage had not been what it was. He was listening to one story only and he missed the second one.

The life cycle continues and the one thing that as a man and father, he was expected to always keep at the back of his mind was that this cycle is played out by children. Two of the children - the girls - have moved away. His son remains and there were duties and obligations for him to attend to as a father for the son.

But he always dragged his feet over any idea of bringing on a wife for their son, Mamu. He left them, these wifely ideas for the boy with the mother. It was a responsibility that he was not prepared to take.

Hoveyau however knew the *tusking boar* she kept was to be used to bring on a wife for the boy. Hoveyau was non-committal to it, and he wished for his involvement to be minimal.

The grunting pigs from inside the house were a surprise to him. He had come down onto the *hauspik* thinking the pigs would have spent the night out in the open.

Someone had brought the pigs back into the house last night.

It made him look up onto the *kaukau* platform that his father had erected a long time ago next to the roof of the house. La'ano used this platform to keep her *bilum of kaukau* away from the pigs. Yesterday's *kaukau* for the mornings feed should have been on the platform but there was an empty space and no *bilum* with *kaukaus* in it. The person who put the pigs inside must have either taken the *kaukau bilum* into the house or someone had snatched it and must have walk away with the *kaukau* and the *bilum*.

He rued the fact that he knew nothing about where the woman got all these *kaukaus* to feed the pigs from.

He need not remind himself that their garden was just a fenced-in-bushland.

His mental snap yesterday was very telling in that there would be no more feeds for the pigs. Perhaps the wayward *Lupiye-Tapiye* pig, if it is freed of the leash on its leg may have gone and would have broken into the same garden again.

Boy! He blew hot air from his nostrils mentally visualising the rounds of further abuses from Kelekele, which may mean more flailed nerves and anger, perhaps another fight again with La'ano. These were not happy thoughts.

He opened the *mehe* door and got in amongst the whining pigs. He looked for the *Lupiye-Tapiye*. She was on a leash in a small enclosure at the back. How did that happen? Someone had attended to the pigs in the night. Surely in all her soreness and bruises, La'ano did not come in the middle of the night to attend to these pigs.

He swore at the deafening noises the pigs made, for food and to be let out.

He would deal with *Lupiye-Tapiye* last.

At the centre post *yakises* he found tied up onto the *hikise* was a *bilum* of *kaukaus,* more than what would have been left on the rooftop. He sighed a relieving blessing to whomever did this.

Where that came from, he could not fathom. It would surely not have been done by La'ano. He knew that he had belted her so badly she had been holed up in the house. Did she send someone out here?

That outing with the towel and soap - was that a night journey to the *hauspik?* And she did that with all the flickering aches that he meted out to her. Her body must have been aching all over now. He felt sorry for her and took stock of his foolishness.

The increasing whines from the pigs jolted him out of his thoughts. He quickly released the end of the leashes where they were tied to the wall posts.

The big pigs made hasty exit with the leashes chasing after them. They did their toileting and moved into the grass areas to see if they can root out some early worms.

The two small ones near the door made enough din to burst his eardrums and he swung his foot at one. This made them a bit quieter, but there were still a lot of noises in the house. He undid the other leashes before he moved out of the house with the *bilum* of *kaukau*.

The *Lupiye-Tapiye* yelled out loud and long knowing that she was kept behind. It gave up after a few tugs at the rope and after trying to jump over the pen. The fence around the pen was little bit too high - enough to keep her in.

Outside the house, Hoveyau scattered out the *kaukaus* near to the outside fireplace. The pigs jostled over each other to get to them. Even after he had got them out of the house, the pigs kept a wary distance from him. He was still new to them. It was only fortunate that all the pigs were on leashes, and he was going to manage. After they were fed, he took each pig by the leash and tied them up in the bush making sure that there was more than enough bush where they could find shade.

He went back into the house.

'If you stupid pig did not go into Kelekele's garden, I'd be comfortably sleeping.' He whacked the *Lupiye-Tapiye* across the snout with a piece of *pitpit* stick. The pig screamed terribly long and very loud. The noise startled him, and he realised that these were the type of noises La'ano put up with daily. It was sobering.

He paused.

When the noise had quietened down, he threw the pig a piece of *kaukau*. The *Lupiye-Tapiye* pig nudged at it with one eye on him.

Hoveyau slipped in another leash to the other leg that was sore from previous leashes and pulled it tight. The pig gave a squeal to let him know it hurt and continued munching at the *kaukau*. The pig was now securely leashed on both feet, and it would not travel far, let alone go frolicking into another garden.

He went out to where he had tied the rest of the pigs and distributed the rest of the *kaukau* to the pigs. The pigs took one sniff at it and returned to their snooping for earthworms.

He had placed *kaukau* for three big pigs and two sows and now put more at the spot he wanted to tie up the leash of the troublesome *Lupiye-Tapiye*. He had forgotten lessons on pig rearing - never to put food near tethered pigs as other free ranging pigs would come in to get at the *kaukau* and would also attack the pigs on leashes during the day and it was going to be trouble.

He then remembered what folly he had committed and reminded himself that he must come back every now and then during the day to make sure that other pigs were not getting at them.

Satisfied that all the pigs were tethered on leashes, he made a fire in the house and put in two pieces of *kaukau* that he had set aside for himself. He was going to have this for breakfast.

After a while, the pigs finished with their munching on the *kaukau* and whined for more. He went out and threw them *ghopoluho* shoots he had collected in the morning dew. The pigs attacked these with vigour.

He then remembered the *worm grass*. His grandfather had shown him the *worm grasses* when he was small but he had not used the knowledge. He had forgotten what the 'grass' looked like now. He may have to ask his brother. The *Lupiye-Tapiye* was probably full of worms and that may be the reason for its erratic behaviour. He'll try looking for that 'grass' later today. The pig needed a big dose of it right now.

He turned his *kaukau* that was burning on the fire. It was good the pigs were tethered to the *pitpit* clumps around the house. If the pigs spent enough time tethered, they could be responsible for clearing and upending all the bush and *pitpit* strands around the house.

After the pigs were through, they probably could make out a decent garden. Talking about work, he could already feel the pain of the morning's sheer work in his bones and tried to avoid letting his mind go along that track.

When was the last time he had made a garden? The only time he had made a garden was at school when they were to make a school project garden. His plot had failed to grow because he had not dug up the soil properly. No, he did not dig at all. All he did was to bring loose soil and pour it over his plot. On top of this he had planted corn which sprouted, grew up pale yellowish, withered in their prime and died.

When the teacher checked the garden by probing under the topsoil, she saw the still impacted grass and soil. She had shamed him in front of the class, and he had simply stopped going to school. He has not to this day made any gardens nor participated in the making of one. Initially, he lived off his parents and now he is living off his wife.

He needed to pull his weight, but he was now going down on the other side of the mountain of life. Two of his daughters had moved off to live their own defacto married life. He needed to ensure that a wife was bought and brought home for his son. It was a tall ask as he knew that he had not one *toea* to his name. Bless her heart, the big boar, and these horde of pigs in the *hauspik* were going to be used for bringing on a wife for their son.

When that was going to happen, he was not sure, and he had no clue. It was the issue of money for the bride wealth that he could not get his head around – he, the father, hardly had any nor did he know where or how he would get the money. Some crazy wife he got, he rued.

A pig grunted and pushed through the *pitpit* brush when another breached its space.

Hoveyau looked over. This was the boar that was on the mind of La'ano; he mused. This pig would make the keystone in the feast when a bride was installed. It was getting too old and La'ano will force the issue.

He was okay with the pigs. From this house that will be six pigs. He could make it seven if only the *Lupiye-Tapiye* was willing to be more docile.

He let out the shout to chase off a passing pig from another *hauspik*. It was immediately followed by another voice from the ridge above. Someone was calling.

'Te'enike's father,' the voice called out several times before he realised that the voice was calling for him. He remembered that her daughter Liivelave was also called Te'enike. He himself never used the name Te'enike so now that she had gone off in marriage, the name was getting lost in his mind.

'Whoa! He replied as he recognised the young voice belonged to his nephew and that the call was for him.

'Is that you, Koila?'

'Te'enike's father, my Ma asked me to call if you were here and they asked for you to come quickly to the village.' She called down from the ridge top.

'Oi, thank you.'

He tightened the leash around the ankle of a pig that had loosened its leash. He had tied this pig to a clump of *pitpit* stumps at the back of the house next to the banana plants. There was plenty of shade there for it.

He found the *Lupiye-Tapiye* stuck in the *nivi-nivi broomstick* grass. He uttered his prayers for wishing that the pig had not being clever enough to undo its leash and escape. It was entangled and straining at its forelegs. The rope had really cut into the skin.

At least this pig was not going into somebody's garden today.

The fact of the matter is that he was good friends with the husband. The stupid pig was putting a wedge in between them. The wife Kelekele had a sharp tongue and would say the best of things - straight and to a person's face. At times she said things that would make you want to shrivel up and disappear. She can be confronting and this time around, their *Lupiye-Tapiye* was contributing very much to the angst.

He knew it was worms and he reminded himself to look for the worm grass. He felt sorry for the hobbled *Lupiye-Tapiye*, and he undid one of the leashes to one leg to let it forage for worms.

Getting the left over *ghopoluho* fronds he threw these at the young pigs, satisfied that the pigs were safe for the day.

He got his *kaukau* from the fire, secured the *mehe* to the door and again looked at the pigs to confirm if he had tied them all up securely.

He knew what they wanted as he ambled his way slowly to his house. It was the gathering for the inquisition of what happened yesterday. He was going to face the music from his family…… He did not let his mind wander over this. He was greeted by his uncle and aunt.

'Morning, you must have exited the house very early. It was assumed that you would be still sleeping but it wasn't so. It is good for you for once to come from that garden road instead from up the village where the people are gathering.'

'*Apo, i-Seliné ne ve*', he cut in quickly to stop any more sarcasms. 'It is good for you people to come visit. Unfortunately, I've had to take care of the wretched pig that is causing a lot of strife for me and the garden owners.'

Everyone frowned at his answer. It was the first for some of them that Hoveyau must come from the *hauspik*.

He bumbled something of a greeting to them all. 'There should be some left-over *kaukau* from last night? We had a little problem last night and the food was not touched. I hope we can heat this up for you lot.'

'Oi, thank you. Yeah, we were given that plus more. There should be some left-over water in the teapot if your good wife can make you a cup.'

La'ano flinched as if she had been punched again as the pains from the bruises came to life. Surely, she was being funny asking her to make tea for the wretched man. But this was her house. And she wanted something done later. She must be resolute for what she wanted done later.

She stood all blue and puffed up. There was a small slit around her eyes that she could look through. Her nose was swollen soft, and she tried her best not to wipe the mucus that ran constantly down her top lips. The pain was a bit much. She however was stoic and was even standing up there making cups of tea for her visitors. She was making a cup, but it was for her own. She squinted daggers at Uncle Tota for his odd humour to suggest she make a cup for the useless wasted muscle of a man.

Nonetheless she passed the cup to her contrite husband and pointed to the freshly baked *kaukau* next to the stones around the fireplace.

She looked ruefully at him. At least he can enjoy the last comforts of having a wife. She was going out of his life soon.

The man grimaced in guilt – what had he done to his wife. He was feeling sorry for her puffed up bluish bruised face. It would turn bluer at the day progressed. He reluctantly got the teacup off her and cradled the cup with both hands like he was trying to warm himself - rather to show his remorse.

He was wanting to say sorry, but he did not know how to say it.

He tried saying he had his own *kaukau*, but his voice got stuck in his throat so in the end he just held his peace.

He leaned against the centre *yakise* post and sipped the tea. It was very right, not too hot, and not too cold and very sweet.

He picked up the *kaukau* on the fireplace, it was his special *Opume*. His morning *kaukau* from the *hauspik* can wait in his *bilum*. He looked at the kettle on the fire anticipating more tea to go with the *Opume kaukau*.

His uncle watched, trying to think how to put the appropriate words to start the conversation. But before he could start, La'ano cleared her voice.

'I want to return to my village where even the pigs listen to the people.'

The sarcasm in the statement was wasted - as the younger of the brothers, Papa Ave and his wife, Mama Heloiseh, walked in through the door with as much noise to greet their uncle and aunty - Tota and Avise.

Word had got out that La'ano wanted something else. Papa Ave interrupted all to ask La'ano.

'*Apo*, I am hearing something that is new to me, but it is a strange statement. You surely are entitled to make that statement after this small incident. *Seghané,* you will repeat it again for me. Let me greet you all first. The man should have been easy on you, but I see you standing with your bruises entertaining Uncle Tota and Aunty Avise. I hope you did not make tea for your husband too. I hope you are not suffering to do this entertaining.'

'Now that I have got my breath back, *'big Mama, Apo ya'*, did I hear you are saying something or are my ears playing a trick on me. You cannot throw words like that around unnecessarily. Your presence here is important to all of us. A woman like you who is already established as a *big mama* here just cannot go back to her village. It will be ridiculous that you go from *big mama* to a new *ghetto* in a blink of an eye. Now, what are you trying to say?'

Hoveyau cut in quickly with his own judgement.

'Just the bashing I gave her yesterday and she already wants to up and leave for her village.'

'Please don't say something more', Tota looked daggers at his nephew.

'Papa Ave, I will repeat it for you. I want to leave this man, this marriage, this house, and this village. I will return to my village.' La'ano spoke with a raised voice.

'That man there, that *pipia!* He fought me like I am his rival and his bruise marks on me are not only to my skin and bones but to my pride. He fights and kicks me like a football, and he thinks these are nothing. He makes me pee in front of my *poromeris* and he waters it down.'

She turned to talk to her husband's face.

'*Lapuluvo ya!* The man wastes his bones, and he wastes his muscles.

He never for once had any thoughts that his *hauspik* and his gardens have been kept by me and me only. He calls that irrelevant. He cannot look after pigs and yet he expects me to produce them at his will and for his egos. *Pipia bilong ol pipia yah!*'

'His house pots and plates don't even say '*daddy*' to him, and yet he thrashes me like a rag doll. I am not his *play-play* thing.'

'Now I say I want to leave him and return to my village, and he brushes that aside like it is a joke – something that I will not take up on. He is not a *humbin*. *Humbins* would understand and know their mistakes.'

Papa Ave laughed at her mispronouncing of the English words - human being.

'*Apo, leva ya*, you are, in your serious speech adding something to make a day funny but that aside, you seem to have some serious gripes against your husband.'

'Yeah, some husband! Some good bones he carries but it is all a *lapuluvo* - a wastage but thank you all for coming. Papa Ave, Mama Heloiseh, Uncle, and Aunty, I asked you all in seriousness to come today, not for you all to hear about my gripes or that we bicker over his footballing me. Like I said and I repeat here, I need to bring on a woman for that useless son of mine before I see the back of this village for my own.'

'That stupid boy is becoming like his father, wasting his bones away doing nothing all day but indulging in bad smoke and chasing girls. It will not be long when one of these girls will bring a fatherhood suit against him. He will marry that girl and it may be one that will give me a lot of headaches. He is going to brandish that *itehetu* title around for nothing. It happens with one father; it should not happen again with the son.'

The house went silent.

The idea to bring on a wife for a son was a big, big thing and the implications weighed heavily on the house.

Hoveyau kept silent. He was already seeing a lonely life for himself.

His mind wandered away trying to reflect on where he went wrong. The fight yesterday was just the trigger only. He was already feeling empty inside.

Uncle Tota did not like the *itehetu* claim and he abruptly left the house. True, his family were the original settlers to lay claim to all the land, he did not like the idea of it being used as a weapon against the family.

His wife Aunty Avise joined him.

Papa Ave too sat in silence for a long time getting his thoughts together.

The *itehetu* claim – that they were the first family in the village was used once too often. He had been disgusted when his father had used it and was very angry that his brother was using it like a right. The claim to be the Adamic family – the *itehetus* in the village - was a bit too much of a burden to carry when they were an unproductive lot.

But that had nothing to do with bringing on a wife for young Josiah. He pushed aside the *itehetu* talk to concentrate on the talk of bringing on a wife for Josiah.

'Mama, we came to discuss this small misunderstanding between you two, but you are saying something that is not on our minds at this point in time. Instead, it is a big, a very big topic you are suggesting for us.'

Papa Ave tried to digest the importance of La'ano rambling now. As an uncle to Hoveyau's son Josiah, he was to actively participate in the choosing of the bride and the collecting together of the bride wealth. It imposed a lot of responsibilities and outlay for him and his wife Mama Heloiseh. They did not readily have the right number of pigs nor the monies. He was not sure of his other brothers; Pilipo and Goi and their wives, Sisi-vena and Ambaii Urr. He did not know what wealth their uncle Tota and aunt Avise have in their house and *hauspik*.

Tota and Avise returned with some sugar and coffee packets to La'ano still lamenting …

'You see these pots and pans,' La'ano continued, 'my good *Apo ya*, they have long gone past their use-by-date. They don't look like pots anymore because this man and his son have been panel beating them every time they feel like they should. They did not buy them, and they are second, or third or fourth hand from someone.'

'You see this house, there is that big leak on that side, the dogs have made holes all over the house and the pigs go in and out of these holes like it is a public house. I have two able bodied men who don't take pride in their own house.'

'I have decided, and I must go back to my place, at least I can die old in peace and at least with all my bones intact. But please, first, we must bring the boy a wife before I leave.'

'Papa Ave, you will listen to me just this once and organise your people. I want to take out a bride wealth for a bride price to find a wife for my son.'

'Mama, *Apo*. That is a tall ask. I don't have any money or pigs to go up to stand in front and start speaking about it. I must speak when I have my own backing. All our people will come when they see me backing up my call. If I don't do a show-and-tell, they will not come with much. I think our people may not have much.'

'Our Uncle and Aunty are here with Mama Heloiseh but my brother Pilipo and Goi are not here with their wives, *Sisi-Vena* and *Meri Simbu.*'

'Papa, your brothers, and my sisters-in-law Sisi-vena and Ambaii Urr can join in the conversation later. You are here, the *maus-mahn* for the family. Your brothers will go along with what you decide and say.'

'*Apo*, all you nice ladies, *Seliné ne'*, Uncle Tota, currently, we have not had any discussions, but I and Mama Heloiseh came along thinking that we were going to talk some peace-talk over the fisticuff but now we are confronted with this big new talk.'

'Before we progress any talk of bride price, Mama La'ano, *Seghané*, you are a *big mama*. What you think and say about your son is true and something that we must do. It is the mother that thinks big about these things, when she wants it done then it becomes public, and we others give assistance. Inside our family, I am the *maus-mahn* and it imposes responsibilities on me that in my current state, I feel constipated when I want to bring this out to the village.'

'That is not to say we will not do what is needed to be done but I must know our combined strength. Having that knowledge, it will give me the assurance to lean on our combined strength of our contributions when I go out to rally the village together. Only then can I speak with authority to the family and rest of the village.'

'Papa, I will need the assistance of the village. I know but whatever little each and every one contributes and brings will add up. For pigs, I have a few in my *hauspik* but will be calling in my pig debts. You must know that since the first year I got married into this village, I have been killing pigs for everyone. You see those two *stick-score ropes* there on the *yakise* post, that is the total number of pigs that I have killed for people in this village. The ones that are inside out are ones for which I have been repaid and that is a few new ones. The ones with the notches are to people whom I have made a new commitment. Pigs that I have killed for families are the red painted ones.'

'I can use the *stick- score rope* to ask those people to make repayments for these pig debts. This will the best time and their opportunity to repay these debts of pigs. There are more than seventeen pigs that I will ask for repayment.'

'For pigs that I have slaughtered for the family are on the next string, you will see more sticks. You will rally your family to see how you can assist as there are plenty pigs that I have slaughtered for the family.'

Papa Ave looked up. The woman was serious.

'It is good to know that we can be pig rich, *Apo, big mama ya*. But I pose this question for the family - can we raise enough of the money for the bride wealth.'

'*Apo*, good man, now for money contributions, you know that at every village gathering and when doing contributions in the village, I have been going with twenty *kina* while the rest of the women in the village have been coming with two or four *kinas*. The village will have to think about repaying that goodwill I have had in this village. At every *mumu*, I have been there even though I don't have a big and good garden.'

'Eh, thank you, *big mama*, we all know how gracious you are in this village, and we know that you don't beat on your chest nor mention all the good that you do. These villagers are good people, they will contribute something big or small. It does not matter. It is only me, Mama Josh, I am afraid to say that I may not live up to the title as an uncle and father to the boy - never mind that I am the family *mausmahn*.'

'Good man, I understand your reluctance, but I have no hesitation to leave this man and I'll be gone tomorrow. You people think that it is nothing that I was knocked out cold. I must live with the humiliation that I did *pispis* and *pekpek* in my clothes in front of my peers. I will not hold my head up here after this incident anywhere in the village and especially at the *kandis*. I am now the joke of the village. The woman Kelekele who threw down that dare will be in my face forever.'

'I will do something about it, and I am leaving this man, don't doubt me on that. My issue now is what will happen then to the pigs I have now. They will go to waste. One is already a pig for going into people's garden. The other - the one that I was raising to do this very thing, is so lazy that it sleeps beside the house all day. This pig can be stolen easily. There are louts out there that indulge in marijuana who will gladly pick off this pig. It will be a shame for it to also go to waste in such manner.'

Hoveyau interjected.

'I think that pig, we were thinking of it was an earmarked pig for a problem that we're going to use it for. You remember someone came to us stating he was taking us to court for a pig that he killed for the old man.'

'Look! You can bring on a new piglet and raise that to deal with your father's debts. You father should have dealt with his *dinaus*. I am not going to worry about a dead man's *dinaus* that I did not see or eat. This is something you and your brothers will worry about. This pig is one that I purposely raised to go into the basket to give to the prospective bride's parents.'

'Oh. Is there a woman we already have in picture?' Papa Ave tried to gloss over the debt that his father owed someone. He too had the same view. His father's debts were his fathers and now that he is dead and gone, those people should forget about it.

'No but it will be a bride of my choosing from amongst my relatives. She can be a good bride for this useless son of mine. She will bring that boy into line.'

'Papa Ave, I hear you about your lack of money- if the village don't come good, don't worry, I think I have a good sum to start with.'

'I've been hoarding some small amounts in these long years even before that useless boy was born and I think I will have *two good asapu - wraps of sticks.*'

Hoveyau's mouth fell apart. This was his wife who hardly went to the market and spent half the time gambling in the village.

The men fell silent.

They each were trying to determine how much an *asapu* was and what did she mean by *sticks* in the *Tok Ples* counting system.

In the *Tok Ples* counting system one *stick* was ten-kina, *one hand,* a five kina and *a wing,* fifty kinas, a *gho'* or bilum was one hundred, and a *ghola* or mountain was two hundred and a *mulise* was a *pile* of money deemed to be a thousand kina. Any of these, when put in a unit of ten would be deemed *an asapu* or a *wrap.*

Which of these was she referring to when she said she has two good *wraps of sticks*?

Papa Ave felt unease about it all. Did she say she had two hundred or was it twenty *kinas*? Two hundred was not sufficient to invoke him to call out to the family and village to start the pooling process to collect bride wealth.

Hoveyau started sweating. He had his own problems, one of them foremost is that he never had any money nor any he would have hoarded away. Secondly, he never had any inclination that La'ano had been hoarding any money all this times. He was silently glad his wife had some monies that would give the credibility to Papa Ave to call the village.

La'ano could read the doubts on the men's faces.

Going to her battered suitcase, she pulled out a kitty bag. She came back by the fire and made out a bed of an old rice bag. She turned the bag upside and the contents fell out.

The three men's eye ogled to see whether money would fall and how much.

Instead, two bundles of tightly tied sticks fell out and down with some bottle top caps.

Hoveyau was dismayed.

'Girl, why the sticks, where is the money? Don't disappoint us men.'

'Papa Ave, you see these *sticks*; each *stick* is what it means in our traditional counting system. That bundle of *sticks* represents what I have hoarded away.'

Papa Ave looked at La'ano and back at her husband and then at the pile on the bag. It must be a joke, he reckoned, but then reluctantly undid the first bundle. It opened to another bundle, this time more bundles made up of bamboo splinters.

These were her two *wraps*.

Uncle Tota stretched his neck to get in the picture of the bundle of splint sticks.

'My good woman, is this real representation of money that I am going to count? I did not think that you would have money, but I am not going to doubt you. And let me praise you first up for these *asapu of sticks*.'

He knew that their parents kept their money and numbering by using the old way of counting and La'ano was good in these old numbering systems.

Hoveyau was still at a loss of words. Hot airs came out of his ears. He was on the verge of tears.

'Papa, you see *sticks* there. I count the old way and have used that way as accounts of my savings. Please count them first.'

'*Big mama*, I can see that you have *twenty sticks* in one small bundle. One stick is ten *kinas*, so if I am right, that would be two hundred kina - what we call a *ghola* or *mountain*.'

'Now there are *five ghola* in this one bundle so that is *one mulise* or one thousand kinas.'

'These five *ghola here* make up one *mulise* or *a pile*. If that is the same with the other bundle, then I take it that you have two *mulises*.'

Papa Ave paused long enough letting the figure sink in. He continued.

'*Apo*, that is a substantial amount that none of us have in any of our houses. *Seghané ve*, the very bundle of sticks that I see here gives me joy and it sure now is powering me as the *maus-mahn*.'

'Now may I ask if I can? What about these bottle top caps?'

'Aagh, those is nothing. They are Swan Beer tops. I liked the shape of the black birds on the top and have been keeping them.'

Papa Ave looked at her quizzically. He was not buying that. It must be important for her to keep bottle caps amongst the stick bundles.

The bundles of sticks were representing actual money that she obviously may be hoarding elsewhere. So, there were a possibility too about these bottle tops. They must mean something more - the black swan on the bottle tops. Besides this beer has long gone out of the country and SP Lager was the prominent drink in the country now.

La'ano sat smug, not saying more about the bottle tops. She was not going to tell what these tops were for.

Why should I tell you what these tops mean to me, you men say I am lazy but that is my reserve money? La'ano raced the line in her thoughts.

Mama Heloiseh and Aunty Avise pinched each other. They just could not believe what they were hearing.

There was something that La'ano was not going to reveal. She was keeping it close to her chest.

La'ano was not going to tell them that over the years, she had been giving money to Unca Holoe for him to keep for her. Each top represented a full bundle of sticks. One cap represented a bundle which in turn was a *mulise - a pile* of money - one thousand kina that she had passed over to the village scrooge, Unca Holoe for his safekeeping. She smiled at her clever thoughtfulness.

Papa Ave looked around. There was a feeling of excitement in the house.

'*Big Mama*, good woman, *Seghané,* you show that you have such a big sum here with all these stick bundles; now, what about the pigs? I don't go to your hauspik and so I don't know how many pigs you have.'

Hoveyau felt he needed to say something and cleared his throat.

'I see that La'ano is doing some serious talk here. Yes, she has six big pigs that she can do several serious businesses with. That is not counting the troublesome *Lupiye-Tapiye.* This pig can be used immediately to announce the call to the *lulu ghehene tolumo mumu.*'

'Okay, you two good couple, I came here thinking peace talks, but it's all a different matter altogether. This is serious business now. I'll send out a word that we will start the first gathering - the *lulu ghehene togessa* or pooling the bride wealth together on the next weekend.'

'Thank you, Papa Ave. I'm glad that I finally can rest easy on this forever pressing issue of getting my son a wife. I don't want to talk about the bash up as I have made up mind that I must return to my village. I must repeat myself that I must bring my son a wife before I go. If I go on about the bashing, what good will it do. You know that man – your brother, he hardly works in the garden, he hardly cares for the pigs, he does not know how to make a house, he does not know how to keep a house and we have not slept in the same bed since the boy was born. Ghitume Monopoliso and Te'enike Liivelave are now both married. I am a forever a *ghetto* woman in my marital village. So, the bash up, yes, my body cries out for revenge, but it will be on my terms, that is, I move myself out of his life.'

'You all know that your brother walks up and down this village and up to the big road looking for people who sit around the *kandis* and he stands *pehe-pehe* there all day, the *Yar Yomba*, the strong posts. His bag of bones has not seen any physical work and his garden does not know him. You must know your brother does not know which side of the spade or knife to use. All my *poromeris* have two or three gardens, I have one half of a big garden and I have had that one garden from day one when I came here as a young bride. I don't have a coffee garden but a lot of bush land that people say is our land. A land that is not cultivated is useless.'

'*Imph iii*,' Hoveyau tried to interrupt with a quick burst of air through the nose.

'Thank you, this La'ano woman.' Papa Ave spoke cutting out his brother.

'Mama, you take my breath away. You want to leave, and you want to bring on a wife for your son before that. The idea of you leaving the marriage and family pains me but you have the right idea. It is a good thing to see your son settled. I had no idea you could have all these money. I knew you are quite good at the cards and *kandis*, but I did not think you could hide money like these. Not that I come to think of it; at all the village gatherings for contributions, you had a sort of ritual of contributing your favourite *two sticks money - twenty kina* and I always thought that was the sum of a couple of days of gambling.'

'I feel so proud now and at the same time rue the fact that this is your start of the preparations for your return - back to your village. Like Uncle Tota said, I came petrified from my *hauspik* this morning, knowing it was going to be a moot court over yesterday's little fisticuff, but it gone a different course altogether.'

'Oh, by the way, is Kelekele going to court over her garden?'

'No, yesterday while she was screaming abuses at me and that useless man, I went over to see the garden. I had to swallow some pride at the dare she put out for me. I also gave her some good money for her troubles. If she is not happy with that money, she can go to court, but I don't think she will as I gave her more than enough, I think. I returned and was sitting there with my first game when I was attacked by the man.'

'Hoveyau, you have something to say.'

'This marriage talk for Josiah is not something that was in my mind but now it is an issue.'

'Pigs, we … I mean she has - but money is not something we … I mean I don't have. But if La'ano insists, I will cooperate and get this done.'

'Eh, now you want to say you're the man you weren't. You stammer for words. You're a waste, even of a good bag of bones.' La'ano could not stop from putting in her bit to sweat out her husband.

'*Lapuluvo ya*, where did you think I got all the *kaukau* to feed the pigs – not from your garden nor from any work that your old wasted and withered bones would have done. I gave you leashes to pigs that you had the joy of dragging these pigs around to kill for other people's trouble. The kudos generated from these acts were all yours, it gave you all the good name and standing as a man, none were for me. I slaved to feed these pigs, not from your *itehetu* lands and gardens but using money that I won at the *kandis*.'

Uncle Tota cut in. He was already fed up with all things *itehetu* and *yar yomba kandis* teasers.

'*Seghané*, when do we want to do this? The next coffee season? We others don't have money now.'

'Papa Tota, you are not hearing me correctly, I want this done now. I am serious in my desire to leave your son and return to my village. I want to go back to my place and not worry over the young man.'

La'ano was forcing the issue.

Papa Ave answered for them. 'Uncle, this coffee season is over long ago but there are some *wan-wan* cherries left over on the trees. The next week, the village can work their coffee gardens to collect these that they can sell. In this way at least we can expect some good contributions at the *tolumo togessa* gathering.'

'Mamu's mother has the money now, that two thousand Kina is a lot of money for a bride price. It is more than enough and that should be the backbone of the collection. The two thousand is the bottom level of the community threshold for a village girl-bride. We the family will support and build up on this sum with whatever little we can come up with. The village as a community will do their part and all together whatever we bring will make it up to a sizable amount.'

'We will give time to those in the village that have coffee gardens to collect these berries for sale. We will also allow time for those who must go to the markets. We then start with a *mumu* the first of the *tolumo togessa* gathering of pooling together towards the bride wealth. I have suggested that the *mumu* not be this weekend but the Monday after the next weekend.'

'La'ano, my good *tambu*, I am at a loss. You put us all to shame. We need to look at how you saved those money and take a lesson out of it. We need to teach our wives and the other village women to be money wise. A lot of them get money, and then chew them up greedily like a *bulmakau-pigs* on grass, even masticating on the leftovers that could be saved.'

La'ano was unperturbed. 'When to do something about this or to start is your – you - men's problem. I have stated what I want done and you have heard me.'

'This bride wealth will be my burden. I am using this opportune time to also call in on my old debts. I have not given any big money to anyone but my contributions in the village is always a good sum. I expect people to do the same thing back to me - that they be generous in their money contributions.'

'But pigs, that is a different story; I have killed lots of pigs for people. Papa Ave, when you send word out, remind people that I will be calling on my pig debts and those who owe me pigs must come good and repay what I have done for them. I don't want any new debts. I don't want Josh and his wife to come into marriage with a huge pig debt hanging onto their marital life.'

'I will call out the pig sticks and most of those sticks must be burnt off as settlement of my debts. I am not giving that stash of *stick rope* to Josh and his wife. They are debts that I created, and I want them repaid at this time.'

'Mama, what you say is true.' Hoveyau tried to feel relevant and contribute to the conversation.

'Hoveyau, my brother, listen, I, Papa Ave, am the *maus-mahn* for the family.' He beat his chest with folded fists to emphasis what he was saying. 'If I was asked earlier today, to be the lead person in this event to bring on a bride for the small man Mamu, I would have hesitated, knowing that you spend your days at the *kandis*. You know your wife is also known to be a *kandis* person. However, on the word of your good wife and Mamu's mother, I am now taking control over the idea of bringing on a bride for my nephew.'

'We will start the *tolumo togessa mumu* that you and Hoveyau can host. The *Lupiye-Tapiye* can be killed then. I hope one of our neighbours do not kill it in the garden before that.'

La'ano turned for something and she let out an audible gasp as the aching pains came full on. She bit hard on it to contain the pain.

Yet she was elated though that there was something of a movement towards her desire to do something for her son. She was also going to live with the aches and pains for the next few days.

She grimaced and turned to face the men.

'Oh, by the way, Papa Ave, do any of you know the grass for worms. That *Lupiye-Tapiye* pig could use a handful. I think it is going into the gardens because it is full of worms. If we give the grass, we may be able to put a stop to it going into the gardens and secondly, it will fatten the pig up for a little while before we use it for the *mumu*. My other pigs could use the grass also.'

'Yeah, that is right. Now the worm grass for the pigs, I think I saw some at the top of Tamtex's garden at Sogopex. Hoveyau, you go to the cemetery area and at the corner under the red *Ghilukalu* tree, you will find them growing next to the old *marrmarr* trunk. It is that plant that has the brown leaves. I suggest you mix it with some tin fish or meat.

It is a bit bitter, and the pigs will not take it without a smell put on it.'

'Oh, okay, I'll try later today to gather that grass for the pigs. I had them tied up in the sun I think.'

Hoveyau now has to try to be helpful.

3

GHEVENA VIISE LO
– CALL THE PEOPLE TOGETHER

Do we know if Josh Mamu has a girlfriend or a girl in mind?

'Like I said, I don't know if that foolish boy has a girlfriend. However, I have a sister-girl in mind who is five times removed from me as a relative. This young lady's parents are related to me through some complicated family tree. My cousin sister is married into their village, and she will talk to the parents.'

'Okay that's it then, you guys talk to Mamu and prepare firewood for that *mumu* two Mondays from now. In the meantime, I will send word around to inform the villagers that we are going to discuss contributions – *the tolumo gatherings* for Mamu's bride wealth.'

'Now before we leave, Hoveyau, let me ask you to keep an eye out for the pigs as La'ano will not be feeling too well to care for the pigs. This means that you may have to forgo having to go up the road to the *kandis* games.'

'You must know that our ancestors over the mountains at Wesan let women do all the work. They were also a lot of single men - bachelors after their wives left them for other men. You know, one of our sisters went in marriage there but came back with her son because she could just not bear it. You have been acting like one. You may have been thinking it was your entitlement - being man-lazy, but it must stop.'

'One day, my brother, one day, those *Wesan* men, our ancestors will appear and when they do, they will *show you the birds*, there …

and you'll piss in your pants. You keep on treating women like rag bags, those *Wesan* men did and then the spirit men - *Ghewos* had to step in and when they did, mark my words, those men that lazed in the house all day and sent their wife and children to the gardens, they *pekpek-ed* in the house. That day is coming when you too will have to excrete in fear. Don't you think they are not watching; you keep mistreating La'ano, and your time to *pispis* and *pekpek* in your pants will come upon you?'

A drizzle fell in the evening bringing with it chill and misery. La'ano checked the corner where the rain fell. A little of the rainwater had seeped in, wetting the blinds and mat. She hung up the mat and swore at the inability of her husband to repair the *kunai* thatch properly. Three days ago, she had brought a big bundle of *kunai grass,* and it was still there where she had dropped it. Some village dog had poohed besides it and the rain had spattered it onto the end of the *kunai* bundle.

Her good for nothing son had been nowhere in sight for the last couple of days. His yesterday's dinner was untouched on the *hikise*. That will go to the pigs later. She should perhaps bring on a *titivis* piglet. Yeah, she will buy one, she resolved.

When Hoveyau came in, he was all wet. He muttered something about coming from a court case. Yes, she affirmed the court case at the village happened in the morning and the rest of the day he spent either in one of the *kandis* gambling or on the fringes of the *kandis* watching the gamblers deal and play with their cards.

'If you did win some, you could do well to buy us some rice and tin fish. I am just about to pot *kaukau*. There is no *abus*.'

'The *kaukau* will be good. I was watching them play', he implied that he had no money.

'We said the *togessa mumu* is tomorrow and I see no firewood, how is that!' La'ano countered.

'I told Josh and the young boys. They went to *Menehetaka* and there is a pile of firewood on the road. They will bring it down at dawn. We will use those three on the *hikise* as the eye piece for heating the stones.'

'Okay, that is good, I need your assistance very early to bring the *Lupiye-Tapiye* up before I go back for the *hetuvo*. I got two bags of *kaukau* from the new plot that I made in the top end of the garden. We'll ask Tolitoli - Papa Ave's young girl down to help me carry them up.'

'I also sent word to my sister *Alu Iyeyo* saying we were discussing bridal issues for her nephew. My sisters and their families want to come the following weekend.'

'Okay, we'll get organised. I am just worried that you are rushing things for you to go back to your village. I am curious to know why you want to return to your village.'

'Don't talk to me while I'm still black and blue and let me not go down that road with you.' La'ano retorted.

'The boy needs a woman to take care of him. Both of you are useless. You have all this land that I cannot make use off. The coffee plot is a laughing matter, and you think I am happy. I will do my thing first to bring on a wife for my son, useless as he is, then return to my village. I am a *ghetto* here already and it will make no difference to me back home. There are plenty of *ghettos* there so another one more is nothing. You worry your bones how best you can be of use to your son and his new bride.'

'*Oi, oii*, let us not start an argument. We have better things to discuss if you will get that *kaukau* pot going. I'll organise the Coleman lamp.'

He pulled down the lamp from its storage and undid the caps and glass. He got the spirit bottle to fill with spirit but found no spirits. He cursed his son. When intoxicated with marijuana, he would look for alcohol and spirits were fair game. He would be happy if his son drank the kerosene too. Such wastage and his mother want to bring on a bride for him.

La'ano put the pot on the fire and going to her side of the house; pulled the spirit bottle and without a word pushed it before her exasperated husband.

So now it has gone to his mother hiding the spirit. He put aside the kerosene that he was going to use as substitute for the methylated spirit.

'Don't leave this around when you know that your son is indulging in *spak-brus*.'

Hoveyau nodded a rare thank you to his wife and went about lighting the lamp. When the lamp was lit up and running, he hung it up at a vantage point. The centre *yakise* post was a good place for the lamp. It shone to all corners of the house except for a streak of shadow lines that were from the *yakise* posts. He pulled out a cut flour bag that he used as a mat for his bed. He then made himself comfortable and from his pocket pulled out a packet of old used cards. He then started playing canasta.

'While you play canastas, let me remind you about the *kunai* outside, the dogs are poohing all over it. Soon they will make a house out of it while the leak to this side of the house will grow bigger. Can't you organise yourself? You must know that my sister is coming, and we will need space for them to sleep. You don't want them to be moving beds in the middle of the night when it rains in the house.'

Hoveyau half heard her but concentrated on his cards.

La'ano tended the fire to bring the *kaukau* pot to boil and then replaced it with an old, battered kettle that had no lid. It was held together by wires and a protruding piece pricked her. She swore at it and hurled insults at Hoveyau.

'Are you as blind as the bats and don't see things around the house that you can fix? It does not need good schooling to properly do up the handles to this old teapot. Unless you can buy a new one, you better man up and fix things around here properly. This pot is like the house, the garden, the pig's house, they tell you a story that you are blind to see. Gosh, and I must harangue you about the *kunai* bundle outside.'

'Oh, you just cannot stop, can you? I just cannot find the appropriate way to say sorry, so you want to go on about it, but you know I am very sorry from the bottom of my heart. I wish I never abused you like I did. I am truly sorry.' He continued with his canasta game.

'You could seriously do something about the leaking roof.' La'ano spoke back as a matter of fact as she dished up the *kaukau* and made sweet tea for him and herself. She had to remind him again and again for the simplest of things in the village. A repair of a leaking roof was something that other men did with ease and as a matter of fact. It was never the same with this man.

The man accepted the tea.

They ate in silence.

Hoveyau wanted to ask her to show him the money that she said she had. He was sceptical over it. He wanted to know how she amassed such a sum.

He looked up when La'ano pulled down her *iye nakavosa* - the string of bamboo sticks tied together as an account of all the pigs that La'ano had raised and used in the village either by herself or given to other people as a pig debt.

She wanted to remind herself who owed her pigs now.

Making herself comfortable, she laid out the strand of tied sticks and started recounting what the sticks represented what pig and who and where it was used. La'ano looked at each stick carefully matching the size of the sticks and to events that stuck out at her.

Hoveyau listened with half his ear cocked to the muttering La'ano. He marvelled at how she could accurately match each stick with a name. She even could remember the type of pig and the colour pig that she had in her time in the village. She could remember the event for which she brought out and slaughtered the pig for. Hoveyau listened and as he did, he pulled out a twig and broke and gathered his own set of twigs. By the time La'ano had finished recounted her sticks, Hoveyau had his own set. He had nine sticks. He tried to match names to the sticks he had collected but after five names he gave up.

These were the ones for which he knew he could go and ask now or remind them it was time that they had to come with a pig as repayment for this debt.

Hoveyau selected a few names that they could approach to call on to ready a pig La'ano had slaughtered earlier. It was not habitual for them to be asking up front nor was it customary. An intermediary would have to mention to each of the names individually that they need to make a repayment.

When she mentioned the one pig that she had killed for the owner of the garden that their *Lupiye-Tapiye* was destroying, Hoveyau became angry.

'Don't mention their names again. Don't dare think of asking them to repay their debt. All these issues are because that woman not being careful in her choice of words. I don't want to hear or see that woman ever.'

'But the argument of the garden has nothing to do with my deciding to bring a bride for my son. Bringing a bride was always on the cards and those that do owe me a pig know that. They know that I have a son. This type of thing is a community thing and whether they like it or not, all the people in the village take part and contribute. We are a people who forget our arguments and fights during community gatherings and take part as one people when we have a death or when we try to do bride price ceremonies. After the event has passed, we then get back to our arguments and fights if we still remember them. Just because we have this situation that you say was brought on by her - that is not the issue. They owe me a pig and now that I need to do my thing, they must repay my pig,' La'ano asserted.

'If that is what you want then you must have an intermediary do that job. I have no tact; I will just go up to them now and ask for it. It is a job for one who has diplomacy and must be tactful to ask them for that pig. I don't want them thinking that their outburst is the reason for the calling of the payment of the bride wealth and we are using that to ask for settlement for the pig that we slaughtered for their cause.'

'Oh, so long as when we discuss the topic of pigs, they can come forward in saying they will contribute a pig. I know it is not easy trying to ask another to repay their debts. It is more difficult when one has a running mouth that led to all of this. The woman knows that she threw down the dare. It was a challenge and when I step up to it, she will do her part and come good on her debt.'

'We'll ask but if they don't come good in repayment. They may, perhaps another time, we'll try some means to get them to repay that.'

'There will never be another time. This is the time now for the settlement of my debts. I am going to my place. You and whomever intermediary that you choose, must impress that upon them.'

'Those who owe me a pig or two, they need to repay my pigs.'

'This woman disparaged me why I was looking after pigs that went into the garden. She questioned why I was looking after pigs and coloured my name blue with her rebukes about my pig rearing skills asserting that I would not step up to bringing my son a wife. That hurts and now I want to go about doing just that, she is obligated to the debt that was made to them. They need to front up and help me bring that wife for my son.'

'She needs to be told that her village high *tok baksait* about me is the start to this call out to all.'

'She issued the dare; she has to step up to it for her part.'

'You also need to get to these other ones to also repay my pigs. I am not going to come back from my village taking people to court because they owe me a pig or two. It will be very funny me coming as a *ghetto* with my own people – people who did not eat of any of these pigs nor know a thing or two about it, tailing me back here in my search for repayments of these debts. This is the only time I am going to ask people to repay my pigs and I have killed more pigs for people in this village. My new in-laws must be feted on a bed made of pork.'

Hoveyau raised his voice. 'We will get them to repay those pigs, but don't go on nagging me for it and you can tone down your insistence.'

'Don't harangue me over insistence. What will you do to make your village people repay my pigs?' La'ano raised her voice.

'Ask your people, ask your brothers, fathers and they must make a genuine attempt to get everyone who owes me pigs to repay these pigs. You make it out like they did not appreciate the pigs. I can remember one family, who put out their dead father and were trying to bury him a pauper's death.'

'Remember, they wanted to bury him in the very dirty blanket he had been sleeping in. They made no *mumu* and showed no sorrow or were prepared to wear the anger of the village. I killed off the anger of the village when I brought that boar with tusks coming through and made that *mumu* and they gave their father a decent burial. This family have not even thanked me for it by repaying the pig nor have they done any work for me. A year or two later, I buried your father and grandfather. Did these people kill a pig in return, no, if fact they did not attend any of your funerals. They could have at least come for your father's or your mother's wake.'

'Now that I want to do something, you must make it your business to call in these pig debts. Don't be a soft mellowed person, don't be like a woman, think manly and do the manly thing to go about calling in on my debts.'

'I have these thirty sticks; the sum of my pigs that I raised and slaughtered for your people. I want thirty pigs tomorrow. Do something or I will go out myself to call on my debts. You know that it is not proper for women to be calling around for their old debts. You men must do the politicking and put out the appropriate words for these people to come around.'

'Wow, wow, slow down. You did not give notice two years ago for them to raise pigs. It was only just now that you are taking bride price.'

'No, man, you know when a debt is made against you, you go out and make it your business to settle it or be on a watch out for the opportune time to repay that debt. A person watches for the opportune time whilst raising pigs - waiting for these opportunities.'

'Now if you *sugar-sugar* on all these people, I will make those calls.' La'ano was adamant.

'Don't be that daft or stupid. The village is not going to like you for it. And you don't have to rub salt into it. Let me see those sticks again and go through the names.'

'Hove-Hoveyau, you have not been listening. There you go again showing your disinterest in what I do. You waste your life doing nothing.'

'What are you going on about? You are just a woman. You came in marriage to me, and you enjoy life here. Okay, I may have some disinterest in you but since when was the last time, I had done things that were normal. I have tried to do things that other men don't do. Like I don't mind what you do all day. You basically have a free reign over your own activities in the village. I don't check your side of the house and you keep your own finances. I don't fight you unnecessarily. This fight is a very, very exceptional one.'

'Oh, is that how you explain your inability to work your big *itehetu* lands? Is that how you explain away your bag of lazy bones?'

Hoveyau swallowed bitter bile and shot back.

'You stop interjecting with your smarty interjections whilst I am talking. You want me to show my disinterest by walking out of the house.'

'Yeah, do so, it will not be anew thing. *Your body is already outside of this house*, what is here is just your shadow so if you want that shadow to join the body out there somewhere, be my guest.'

'Why do you *ne'ghe-ne'ghe* so much. It is stupid women like you that *ne'ghe-ne'ghe* to much and send their husbands out to go walk into other women's arms.'

'Ha, you want to fault my *ne'ghe-ne'ghe* to go shackle up with another. *Ha*, stupid impotent man. It's been a long while since you have come over to my side of the bed. I did not come to marry an empty house. A woman must be married to a man. You have a total disinterest in me, my house, my garden, my pigs, my children,' a tear fell down her face as she did a bitter recall.

'And where do you walk out to? How can you walk into another woman's bed when you have not warmed mine and that is since the boy was born? You already look like a shrivelled dry bush, an old leaf with a use-by-date that has long gone past.'

'Don't you *use-by-date* me, otherwise I will walk into the arms of another lady.'

'That's a joke. You … seriously! *A dry bush* like you has its overused-by-date. Since when did you get it up all strong when you *carry a perpetual limp one*? You want to bring on a woman to what - what will you do with her – a cold bed and a *holey house* and bushy garden? I am known as the *ghetto* here in my husband's house and village. You want to bring on another *ghetto* again, but it will be a joke - as to what bed, what house and what garden, ha!'

She jeered through her teary face. She swallowed hard too. It was the first time she had mentioned his manhood.

'It will be a joke when your house has holes like your backside, your garden is half planted, and your *itehetu* land is still bushland and your coffee garden looks like yourself. All these needs a man's attention, and you think another woman is going to fix it. *Aa'hai-ye* to you. It is a joke. You have all these *man bones* that you waste – *lapuluvo* it, going up and down the road looking for *kandis* places and you waste it, your energy, your bones, your land, your wife, and your life. *Lapuluvo-oh, hai-e-hi!*'

'Now you want to be smart. Don't you dare to walk out on me at this particular time when I am suggesting that we bring on a wife for that lousy Mamu boy? If we don't, he will turn on us and more so, I will turn him on you. The least you can do is hang around and bring on a wife for him. You must also remember that I seriously want to return to my village. That spells out that I am leaving you. You can walk into the arms of another woman when I am out of your life but not before that.'

'Okay! Okay, I am not apologising but can we serve some peace meantime. Can you hold on to your cynicism about me and please stop the *ne'ghe-ne'ghe*. These naggings from you are getting the better of me.'

'Yeah, but say something civil instead of being such a cuss. Also please do accept what I say to you because I am going to have my day throughout this short time to bring on a wife and until I go home.'

'And you must know that what I do - is to bring you kudos - like you say I am nothing but a woman. In your name, your village, it is all for you – to give pride to your name and status. I was nothing but an appendage that will have to go.'

Hoveyau bit his lips and remained silent – at least for the moment. The pause was pregnant.

Sensing no reply from her husband, La'ano picked up the sticks, she repeated in a voice only audible to Hoveyau. She was mindful of persons outside the house who may be eavesdropping. She recounted the pigs to the sticks and names.

'This morning at the *tanget* plants, I counted the seventeen pig jaw bones. That is the pigs that I have killed that have been eaten in this village. It does not include the pigs that were taken out of the village on the day we slaughtered them. The knot from the leaves for recording such have dried and shrivelled up. I did not renew these knots and I have forgotten a few of them. My record with the jawbones and the sticks however tallies up. There is only one that I could not place. I think it is the old pig that we killed for Hololu and somehow, I think it is for another person. Now on the sticks I did say it was for Maria's daughter Tolina. You remember Tolina knifed her *meri poromahn* and they brought the case against her for causing her *meri poromahn* to lose that baby. I not sure if that is the jaw of that pig that was contributed for the compensation for Tolina's knifing problem. I am sure the slaughtered pig was taken away by her *meri poromahn's* relatives. I am stuck as to whose jawbone is that?'

'I think it was the one that you killed for the old man when we did that *seme'ne mumu*. You know that time when we thought the *Ghetolisos* had done their *puripuri* on him and that *seme'ne mumu* was to break that curse.'

'Oh yeah, that may be right. I forgot all about that. Let me go and remove that bone. The family line is the next row of bones.

'No, leave that where it is. Just mark the stick here by an 'x' or scratch on it. Now that reminds me. Are there any more sticks that represent pigs killed for the immediate family?'

'Yeah, there are ten but that is the other strand of sticks that you see behind the centre *yakise* posts. Also, underneath them is the pigs that I killed for the children, seven in all.

'Whee, that was a lot of pigs.'

'You know that, and you must remind yourself that you rarely put a hand in raising them. I raised them all from that one garden and with money I won from the gambling around at the *kandis*. The village knows that I raised these pigs with money – buying *kaukau* from other villagers.'

Hoveyau cocked his head and squinted his eye at her. He wanted to ask her where she got the pledged money from but thought otherwise. If he asked, she was going to throw aspersion on him. He knew that he hardly ever put a spade to dig up the ground for her to plant anything or fixed up the fence to the garden. He was lucky that when La'ano came in marriage, on the settlement day, her relatives had come to build her that garden and they also put up the first wire fence in the village. The posts were from her village, all hard wood *Yomba* posts that thirty years on still stood strong today.

They continued again murmuring in voices audible to themselves whenever he disputed the names La'ano put to the sticks.

Hoveyau realised that La'ano had killed four big boars for his family. He silently tried to remember his visit to his three brothers pig houses to determine if they had boars. He could not recall seeing any and if he did, it was a long time in between his visits to remember them accurately. He hoped that La'ano would not insist that the brothers repay the boars. It would be the start to bad blood coming into the family. His brother's wives hardly kept any pigs, even one citing religious affiliation that barred them eating pork and that meant even rearing one. It was a sacrilege.

La'ano was packing away the sticks when there was a rap at the door.

They looked at each other wondering who was at the door.

Hoveyau went and undid the latch to the door. It opened to someone with a bright Tilley lamp.

Hoveyau looked back at La'ano enquiring if she had asked the lamp for a visit. La'ano shrugged her shoulders. He let in Ambaii Urr who preceded her husband into the house.

'Iii' *Meri Simbu*', La'ano greeted her sister-in-law Ambaii Urr.

The light from the lamp flooded the house as his brother-in-law followed his wife into the house.

'*Seliné ne*. It is quite late, and you visit us with your Coleman.'

Ambaii Urr and Goi spoke in unison. 'We heard word of you wanting to return to your village. We thought it was strange, so we decided to ask for ourselves if this was true. We came to see if we can determine the reason for you wanting to leave. It is strange that you are the *big mama* of the family, and you want to throw that title to the wind.'

La'ano nodded as she went about to find more firewood at the side of the house where a small pig was tethered.

'The children have left the coop, and you want to leave too. We find that disconcerting and we'd like to come talk to you about it.'

'*Meri Simbu, Seghané,* your sister here is putting me in the public spotlight and we ourselves are trying to work out how far our little scrimmage will take us. Please come sit down.' Hoveyau tried to be jovial.

He gave her a complimentary hug and let her go sit at the women's side of the house. He let his brother take his spot and he moved by the fireplace. He put on the kettle and rekindled the fire, adding some more pieces of wood to heat the warm water.

La'ano checked the cooking pot, she took out two plates and put on them a couple of pieces of boiled *kaukau*. She proffered it to them.

'There is only *kaukau*, we have no *abus*. You can have it with tea.'

Ambaii thanked them for it and set her plate beside her to wait for the tea.

Hoveyau cleared his throat and began conversation.

'This woman wants to return to her village and is turning the whole house out. She wants to empty the pig pen and clear out the garden. She wants to bring on a wife for Mamu which is a good idea as he does not listen anymore to good advice. The mother is scared he will impregnate some woman she does not like and that will cause tension for her and me.'

'Okay, we agree that going home for Mama Josh's is not a good thing. We may have to discuss that at some time in the future. But a wife for Josh, that is timely. You know all these young people are having free sex everywhere. They are not even properly spoken for, married or being friends. They take this sex thing very casual, and they play around like it is a *play-play* thing.'

'We are people for having sex in the house, in a proper bed, but this new generation are doing it in every other place except the bed. They are doing it standing up, on the road, in the coffee gardens and even in the pit toilets amongst all the smell.'

La'ano burst out in painful giggles at Ambaii's burst of worldly truths.

'Now these young ones drink this homebrew or *spak-wara* thing, combine that with *spak-brus* and they lose all their senses of reasoning. They remove their private things and show it to everyone. Even the girls wear small tops and roll down their skirts to show everyone their pubic hairs. These people are in a rush to get married. The girls, very young ones just because their breasts fall, they think it gives them the authority to be mothers. Babies are creating babies. Gosh, just count the number of baby girl mothers in the village, try the next village or the next. It is all the same, young girls becoming mothers very early and all these children without fathers. All these girls have seen men already and there is none that we cannot say have not seen a man. They are sexing before they are even ready.'

'*Apo*, Ambaii, that is true, these girls are really wanting to be mothers and in such a rush most of them were yesterday's children and still are children when they are mothers. We have babies making babies. The boys could not care less. It is not a surprise. They think it is a game that children play. The baby mothers do realise rather late that it is no longer a game when a child is bawling for food; what does a baby give to a screaming baby?'

'Those baby fathers are not wanting responsibilities for the baby they create. They just want to make a name for themselves without owning the responsibility. They are all in league with all these sexing of the girls. The more girls they can sex, the more girls they can mount, the more kudos they get.' La'ano put in her observation.

'It is the *spark-brus* and the *spak-wara* combination, all caution has been thrown to the winds. This new sick, Aids will soon be upon us.'

Ambaii Urr looked into the rafters. She shook her head and replied with some alarm.

'Apo, Big Mama! No, it is already here. We have had it in the village for a long time. In recent years, we have had seven young people die already. These girls; *Ghutalo, Ghaliho, Siovilo*, all slimmed down and died. *Guminoh, Toneme*, and *Sipuno* had mouth thrush and they too died of starvation. That young man, *Hulo* had that ulcer on the leg that grew and grew, and it downed him. Three of our young men now are showing the same signs that these seven had shown.'

'Rather than going to the hospital, they continue to seek out the medicine man and all the associated stupidity of his *puripuri works* and *lusowaso* with that *bamboo bursting speciality*. And we keep on blaming the *sangumas* for these people dying from this new sick.'

'Gosh', she wondered aloud.

La'ano sat pensive, Ambaii Urr was trying to say in a roundabout way that Josiah was playing with the prospects of contracting AIDS. Was Josiah into it badly? Was he sexing the girls in the village too? She had thought when he was still a child, she had talked to him about girls and on babies but not about sex. It was a taboo for any discussions so they could only make inferences.

She gave the cups of tea she had made to Ambaii Urr and her husband.

'Sorry, we did not come to talk about Aids or the sexual prowess of our teens. We came to ask about your desire to bring on a wife for Josiah. Papa Ave and Mama Heloiseh said something about it in passing. Is it true you want us to gather?'

'Yes, that is right, La'ano wants to drop everything here to speed back to her village, but first she wants to bring on a Mrs Josiah first.'

'Would you stop phrasing that statement like that? You want me to look bad when you put it that way. And let me tell you to your thick head regardless I am dropping you and everybody in between to go back to my village and that spells - I am leaving you.'

'Hey! Hey, we did not come so that you two can get on with your arguments. That is something you two can discuss under your dirty blankets when we are not around.' He joked.

'Yeah, that man of your brother has been saying these types of words these last two days that does not give me peace. He even forgets his football practise on me - never mind me sporting all these blue and black spots. He does not think it is his manly responsibility to be talking bride wealth as a man. He should have a choice of words to state his statements. And for the record, I am a *ghetto* in my own house, I don't share my blanket or his dirty blanket.'

'Now do you have a choice of a Mrs Josiah?' Ambaii Urr asked with a smirk over her revealing blanket statement. They were deviating into unhealthy grounds.

'I have a girl in Siametoka village that one of my cousins think I should consider walking around the bride price for. She thinks this girl is ideal and she has already broached the idea with the girl's parents. The parents say that they want to marry off the girl early so that she does not get into the dilemma the other girls are having.'

'Do you know the parents?'

La'ano mentioned a name.

'Oh, Timothy's daughters; which one of the girls? Timothy has several girls, which one exactly.' Ambaii Urr was from a village that shared borders with this Siametoka village and girls.

'I don't know them, but Ghitume has seen her and says she is a light one with a tattoo on the right biceps.'

'Oh, okay, I think that is the third girl. She is barely out of primary school. She may not have continued onto high school.'

'Yeah, that may be the one. Ghitume said she left in grade eight and if we can get her to be the bride, we will do well for Josiah. We don't want to bring on a wife who has all these sexing savvy.'

'Good, that settled on the choice of the girl.'

Goi looked at Hoveyau.

'Now what is the next immediate thing to do?'

'I think we are knocking that *Lupiye-Tapiye* pig that seems to like gardens; two Mondays from now. We start doing the *tolumo togessa* and collection of contributions for the bride wealth. La'ano here says she has some money. I have not seen any yet but when Papa Ave and Mama Heloiseh were here last, she showed us bundles of sticks that she says are money that she had hidden away. She says she has a good pile of money.'

'I don't understand sticks and piles.' Ambaii Urr interrupted him.

'No, sticks are normal sticks that you tie together to show some value, it is our counting system.'

'One *nakavosa* is a *stick* representing ten-kina.'

'One group of five of these sticks is a *holokena* – a *wing* - fifty kina, two group of them equals to one hundred kinas.'

Then you have a *ghola – mountain or mound,* which is say one hundred kinas. Two *gholas* make up one *gho'* - a *bilum* - two hundred.'

'Five of them make up a *mulise* or a *pile* of money which is one thousand kinas.'

'Any *asapu* or wrap of money has ten pieces in it. If La'ano has a wrap of sticks that would be one *asapu.* '

'Oh, you confuse me. All these *nakavosa* and *sticks, holokena* and *wings, ghola* and *mounds, gho'* and *bilums, mulise* and *piles,* why don't you people use modern counting.'

'We had our own counting system using our hands and feet and other things. We went one, two, five, ten, twenty, fifty, hundred, two hundred and then thousands. We had for fifty like we had one wrap of a hand, or two wings is equal to one hundred kina.'

'It is still confusing to me. What does an *asapu* or bundle have to do with the counting ... oh never mind, I guess I may have to learn all these sometime.'

'Yeah, it was confusing all alright when your sister here gave us a bundle of sticks and bottle top caps to say it was money with no money. She kept her stick records using that counting system.'

Hoveyau piped in further. 'Just now, we are looking at a bundle of strung sticks to remember pigs that we took around and killed to assist at people's problems.'

'I cannot follow with that, but your sister can, and she is reading off people's name that she associates with each stick.'

Ambaii Urr and her husband looked at each other. La'ano had been investing in the village affairs for a day like this when she could call on all these debts.

'My *tambu,* I am finding that all too intriguing to say the least, where I have very little input in all of these. All we have are these stick items and I have not seen the money, nor do I know where she got that money from.' Hoveyau quipped knowing it was going to get a bad reaction.

La'ano became angry at the aspersion.

'Do you want to say something about me? Are you implying that I got these monies by selling myself? If you are implying that I am a *pamuk*. The amount of money that I put forth would mean that I would be the most sexed and talked about woman in this village. Don't you dare think that - as yours is shrivelled up that I may be forced to go out there looking for this sex thing?'

'Iimpph', Hoveyau forced down his anger. It wasn't going as he intended. He did not want his ineptitude in the house broadcasted.

'Now the bag of lazy bones wants to have a say. If we had it your way, I would not have any of these *piles* and *sticks*. I have always been on my own yesterday and all my marriage life here without you in this bed and village and will be on my own tomorrow when I go back home. I will lose nothing by leaving you. So, if you will, we have guests and an agenda. We'll stick to the agenda and see to our guests.'

'Oi, oi', Goi cut in. 'Thank you for letting us know of your hanky pankies under your dirty blankets', he smirked.

La'ano was not having it. 'Let me repeat myself. My side of your brother's dirty blanket is still dirty new. He does his hanky panky if any at all, up at the *kandis* places.'

Goi looked at his brother. He had his own thinking and wanted to say something, but he buttoned up.

'Yeah, that brother of yours, the laziest man in the village wants to know where these monies came from. He wants to believe that I brought out all these monies from a side hustle business marketing and selling of myself, ha.'

'I am going to have the last laugh.'

'This is his house and place. He is the man of the house and if he has anything, I am suggesting something that will be all to give him kudos – something that will give him big name. He should bring his material wealth out. He is a *yomba tree* in the village with an *itehetu* name and is always at the *kandis* like a moneyed man. If he has something to bring out, then he should say so. If not, he might as well stand at the back and crawl under the beds - into the *sepeku* that is where he should find his station in life.'

'I started hoarding money from a long time back, in fact a month after I was brought in marriage to this village. He's doubting me like I don't have money.'

She stood up angrily and went to her side of the house. In the bright light of the Coleman, she started going through her battered suitcase.

She then shoved the suitcase to one side and found a slit in the *pitpit* bed. She parted the *pitpit* around it and put her arms through a slit to the ground below. She hovered over it for a few minutes and then pulled out from under the *pitpit* canes, a dusty and dirty used rice bag.

Shaking off the excess dust, she bought it to the front with a stern face and dropped it before Ambaii Urr.

Ambaii Urr looked up with consternation.

When the word got around that La'ano was contemplating putting on a *Tolumo mumu*, the village was rife with gossips and quite a few snippets of sneers and aspersion.

How was La'ano calling for a collection of bride wealth when she was without any money to her name? A lot of bad words were raised about her sitting down all day at the *kandis*. A few jokes were that she would take the cards and add the number on the cards as her contributions.

As it was with La'ano virtually having no garden and with Hoveyau being known as the *kandis yomba post*, there was a belief that the two couple would not have the ability to put up the main start-up money to begin the pooling of the bride wealth or any pigs for the bride price. It was a known fact that Hoveyau was the laziest, and La'ano was the gambling queen. He was the *yar yomba* and she spent considerable time twenty-four seven at the *kandis* place. These aspersions did not mention her ability to provide pigs for anybody in the village when it would be desperately needed.

It was also thrown around as a jeer that perhaps La'ano was forcing the issue as a revenge for Hoveyau bashing her up in public. It was customary that Hoveyau would be supported by his brothers who were to come up with the core of the contributions. Perhaps La'ano was relying on this customary practise and asking the family and others to bring on a wife for Josiah.

Ambaii looked again and again at La'ano. What was the meaning of pulling out a bedraggled bag before her?

Goi was incredulous in his disbelief. The mere sight of the dusty old rotting bag pulled from under the woman's bed was some messaging that evoked of mystery and intrigue. What was in the bag? He was witnessing something abnormal.

He hoped there would be no disappointment.

'Woman, that's an extra ordinary show. What is it all for?'

'This man, this lazy husband of mine doubts my saving ability. He has all these land and muscles and bones like those big elephants in the books, but he hardly put it to productive use. Each morning, he gets up and goes looking for a people to hold conversation and tell stories like he was a small boy, and it leads to people gathering and to start gambling. Where there is a *kandis*, he is there like a *Yomba fence posts*, ramrod straight. He has been doing that from the first day I came here as his wife and now he is all salt and pepper – nearly becoming a grandfather.'

'Every day he asks me for money like I am a working-class girl. It never had entered his two peanut sized brain to ask me where I got my money in the first place. He assumes that I just have the money.

And at all the talks in the village, I have given him good money to contribute towards all these gatherings. I prop him up so that he gets all the kudos. People know the money that are *dropped* are for and in his name. I earn this monies from gambling around these *kandis*. I have no business to prop up his name but time and time again, I do it because it must be done. Otherwise, he and I will be fit to be people who should live way at the backsides, near to the *arere* and *sepeku*.'

'I know I cannot end the day without gambling, and I have my fair share of sitting in the *kandis*. But I always make it my business to go to the *kandis* place with ten kinas. I play with my first five kina and if I don't win, I quit that *kandis* and look for another *kandis*. I must win enough to buy *kaukau* for my pigs and if I am lucky, some more. I try to leave the *kandis* with my ten kina and extra five for the *kaukau*. The ten kina I use that for the other day. If I find Hoveyau there in the same place, I don't join in the group like what other couples do. I play in another area so that I don't have to share any of my wins with him. In that way at least I have some money, not plenty but a little bit enough for my pigs and me.'

'The *kaukau* money for the pigs is always a priority for me. When I have more than fifteen kinas, and if I am lucky, I try to make it to twenty kina that I win, apart from my ten-kina *spia money*, then I quit playing for the day. That twenty kina I split in two, one for the *abus* and the pigs *kaukau* for the day and the other ten goes into that bag you have before you.'

'Both of us stay around the *kandis* every day so if the man has any, he will add to that money.'

'*Apo, Meri Simbu,* you count what is inside the bag and take it with you for safekeeping for the time being. You keep it for that *tolumo togessa* gathering. I am serious and the money that you find inside there will be the spine for the pooling together.'

'*Eh, ugh,* what!' Ambaii stammered.

'*Oi,* thank you, *Seghané.* I don't feel comfortable about your suggestion that you want me to take care of what's inside this bag. We all know that you have one garden, a small coffee garden that our father planted. Hoveyau has taken control over it, and we know and say, you twos gamble too much. Yet we also know that you look after pigs and slaughter them for our benefit in the village. I always wondered how you could gamble and still raise good pigs. We assumed that you had some *puripuri* for looking after pigs, but it is you, feeding them every day from the money that you win to buy *kaukau* with. You can afford to care for them with such cleverness.'

Hoveyau had his back turned as he knew he was going to be shamed.

Goi took the bag and shook off the dust. He and all his brothers had earlier today discussed the issue and had been doubtful of her, whether there was actual cash attached to the bundle of sticks that she had brandished before Papa Ave, Mama Heloiseh, Uncle Tota and Aunty Avise.

Ambaii found another cut bag and after shaking off the dust on it, she laid it out as a bed of it.

Goi then held up the end of the old rice bag and sneezing off the dust that had got into his face, he tipped the contents of the bag down on the bed of flour bag.

He gave a low whistle.

The notes all tumbled down. It was quite a sum. Wads of twos, fives, tens, a lot of twenties and some fifty-kina notes, very crisp and new, fell out of the bag.

Ambaii looked from the bag to La'ano and mouthed a - how did you get all these moneys?

She waited for the dust to settle and her own stomach to settle before she separated the notes and lined them up in piles in their denominations. She went through each pile and made a wad of each ten notes and folded them like they do in the banks. When she was finished, she looked at La'ano who was wearing a frowning face.

'Is this *a pile, a mulise?*'

'*Apo*, there is more than that. I can see some *nakavosa*, a *holokena* and perhaps two *gholas* and a *mulise*.' Goi laughed.

Ambaii Urr pulled up a face at her husband. 'There you go, you people want to be primitives. I like the white people's counting and we learn their counting ways but then okay, I remember that we forget we had our own counting ways too. Yes, thank you, I think I have counted a bit more over two *mulises*.'

'You see these two-kina notes; you have put them in piles of *two sticks* and you have used the bank system of counting to have them in twenty kinas worth. Our village counting would be *one wrap* or *bundle*. A *wrap* or *bundle* always has ten pieces to it. This is *one wrap of ten sticks* and that is *two wings* over there which equals to one hundred kinas.'

'Now you confuse me on that one. I will stick to the new counting ways. think in the bank they put in certain number of notes to make one wad of money. For two kinas, I know they use ten notes to make it twenty kina and ten wads of twos would make it to two hundred kina. I hope it is the same with the others. I had put each denomination notes in the same format so one wad is ten notes.'

'For that hundred it is ten notes and that is different.'

'Yeah, that is correct, if the wad has twenty ten-kina notes that will make it one *bilum* or two hundred kina.'

'Whee, what! Stop confusing me with your counting system.'

She then looked at La'ano. 'Whoa! Now good mama, how did you amass all these money?'

'It was from the year before the drought. We were told there will not be enough food the next year. I had a big pen of eight pigs, and I had to sell off six pigs otherwise the pigs would die of starvation. We negotiated with the primary school Headmaster when they had that party to open the new classroom to buy our pigs. The headmaster and chairman of the Board of Management of the school agreed that we sell these pigs to them at a negotiated price. We undersold them but if they starved, we would not have got any money and we were afraid that I would lose all these pigs.'

'Hoveyau will remember we sold the pigs to the school for the opening of the classroom party. I had sold the pigs for two hundred each. They gave us cash for three pigs and each year for three years the balance. The first batch they gave us, Hoveyau got most of it. He gave me a hundred kina. I don't know what he did with his share of the money. He must have given it to the village at the *kandis*.'

'My hundred is the start to growing these piles. That is when I started that collection.'

'That new fifty-kina note was changed by that coffee buyer Ghutamo when he was drunk and wanted to buy some banana and the seller did not have change so they asked me if I could change it and I changed it. That was years ago.'

Goi cleared his throat.

'*Apo*, we don't have that type of money in our house and it is a great compliment that you have these. Now these brothers can stop doubting you and go ahead with the *tolumo mumu*. Your money will provide the basis or spine to rally the village to do their part, contribute to bring on one of their son's wife.'

'Mama Josh, good mama, *Seghané*, you have turned the tables on my belief in you. I was always critical of you gambling and your spending long hours at the *kandis* instead of working the land. You are fortunate that your garden posts are made from *Yomba tree* and is still as strong as the first day they put it up, but your garden is three quarters bushland, and you make garden on one side.'

'I have always had these bad feelings that you follow your husband in being lazy. I am going to get back my wrong thinking about you. I have also always believed my brother. I now will start to disbelieve him that he cannot work the land.'

'Our family is the biggest land-owning family, we boast about being the *itehetus* and we men in the family, carry on like a cockerel walking around a brood of hens. I and my brothers work our own portion of land and have not looked over our shoulders at our big brother or how he deals with his land. I know his portion is still grassland and he is not doing anything about it. My nephew Josiah needs leadership and direction. This idea of getting his wife will bring him to the land. Thank you.'

'The coffee garden is still the same trees that my father planted, and I can lay claim to it, but we all let Hoveyau control it and you have overseen it. I and my brothers too have been lazy and have planted small plots when we could have big coffee gardens. It is a shame that each of us brothers maintain the garden our parents had. Our father had three boys and four gardens which we all have and still use. You were made a garden on your marriage, but Ambaii and I still have our mother's garden. I have not made a new garden. I know I am lazy too in a way, but I work as the town council's cleaner boy, so I don't have it bad. What little I make we spend most of it in the village.'

'We say we are the richest family because of the land but if the land is not put to productive use, we are as poor as the next family. We, this family should be as rich as our land, but our land is lazing out there and everyday soaking sun like a lazy dog, its tongue out panting for air. If it is still panting for air, then we are useless. You ladies can only work the land as long as we men show interest, and you need direction and assistance. Where that is missing, we cannot blame you for not being productive.'

Hoveyau was feeling like all this talk by his brother was to shame him and he felt ashamed. He bent lower and lower until his back was level with the bed.

'We blame you girls for not being rich. We are rich in land and bones; we brothers are men but are nothing if the manhood that we pride on is not put to good use. We should have big coffee gardens instead we are content with the small ones our father planted. We will pass these same ones to our children and lucky you, you have one boy only. Pilipo has three boys and that is a worry now.'

'Sorry I am saying other things here. It is good that you have these monies, it will be the backbone to what we contribute. I am hearing you have pigs and I also know that you, being a woman who raises pigs well, have been slaughtering pigs for everyone in the village. Are we going to call on the people to repay these pigs debts?'

Hoveyau nodded.

He was looking like the slob he was. All the time, all the decisions of contributing a pig to each village event was done by La'ano. He had passed over that responsibility to her and while he was named as the pig owner, it was her pig, and she was right in calling on these debts. He wanted to say something, and he tried to clear his throat but the phlegm that was there stuck fast. It took a while for him to forcefully dislodge it with hard coughing from the throat and then he could add his bit.

'I think that we have slaughtered a lot of pigs for events in the village and for all manner of people, both family and otherwise. We will start tomorrow sending word to all those that owe us a pig that at the *tolumo gathering* and *mumu* they will have to pledge us a pig in repayment of their pig debt. We will try to size up those pigs. We were in fact in heated discussion before you two arrived. La'ano if you can please bring out those sticks and tell these two about them.'

'It is late, and you don't want me to bore them to sleep recounting them. Continue with what you remember from what I said earlier before they arrived.

'There are ten that we can immediately ask to repay as those were new *dinaus* she made. The rest are for family obligations and a few *dinaus* that we repaid.'

Goi looked up La'ano with new respect. 'That is good, but I don't want to know the details about La'ano's pig killing debts. It is best that you two should be the only one to know about it. Otherwise, I will force reluctant people to bring a pig in settlement and not be popular for that. I will be shaming some people who would have no pigs or the money to go out and buy a pig.'

'*Apo*, you two good people, we will take care of this bag of money. For the pig debts, I suggest you engage intermediaries. These intermediaries must be neutral so as not to forcefully demand the repayment. Our custom is such that if a person can be able to repay now and if he has the means, he can elect to do so now. If he does not, then that will be done some other time, and we will not make the person owing us the pig feel bad. That person however must be in the village to contribute in other ways. You don't want them going on a trip during these times or we will be short of people in the village.'

'Ah, thank you.' Ambaii thanked La'ano for another cup of tea.

'We have nothing to contribute.' Goi added. 'In our discussions earlier today, Papa Ave and I think we will need ten dead and *mumued* pigs on *kaka stretchers* and ten live ones for the *stakes*. Between us, the four brothers will come up with seven pigs excluding the head pig and side pigs that you La'ano will slaughter. That is seven pigs that will go on the *kaka-stretcher*. So, when you call in the debts, it is to fill those gaps. We will need thirteen more pigs.'

La'ano interrupted. 'We have that castrated boar that will be the head-pig for the bride's mother and some other that are near in size to that boar. Two of these will go to the *stakes* as they are not big enough.'

'We are not counting the small ones that the villagers will kill to feed themselves and their children during these times. You must be careful that they don't include those ones in the number of pigs for the bride wealth or you will be starting new debts for Josiah to take on. He should come into marriage with a little debt but not plentiful to swamp him under.'

'Mama Josh, you have knocked the breadth out of me.' Ambaii Urr uttered. 'I am still going to ask how you can amass all these monies. Lucky you that Hoveyau does not check your side of the house. There are some men who do that – check the side of the woman's house including going through women's undergarments and panties. Think how they would feel if they stuck their hands into our used pads. I leave mine, the ones that I remove during the daytime there and dispose of it in the night.' She rolled her eyes up into the rafters of the house.

'Golly jolly, *U-Lala*, think how the man will react to that.'

La'ano laughed. 'I think Hoveyau did that once when we were newly married, and it sort of frightened him away from this side of the house. It was one coffee season and I had won heaps from the *kandis* game. He was looking to steal from that heap. We'll talk about that later at some other time.' The two ladies chuckled and laughed.

'You think that will be one good story to tell, oh,' Hoveyau said lamely as he sipped at his tepid tea.

After Goi had rewrapped the money, two thousand kina - and handed it over to his wife. He refilled back a few residue notes and handed the bag back to La'ano.

She accepted the bag and said a jaw dropper.

'Eh, thank you, now I can feel a bit freer to go long places. I was scared somebody would break into my house and dig up my bag, but you have all of what was usually in it. It kept me a prisoner in and around the village for too long.'

'I still cannot fathom how you can hoard all these monies and still cry-poor-me all along these times.'

'Like I just said I won some big money during the coffee season in my second year of marriage. That money, and any money afterwards, I gave to someone to take care of it for me. I will draw on that money and that is my private money. I will spend it anyhow and anyway that I want to, and I don't want to be accused that I got it from *pamuking* around.'

'Who's saying you *pamuking* around?' Hoveyau tried to put in a defence for himself. The notion that his wife still had some more money somewhere sent shock waves through him.

Ambaii too was shocked. Her cry-me-poor sister-in-law was saying she is richer than she was putting out to be. It was incredulous that La'ano has hoarded more money elsewhere.

'Eh, you think I went *pamuking* to bring all these monies.'

'You look at the notes, some are very old. The very first day I married into this village to your brother and at my first *kandis*, I won thirty kina. I held back twenty kina and hid that ten kina as it was a very crisp note that the coffee buyer gave to someone. They ended up gambling this and it came into my possession. I tucked this away and every time I started adding to this one note, ten kina at a time. At the end of that first year, I had saved four hundred kina but at *krisimasi*, I bought things for my dead baby using two hundred of that. When I should be crying for my baby, instead, I cried for that two hundred kina and since then have not put my hands into the savings again. And oh, I still have that first ten-kina note.'

She moved to her clothes pile and from inside it, she took out several bags and investigated one of the very recesses of the bag and pulled an old Cinderella story book, in the middle of the book was a crisp ten kina note whose blue colour was still crisp clean from being hidden away for a long time but the whites of it had taken on a calico hue.

'Now if all the brothers are thinking that I am a *pamuking* one, they have my thank yous. Now that I am an old stuck-up woman, you think otherwise of me and going forward, these brothers of yours must know that I will be doing it on the side.'

Ambaii Urr rolled her eyes.

'It is true that a lot of young women have clandestine lovers on the side for money or otherwise and I can name names for you of people from the village, but I might get into trouble now.' Ambaii added her take on the many rumours of illicit affairs that ran freely in the village.

'You know I gamble and spent time at the *kandis,* but it is enough time to earn enough to buy *kaukau* for the pigs and if I am a lucky to win a bit more, then it is saved. I have a *hauspik* with pigs and no garden to feed them, so I gamble now. You brothers will go on doubting me, good for you people, tomorrow, the bride comes, tomorrow, this old woman goes back to her village.'

'Ha ha ha, good one.' Ambaii Urr cut in with a big laugh. 'The men should have bought us chastity belts they can lock our things and keep the key with them. It is all lies that they want to believe as true. My sister, these men can believe what they want. Tomorrow the bride come, tomorrow we go.'

'Now you two ladies stop it. Say something good to end the good night. We just had a night where it was something for a *ganine whoop* to be had but it is the middle of the night, and I cannot say the *ganine*.'

'My blood was warm and now you two say something that is making my blood go cold.' Goi registered his displeasure that this *pamuking* talk was going to derail the night.

He forgot that he was the one that started the doubting story. And he was however told from reliable sources that one of their wives had a clandestine lover on the side. It was a long shot that he was thinking it was La'ano, but he could be wrong. It was best unsaid and there was no need yet to put the wives under scrutiny.

'Ambaii, secure that money properly and let's be going. We don't want to sour the night.'

'Okay, no, it is going sour because you asked for it.'

Looking at La'ano and to Hoveyau, Goi tempered his growing annoyance.

'Thank you for having us. I think Ambaii confirms that amount she now holds at *two piles* or *mulises* and we can now plan for the first *mumu* for the *tolumo togessa*. The *mumu* will take place on the day after tomorrow and we will rotate the gatherings between this house and with Mama Heloiseh's house. We will hold these *togessa gathering* for five nights and on the sixth night thereafter take out the bride wealth for its first walk to that bride of your choice.'

'Mama La'ano, *Seghané*, I now speak for Ambaii and me. We have nothing at this time of the year and may not come good. We will see how we pan out in the week. The first night is the family's night. That is the time we the family will come to the front and centre. We will see if the talk of us being the village's rich family is going to be true.'

'Tomorrow night, Papa Ave and I will come over. Pilipo is in Lae now with his *kaukau* and he may return in a couple of day. He plants *kaukau* at his wife's place to sell. Like we don't have land and he works his wife's land to make a garden.'

'He went to his wife's land because of you lot. You brothers argue with each over bush land that you cannot even want to work.' Ambaii interjected.

'When I tried to clear that *pitpit bush* land after the bush fire, Mama Heloiseh, and you, Hoveyau argued with me. When Pilipo cleared that *kunai patch* at Namasu, Goi said no - for the *kunai grass*. He wanted to build a house and he would need the kunai for his roof, so Pilipo ends up with a garden at his wife's place and you complain about him going to Lae. You boys have your heads screwed on wrong. You could cooperate and work together, and big things will come our way but you all grumble and get in each other's way. I hope this *bridal tolumo* will open your eyes and your children should learn some lessons from this.'

'Come on, let us go. All these talks are making me say things that I should not be saying. Sister girl, La'ano. This is an uncomfortable area of talk for us women married into this family, and I hope you don't mind my saying so.'

'My sister, I think we are waiting for someone to talk to us, but nobody will. We keep on shoving it into the villagers here and there that we are the *itehetu*, the original people, the *Atamu ko Evako* - Adams and Eves of the village and will not take any advice from these people here. We, in doing so, are self-destructing our own family.'

'That is an unfortunate chapter of our family life. We can discuss that sometime. Tonight, we came to confirm things and then we get more - to know you have the *iye nakavosa* - pig sticks and to select our emissaries for talking to whichever people so that your debts are put properly to people's ears. We don't want them to feel like we are hounding them for the repayment of the pigs. We still have a long way to go.'

As they stood up to leave, soft light knocks on the door disturbed them. This was followed by a low whine from a girl or woman and harsh sultry talk between some people.

La'ano looked up to Goi. Goi looked to Hoveyau, and all looked at Ambaii. Ambaii was the one nearest to the door. She stood aside and moved closer to La'ano who was furthest from the door.

'Now who is there?'

A murmur and grumble followed from outside and through the thick of it, Goi recognised his nephew's voice. It was Pilipo's son Robin. He went and opened the door.

Robin sheepishly staggered in dragging a young lady by the *bilum*. The end of the *bilum* was wrung up tight around the neck of the lass.

He brought her to the women's side and sat her at the end of the *pitpit* bed. He then looked up at Hoveyau and Goi.

'Daddy', he slurred and stuttered. 'Daddy, I've come home with a woman. This, this girl is Ateyo.'

Goi had his heart in his throat. La'ano and Ambaii looked at each other. They were now put on the spot with a new prospective daughter in law. Another one where again bride wealth would have to follow suit.

However, La'ano turned her back on the group.

La'ano had immediately recognised and was horrified that this young lady until recently was living in marriage to her nephew in her maiden village. That was some two weeks back when she went for that day trip for the *mumu* for one of her nephews. She had seen this lady there and was told she was the wife of a particular nephew. Now, either she was kidnapped from that relationship, or she had left the relationship and had gone back to her village and then to come with this young man Robin in a new relationship.

The young lady too had realised that she had seen La'ano at her last village and was in the most embarrassing situation of her life. If she could have been blushing, she would have been literally red. She assumed that they were going to someone else's house, but they had come to the house of the aunt of the last boy that she had gone into marriage.

Ambaii read the body language of La'ano, and she kicked her maternal instincts.

'Young man, we are just about to leave, and you've happened upon us. Why don't we go to our house? We have finished eating here a long time ago and there is no food. However, we left a pot on in our house and if you will, we can go up.'

4

TOLUMO TOGESSA
– GATHERING TO POOL MONEY

But as she said it, the young man rolled back on the bed and fell into a slumber.

The young lady whispered. 'He was drinking when he pulled me from the market in town and brought me along, and we spent the afternoon at the black market and darts game up the road.'

Goi spoke to her. 'Let him sleep. He is in his house. You, young lady, come with us and we'll put you up for the night.'

He led the way out with the Coleman lamp and the young girl followed, relieved that she was not going to spend a rather terse night in the house with La'ano or explain herself why she was now in a new relationship with Robin.

Ambaii followed quickly after Goi and the young lady. She was in a lot of thought. We are discussing bringing on a wife for one boy and the next one brings a woman. It will be now a competing thing between brothers, and this will stretch their small resource.

La'ano shut the door and immediately challenged her husband about the conjecture of her *pamuking* to have hoarded such a sizeable sum of money.

'Eh, you tell me again, where do you think I got all these monies from. Ah, you tried calling me a *pamuk*. Ahh, did someone tell you that I was marketing myself.'

Hoveyau had however tucked himself into his old blanket was not going to be drawn into any argument.

La'ano rambled on but then stopped when she realised that she was not going to get an answer and secondly, she now had a nephew to worry about.

She lifted Robin's feet onto the bed, put a pillow under his head and then covered him with her tiger blanket. She then found a spot near to the fireplace with her thin bed sheet. She kept the fire going and waited for the cold of the morning. When it came about, she put on more firewood and then moved onto her bare bed. The heat of the fire kept the morning cold outside.

The village was now gearing up early for the nights to start when they will pool their resources together in making contributions towards and for the bride wealth.

A cluster of laughing noises woke La'ano. A thump of noises followed the falling of firewood timber. There was loud shrills and hoops as a cheeky voice tried to put in some humour.

'Eat that bad side of a pig's thing. You're throwing the fire on top of me.'

The aspersion in the voice and tone of the alarm made the men go into overdrive.

La'ano opened the door. She looked up into a group of young men who jostled to say the first word to her.

'Have you been cuddling that old man of yours, Hoveyau? Stop keeping him in bed. He should be out here early in the morning to bring these wood in.'

She looked on sheepishly and thanked the men vigorously. She knew where the pun was directed to. It was to the man that she was married to. The village boys were coming to her for help because they knew that La'ano was the instigator of the events that were going to unfold. This level of keenness was going to be hard to bring about if it was asked for by the men.

'Thank you all very much. If I knew there was going to be a work party this morning, I could have woken up early to make sure the teapot was on the fire. I will put that on if you will all wait.' She looked for her neighbour's daughter.

'Small girl, can I ask you to see if Keko is cooking scones for the morning.'

She replied, 'He was turning the flour when I went to fetch water from the stream. He may be cooking flour ball now.'

'Eh, good girl, go see him and ask him to give me five-kina worth of scones.'

She sent the girl along with the money and made fire. She realised that Robin had also left early in the morning.

She had her biggest pot full of water on the fire and was checking to see if she had enough sugar when Ambaii came in through the door.

'Sister Girl, morning. I had a bad night and came to talk to you about Robin. And I also brought you our sugar packet. Our father organised the boys yesterday to bring the firewood for tomorrow and I knew that we had used up your sugar last night.'

'*Apo*, right girl, I was in fact checking for that sugar packet. Those men must have left at predawn to get that firewood from *Turuku*. I had a coffee packet hidden away for tomorrow night, but I will break it for those men. They must be ravishing hungry too.'

'Oh, I also put in another five-kina worth of scones so old Keko is getting that ready.'

'Thank you, last night I gave my back to the young Ateyo lady that Robin brought along. She is a married woman. She is married to my nephew in my village. Now I got two nephews in two different villages and a woman between them. That's some nice situation for me.'

'I read your body language and so asked her if there was something. She said she had been until two weeks ago living in your village in marriage to your cousin's son. The lady admitted recognising you. She said she knew you were married here but didn't know Robin was your family.'

'She must have left the house in the wee hours of the morning as she was not in her bed when I woke up and I woke up very early to get our father to go with this firewood party.'

'Robin too was gone by the time I woke up so they may be a pair somewhere or she has gone back to her village. Ateyo is a married woman and Robin really is asking for trouble.' La'ano replied to her *wan marit*.

As they spoke, however Robin came in through the door. He went and sat by the fire.

'Eh, Ma, I brought a woman here last night. Do you know what happened to her?'

'*Apo*', Ambaii looked at him. 'One, we were happy that you brought a woman. Two, we were crooked that you were very drunk and lucky you, none of the other men of the village thought of stealing your woman but more importantly, she was a married woman to your mother La'ano's nephew so now La'ano is having a fit. How is this happening?'

'I don't know. Ma, I am sorry. I did not mean to cause you any trouble. This lady, I smiled to her at the market in town, she smiled back at me, and I told her not to go anywhere. She stayed with me while I threw darts at the market dart board games. I was already drunk then from the bottles that I had won shooting darts. We then left town to come to Trikona for some more dart games and I don't remember much after that. And for her being married I don't know. She was in school when I was at school. I had one time protected them when there was a fight amongst several boys from our side and their side. Our boys were targeting everyone including girls who hailed from across the Asaro River. She remembered me from that incident. So, I recognised her at the marketplace, and I smiled, she smiled back, we pair, and we came here. Where she was before that I have no idea.'

'Oh, Oh! She was living in marriage to my nephew back in my village. I think she must have been in that relationship for some five or six months.'

'Now my other nephew from this village has the same woman in tow. I have two nephews and the one same woman. I am not saying anything, and I don't want to be involved.'

Robin kept his head to the ground.

'Ma, I am very sorry. But where is she now. I wake up here and she is not here.'

'You came in and fell down dead asleep.' Ambaii replied. 'We let you sleep here, and your father and I took her with us, but I don't know if she slept in our house. She wasn't in bed when I woke up and I woke up very early.'

'Our suggestion is that you forget the woman. She is a married one. Just keep an eye open in case her husband comes looking for her. I am sure La'ano is going to pretend that she knows nothing about it and will not talk to her nephew from her village.'

'*Apo*, my son, if you wanted to bring a woman to my house, you should have done your research. One nephew cannot steal another nephew's wife and bring her to my house. What would that make of me? I would be in trouble with my nephew and his kin from over in my maiden village and with my nephew and his kin in my marital village. You put me in the most awkward situation.'

Robin's head went lower and lower as the enormity of his actions dug into his head. He then stood up abruptly and left to go outside. He must have been troubled that he was bringing trouble into the village and especially when there was a thing going on for his cousin. La'ano put a good portion of ground coffee into the pot. She was not going to make individual cups for the working party from the sachet of instant coffee. The small girl had delivered the scones from Keko. La'ano asked her to stay on for a few minutes to assist her with taking the cups of coffee out to the men.

She put the scones in her only bowl and in another battered saucepan, she collected her motley collection of cups, most of them with no handles and a few chipped ones. She asked the small girl to take out the cut bag to make a bed of mat and after putting away some scones for themselves and black coffee in the few good cups, they brought out the pot to the jovial men who had a fire going over the still-ground-covered *mumu* hole.

The men had new vigour and had found some merry moment that sent reverberating laughter around the village.

Hoveyau cleared his eyes. This was one of the rare mornings that he slept in. Normally he would be up there on the road around the time when children would be going to the creek to wash to go to school. He sheepishly walked out to the milieu of men clearing out the *mumu* hole for tomorrow.

His brother Papa Ave was there, and he was down in the *mumu* pit removing stones out of it. He was also in a jovial mood, laughing away as he threw up the excavated *mumu* stones.

'You should be up doing this. Why do strangers have to be here first to do our work for us? Your angry wife was up a long time before you so whom were you hugging inside that old blanket of yours.' He rebuked his brother with some glint in his eyes.

'*Egghe*, I am sorry. I am usually the first man to wake up on this side of the village but today I found it not easy waking up. We had visitors who visited late with us last night so it is the combination of the last two nights that might have knocked me out.'

Papa Ave looked up to his brother with his mouth agape.

He was glad that his brother did not mention their nephew's jaunt in the night. It was not going to be news that would be received well and it will bring unnecessary stress to the village. Secondly, as the couple were seen in public at Trikona there was a possibility that there may be a challenge from the husband. It was unfortunate that the lady was married to La'ano's nephew *Tomatutu*.

Papa Ave paused midway and asked for a cup of coffee. He accepted one that was proffered to him and as he did so, he looked up the length of the village. There was an expectation that Ateyo's husband - *Tomatutu* and or his people would force themselves on the village for the wrong done by Robin.

A man does not steal a married woman for free. There are repercussions, probably a raiding fight and that *Tomatutu* and his village will be emboldened by the fact their daughter La'ano is married here.

Young people do things without thinking too much about the consequences. This may be one such day when there will be many bruised bodies if they are not careful and take precautions to be ready for any intrusion into the village.

He stood and got out of the *mumu* pit. Another man moved in to continue what he had been doing. Papa Ave sidled up to his brother and in a hushed voice enquired about Robin.

Hoveyau cast eyes around the jostling men and boys and replied in a hushed voice.

'He brought that woman in and then collapsed in a sleep. The lady went out with Goi and Ambaii. I am not sure what happened this morning as Robin is not in bed.'

Papa Ave showed some anxiety. 'Just keep your eyes on the village road. I am sure *Tomatutu* will be here seeking revenge for someone stealing his wife.'

'I overhead La'ano and Ambaii asking Robin how he brought the woman. He just said something about her staying with or near to him in town yesterday and then coming with him to the village. I think it was just one chance encounter and stealing of the woman afterwards.'

Hoveyau was trying hard not to show his apprehension.

'Do we tell the village?'

'I know we are trying to do something else, and we have this incident cast onto us. But it is still within the family and these villagers will not feel too enthused about attending to problems engulfing two different boys from the same family.'

'Well, I don't see Robin here and he may have gone looking for this woman. Her village is further along the road and the husband is La'ano's nephew, the son of her cousin.'

'Boy, he will be mad, and he will come here knowing that this will be no strange village.'

'The boy is not going to hesitate to come to this village. He has relations here. I might as well inform the boys to be ready,' Hoveyau intoned.

Papa Ave did not want to involve the village boys.

'No, tell them that they watch only and try not to be involved in it. If there is going to be any fighting, it is Robin's own, and he will have to face up to it.'

Hoveyau coughed to get the attention of the boys.

'Young men, you all should be on a lookout as one of you brought in a married woman last night. It is not a thing we normally do but when we do, we stir up a hornet's nest. The husband and his family will come looking for her.'

'I will not say any more than that. Just spread the word to all the young men. ....and you young men, *Seliné ne ve*, I will say thank you, we can rely on you.'

Before the men could throw in a ribald comment or make challenging statements, he looked around for his son. 'There, Mamu, can you go split wood for your mother.'

'And Mamu, there is a pot of *kaukau* on the fire. Your mother has that on the fire too. If any of these young men are still hungry, they can go with you to help themselves. Get these young men into the house and they can have it.'

Another of the young men looked up to the mountains. The morning was going to be clear.

'When the sun is up there, indicating the a spot on the many casuarina trees, we'll fire the stones. It is a pig *mumu* and you wait until the pig is slaughtered and cleaned. It is hard work, and you wait for the men to complete operating on the pig and the women to clean out the innards. We then light the fire to the stones. In this way the stones are at their maximum heat when the *mumu* is started.'

'Uncle,' one of the small boys asked him. 'When we want to make a *mumu*, the men fire the stones as soon as they can, and the women scramble to get their baskets ready for the *mumu*. In this case you want the pigs slaughtered first and then you want us to fire the stones. Why is that?'

He looked down at the young voice. He was irritated that such a question should be asked. He was slow to answer, and another elderly person answered for him.

'Oh, young man, to kill a pig and operate it is hard work and besides the ladies must clean and dress the intestines. All these takes time and if we fire the stones early, we then must wait for the ladies working on the intestines. Most women also take their time to ready their basket of food so we try to make sure that they are all here before we can cover the *mumu*. The heated stones will start losing the heat that they will retain and not produce the necessary steam to cook all these things in the *mumu* mound. We must wait for all those cleaning to be done and in the meantime the stones go cold resulting in uncooked food. Now if the pig is prepared before the mumu is fired, then we can have very hot stones to make a good *mumu*. That should answer your question. Now if you will run along that will be just fine.'

The small boy pouted a thank you and ran off. Adults did crazy things; he must have been thinking.

'Eh, you stop talking to children, their parents should be teaching them these.'

'Some of you parents only produce them and teach them to be around the *kandis* games all day. You are teaching children to be lazy people. You leave the teaching of quality village life up to these children themselves. It is a disaster in the making. How will the children learn to live in the village when the only learning we are giving them is to stand around the *kandis* place.'

Later as the morning drew on, *Sisi-Vena* came by with a bundle of banana leaves which she deposited beside the fired-up stones. She was followed by her husband Pilipo with the biggest bunches of cooking banana. He stood up the bananas beside the leaves with some gusto and flourish. He was going to impress people and he did it with some effect. He stood beside the bananas for those recording it in the recess of their brain for mention later. A lot of praiseworthy words were thrown his way. These cooking '*penne*' banana, were indicative of a person who was a gardener.

It was said that if a knife or spade said, '*daddy to a person*', the results were bountiful. If a man did not know what side of the bush knife was sharp or how deep to dig with a spade, he was forever a *ghohove*, a poor man.

A voice piped up to the beaming Pilipo, '*Oho, Seghané*, this is a man to whom '*the soil says daddy*'.

Hoveyau and his brothers literally lived these sayings. The spades and knives called Pilipo and Sisi-Vena their parents whilst Hoveyau – a *ghohove* who hardly knew what a bush knife looked like was said to be the village busy body and a poor man.

At the village gatherings, the man of means was always the man or woman who knew how to make a garden. At gatherings, cash could be produced and contributed but they mattered little. It was the gardener that produced that was praised endlessly. You still would take the cash to go buy the garden produce. Some of these produce especially cooking bananas are worth up to fifty kina at the market. If two or three people were contributing twenty kina each and a gardener produces one product that would cost three times more, that gardener would get better kudos.

Hoveyau made a mental note they should start recording who contributed and what. How to repay any new debts was going to be his, no, his wife's responsibility. He would mention them later to her.

Greenie, the village herald, and ballad rolled up shouting out urging people to hurry up.

'*Seghané ve*, thank you La'ano, good woman, we give praise to La'ano. There are too many young men here in the village, some with wives and some without. Bringing on a bride with the bride price paid beforehand is a dying practise. All these boys are marrying and separating like they are wearing a *laplap*. These young people are doing it so often that it is tricky trying to remember who is married or not. They are practising something our fathers never did and us, never do also. But this new generation; either our boys are not competitive enough, or their women realise we cannot afford to put out bride price for them and they leave. It is worry that we have this revolving door where young women come and go.'

'*Seghané ve*, La'ano, you are a good woman; you are worried about your son and confront yourself to talking about bringing on a bride for him. At least you are trying to put a stop to this revolving door.'

'We'll make a *mumu* and talk about the bridal contributions later tonight.'

'Hoveyau, good man, has somebody gone to get the pig yet.'

Hoveyau nodded a yes.

Greenie started yodelling.

'*Ohe! Ahe!* I am about to light the stones for the *mumu* now to call in a new woman. Don't you all continue to keep one-eye shut eye? *Ohe! Ahe!*'

A voice from the back of the village shouted a yodelling reply that rolled up the ravine to the village.

'*Oi ii oho!* Thank you, your voice is good music to my ears! I am coming. There now, I am coming with gardens for you. We've being marrying our women without paying for them. *Seghané ve*, tonight we start the paying process for one.'

'*Ohe! Ahe! Ohe! Ahe!*'

'*Seghané ve, Ohe! Ohe!* Please continue to come. *Ohe! Ohe!* You at *Garanaku, Ohe! Ohe!* You still sleeping. The *Laheko* man has come, *Ohe!* You at *Frigano*, you've gone somewhere oh? *Ohe! Ohe! Ahe!*'

The village was a hub of activity with people coming and going.

A squeal of a pig was heard from the end of the village. In a short time later, La'ano pushed through trying to pull the reluctant *Lupiye-Tapiye*. It somehow had a frightful feeling that its hours were numbered. A couple of boys ran to assist her.

'Now hold on', they called to her. One of the boys made a jab with his foot that toppled over the pig on its side. The rest of the boys, making sure that they never got near to the mouth of the pig, grabbed at its front and hind legs.

'One! Two! Three! Up!' They shouted and made a run at the *mumu* place. The village cheered them on. It was fun as they ran the heaving and panting pig. They dropped it at the *mumu* place with much aplomb of heehaws and screams of ecstasy.

'Stupid woman, you should have told us in the first place to go get the pig. We were wasting our young bones in the village, and you had to struggle with the stupid pig, wasting every body's time and holding up the *mumu*. Now, is there another pig? We have energy for two more or three.'

'Now you ask, where were you all in the early morning? Most probably smelling the dirty grass skirts of ladies. When we needed you early, you were not around, when the sun is up, you show your face here and ask what have I being doing? Thank you all very much when I struggled to bring on the tethered pig; you tether up on me with your crass jokes and make shame of my struggles. Ladies' skirts are good for you men, but work is as important and community activities are more so important, so you need to show some muscles early up. Sleeping in the morning is never going to produce a good man. Stop sleeping in; enough of this holding onto your young wives like they are silver and gold. I am sure they are not going to run away.' She smiled through her rebuke towards the young men.

'*Egghe*, stop rubbishing us men with *ladies' skirts*. You are talking to us to show some muscles – yes, thank you, we will knock down this pig. And lady, mind you, you will not stop us hugging our women in the mornings. They are close to our hearts besides someone might steal them during the day but here, hey, bring on the club. We are going to be men.'

'You say you are men, then you should wake up with the roosters like real men. We are now engaging in activities that will bring other people and your *poromahn* – peers, to your village. You will end up feeding them uncooked food and they will ridicule and shame you for it. It will show the world how lazy you are. Here, get it into your thick heads and make it your business to show face at all these community activities with gusto and be attentive to details.'

'*Whee*, woman, stop schooling us. It is in the blood, and you still want to school us.'

'Stop talking to the mama hen, who is still worrying about her brood,' Hoveyau cut in with a wooden club held out to the young men.

'Oh! It is you. You let your wife go to do the dirty work while you cocoon up in your dirty blanket and play with your balls for warmth. Shame on you for letting her go get the pig on her own. Now hold onto the pig while I get the club to it.'

'Watch it, if you talk too much, your skull may get in the way of the pig's skull.'

Hoveyau gave over the club and the young one raised it up to clobber square down onto the skull of the pig. It let out a squeal and fell onto the bed of banana leaves. Its feet started kicking as the last of its life ebbed from it. A dog ran in amongst the kicking leg to get at it and earned the wrath of the men surrounding the clubbed pig.

When the pig had stopped kicking out its legs, it was dragged to the side where there was a bed of fire made from dry bamboo poles burning briskly. The carcass of the pig was trussed over the roaring flames to burn and singe off the pig's hairs. A bucket of water appeared beside the men as they washed and scrubbed off the top skin - the dermis. After a short while, the men were jovial and with a lot of banter had the pig looking very white. They removed the finger hooves of the hands and feet and then heaved it to the butcher boy who sat smug with a cigarette in his mouth. The butcher had been enjoying the boy's banter and banal jokes. There was a lot of swearing that nobody minded. The swearing was not aimed at anyone.

'Hey! Fire the stones, the butcher's gone into the pig.'

A young man stood perplexed as there was already another set of stones being heated.

'Young man! Get out of the way! Go to the side with your perplexed look. That *mumu* over there is the *'hand' mumu*. It is the small one to prepare for the big one. That is the one where that food for the gods and spirits will be cooked to call for their blessings. That is not where you *mumu* such a pig.'

'Eh, take your schooling to the classroom. Don't they teach that in school? If not, you need to stop wasting your time going to school. Oops, sorry, no, continue going to the white man's school but remember here in the village, this is where the real school happens. You learn by doing it.'

'We set fire to this new set of stones prepped ready.'

'Isn't that too late?'

'No, take it easy, we want the butcher boy to operate on the pig. Let him take his time. It is tough work operating on a pig.

If we lit up the stones earlier, by the time the backbone is taken off the skin, the stones would have been all heated up and be smouldering. The longer these stones smoulder without any more new heat, they lose their heat retention just waiting for the butcher boy to finish his task. Not only that, but the poor women also who must clean out the intestines take forever with their tasks too, so it is best to wait until the innards are taken out before the stones are fired.'

'Don't be ridiculous, the pig will sour by the time you put it in the *mumu*,' someone quipped.

'Okay, fire the stones then and since when did you kill a pig and also *mumu-ed* it. Listen to your seniors and one who has killed as many pigs as the fingers on your hands and feet.'

'Eh, like I should know, you want to school me. You could do so without boasting. I hear that the pigs in question were skinny hairy ones that the woman had difficulty finding the real intestines as the worms were as big as the intestines.'

A stone thrown in a crude manner towards him stopped the young one from further aspersions about the type of pig the man cared for. Wormy pigs were not something to boast about, and the villagers knew the type of pigs he cared for, but it was not best said aloud in his face.

This sort of soured the banter and the men drifted on in a muted way.

Some people had the habit of being kill-joys.

'*Ohe! Ohe-ahe!*' Greenie yodelled.

He shouted and heralded that the stones were already being heated. He shouted into the trees and the voice echoed out to the gardens beyond. Those on the fringes in the gardens and for those who elected to live away from the village, the yodelling was a call out to them. And the women came, covered in banana leaves for the *mumu*, on their backs a *bilum* of what they wanted to cook for themselves, their children, and their pigs.

'*Ohe! Ohe! Ahe!* All you good people, there is a *mumu* to take place, come on, roll in, come roll in. *Ohe! Ohe.*' His voice echoed through.

Mama Heloiseh presented him a hot cup of coffee which he accepted with glee.

'*Seghané*, you are bringing this from your house, oh.' And she beamed him a broad smile and showed him the new thermos.

'It is all in there, the hot water, no need for me to go back to my house.'

'Ahh, *Seghané*, the good contraption that the white people bring. You now carry hot water around. Why, we can stop whipping up a fire here and there. Boy, I can never go hungry or chop down my young sugar cane plant for getting to a sweet drink. Thank you, please remember to buy my one when you get into town, good woman, *Seghané*.'

'Don't *Seghané, Seghané me*, the *kongkongs* sell it for a simple twenty kina. You can stop drinking six bottles of beer in exchange for two thermoses.'

'Eh! You are not going to buy me beer and remember I am the only one here in the village that everyone knows that when they hear my voice, there is a gathering. You want to keep your things of value and I am one of those things of value.'

Mama Heloiseh turned to the women around the heating stones and called. 'Eh, girls what if we bought Greenie a thermos?'

'What? Next, he will be asking us to buy his coffee and sugar.' A voice called back from amongst those sitting.

'Seriously, we need him and when you think of it, he is the only herald in the village. It will not be long before we will be borrowing the churches' loud hailer to make all these village announcements. When I think of it, I think this man is value for the village.'

'I am putting out one five kina for him.'

She pulled out a market bag-mat and put her money on the ground with the thermos on it. Her one note paper with some loose coins was enough to kick start the collection. If the women at the *mumu* contributed enough of their loose coins, they could pay for a thermos or two for Greenie.

Those few women who were there searched inside their *bilums* and came up with some more kina notes. Mama Heloiseh had influence in the village and usually any call from her would get an immediate good response. However, this time it was a bit of a struggle to get the twenty-kina needed. It was telling in the reluctance to be contributing their money to buy something for the village drunkard. They knew their money would be wasted.

Greenie took it in his stride. He was the village herald but also a very troublesome drunk who would take on a fight with anybody and anything. The women were sure that the thermos would be the first thing to be hauled at anybody with whom Greenie was fighting.

La'ano had dropped her *bilum* of *kaukau* and was looking inside her purse bilum for her peeler and a ten-kina note fell out. Rather than putting it back she pushed it to Mama Heloiseh's appeal mat. She voiced the village's reluctance.

'He's always breaking beer bottles and having them for breakfast; are you sure he won't do the same with the thermos.'

Mama Heloiseh saw the proffered note and made a small dance for it.

'*Seghané,* La'ano, you've got a *big bilum* and a big heart. We buy him this and he will sing out more for us. Don't worry about his drinking or him breaking the thermos. We are blessed to have him as the village herald. That is important. One thermos is a small price for his free heralding service.'

Papa Ave had come in then and he called out.

'Eh, give me the rest of the coffee in the thermos.'

He looked at the smug Greenie. Greenie nodded his head with some cockiness towards the small bed made of the off-cut bag that Mama Heloiseh had laid out in front of her. The small pile of money was slowly building up.

'*Whii* – you guys trying to market this village herald. We are here because he is the thread that runs through our village. Any herald in any village is treated with respect. Last month he went to Lae to market his *kaukau* and we had that small gathering. Did you guys notice that we sent all those small children here and there trying to get everyone to the village? A herald would have got us together in a jiffy. Don't rubbish Greenie because he is a drunkard fighter. Greenie wants a thermos; Greenie must get a thermos. I will get him one, no, two with your contribution so that he can throw one at me when I next fight him and still have one to make coffee and call the village together.' He punned and winked at Greenie.

'Greenie, you see my wife, she bought these thermoses two years ago and she opened the box to remove its cover this morning. You were the first person to get a drink out of it. It stayed in the house for two years and it will do so for the next two years. So, when we get you one, you make sure that it stays five years, but you can use it right away.'

'*Seghané*, I know you, young ones like the white man's contraptions and crave after it but us old man know nothing of it. If the *big mama* wants me to have one, she will make sure I have one.'

'Eh, Greenie is a man of the village, so is that talk only or are you actually buying him a thermos.' Mama Heloiseh asked her husband.

'I am going to town now, if you give me your collection and tell me which store, I'll buy him two.' At which, Greenie gave a whooping whoop.

'Greenie don't shout your happiness until you get the thermoses. I might not buy you thermos but beer for myself.'

'*Seghané ve*, that will be better still too, and it is close to my heart but whatever you do, buy me the thermos and the beer too. These women and this *big mama* wants me to have a thermos, I think it is a good idea. The women put the money up for the thermos, my son, you put the money for our beer. I am getting old and won't go around looking for firewood to boil the old teapot. I boil it once and carry around hot water. It is definitely a good idea especially out on a cold rainy day.'

He grinned a wink at Papa Ave. 'It is going to rain this afternoon and I will need the thermos and the beer. Now if you will get going or we won't have this *mumu*. Yes, and my thank you to your wife.'

'Yeah, that is the result of going to church camps. She went to this *mama lotu,* and they teach her a few good things including storing hot or cold water, but it is two years gone for her to practise this teaching. It is going to be another two years for her to practise the other things so let us get the thermos now and wait for the other things,' he joked as he shuffled out of reach from his wife.

'Don't joke at the expense of a good woman.'

Greenie rebuked him as Papa Ave ducked the first piece of rubbish, a part of the stem of a banana leaf thrown at him by his wife.

Greenie smiled and put the cup of the now tepid coffee to his mouth. He took a long sip savouring the sweet water to warm his heart. Women were good if they got to your heart. Mama Heloiseh surely did. She was an asset in marriage, and he hoped the new bride would be in the same category.

He took to his heralding with a gusto knowing that he was getting two thermoses never mind they were *kongkong* cheapies.

'*Ohe! Ohe! Ahe!* All you good people, there is a *mumu* to take place, come on, roll in, come roll in. *Ohe! Ohe.*'

'I am coming, I am coming with garden things for you. *Oho, oho!*' a muffled call came back from the end of the village followed by a heap of moving banana leaves.

'Make more calls! Call the others over. *Seghané*, we have been marrying women without putting up a bride price for them. Tonight, the village starts the paying process for one, *ohe ahe,* call out like that for the whole valley to hear. We start with one and perhaps can do the others.'

Seghané ve, ohe ahe! Please come quick, *ohe ahe,* you at *Garanaku,* are you still sleeping oh! The *Laheko Somme* has come with the morning dew. *Ohe ahe Firigano Mahime,* you are gone somewhere, and I am wasting my breath oh! *Ohe, ohe ahe!*

The village was now a hub of activity with people coming and going. A squeal of a pig heralded another woman pulling the leash of her pig. It was also putting up as much resistance as it could. Again, the boys ran at the pig and tackled it. They made as much ruckus as they could as they ran back with the tackled pig screaming murder for the *mumu* place.

Greenie stopped his heralding and gave a mighty whoop.

'*Mita ghoiha kupiiii.*'

La'ano gave the womanly touch to the whoop by screeching the woman accompaniment.

'*Ou-Ou!*' she screeched loud knowing that she had made a call where everyone of her family were going to scratch the bottom of any barrel they'd keep. She knew that they were going to put up their reputation as the *itehetus* and ride the ridicule if they did not step up. But she was glad.

'Thank you, it was Sisi-Vena. She has brought a small pig and is contributing for this *mumu*.' A man acknowledged her.

This was not what they had planned but last night, Sisipulime felt that she had to bring that pig.

5

NAMA LOH – SING SONGS

The pig was slaughtered and operated on in quick time so that the women could take away the innards to clean it at the creek. It was then that preparation for the *mumu* started.

Later in the afternoon when the *mumu* was done each one took their own baskets of *kaukau* away, but the pork was brought to Papa Ave's house. A slight drizzle dampened any more activity for the rest of the evening.

Greenie took his food and his new thermos. He looked up pleased when the three bottles of beer that he was given made noises as he retreated to his house. He was undecided whether to start his drinking them now or to wait till the gathering. He decided if he started now, he would not sing well. He would start midway through the night. He was sure that someone would continue to buy him beer if he sang well.

The sputtering rain fell heavy as the first sound of singing gushed out through the *kunai* eaves and *pitpit* walls of the house. The light from the Coleman lamp lit up the inside of the round house and small smoke was rising slowly through to the pinnacle of the inside of the cone of the round house. One man shouted to another smoking *brus-smoke* to take the rank smoke outside. The man hastily cut off the smoke amidst a grin in reply.

'There are plenty of us here in the house, the smell of your strong smoke is irritating.'

The interruption made the singing pause, and an announcement was done.

'*Seliné ne ve*, thank you for all coming. The house is crowded now. If you must smoke, please remember there are others here who don't like to smoke and will appreciate it if you take your smoking outside. Also tell those sleeping they should be careful not to *kapupu*.'

The people laughed at the silly announcement. How do you tell a sleeping person not to fart?

There were a lot of people now. A head count showed that it was just the neighbours only. Hoveyau and La'ano have not yet come in nor have the two brothers Goi and Pilipo. This first night was slated as the family night for the Solepano family. It was assumed that the rain was holding the family up.

Mama Heloiseh was there first to give *wan marit* support to La'ano and she was busy with the tea pot making tea for those that were there. This was the first. During the week, she was going to go through a lot of cups of tea and sugar. Some nights this was going to be supplemented by sugar canes.

Lucky for La'ano, their elderly neighbour had taken liking to Josiah. Josiah ensued that the old man had fresh water and firewood most days. Now that this gathering was in the name of Josiah, the old man was committing his sugarcane garden to the cause, and he had row and rows of sugar cane bushes. Already he had cut ten bundles for the night. He had promised Josiah two of the rows of sugar cane bushes and that would yield some hefty bundles of good chewing canes.

Mama Heloiseh thanked Josiah for his kindness to the old man. Sugar planting was something that the young generation did not get involve in as it required a lot of attention to grow it properly. The old man's contribution will defray the costs of sugar and tea.

Yesterday La'ano had bought a full bale of sugar a big box of tea and several bottles of instant coffee. While these could go some ways, she was expecting other members of the family to help with a few more packets for the night. She also had put out some fresh coffee beans that she would get her husband to roast and grind if they ran out of the instant coffee. There were enough tea packets, lemon leaves and *mapanuho* plants in case she ran out.

Two young girls were helping in cutting up the *kaukau* into manageable pieces that were to be distributed. Somebody was cutting up the pork into small pieces too. La'ano had asked that one hind leg and the backbone of her pig not be cut up. Sisi-Vena had not made such request for her pig, but it would be best to do the same.

The lull in the rain outside brought the first of other non-family visitors. A person bearing the first bundle of sugar cane pushed his way into the doorway.

'*Seghané ve*; those canes come from a person who works the land. The man of the garden, thank you. Again, a thank you to you all. You have heeded the call early and have come to this first night. *Seghané ve*.'

Greenie was the herald but also was the main balladeer and a composer of songs. He gave praise to the man bearing the bundle of sugar cane. He was also looking for something extraordinary for which he could compose a song. The idea that the young of today were abandoning sugarcane growing was very acute. The man who brought in the cane was one of three old men left who grew good juicy sugar canes. Would they move to substituting crates of coca cola for sugar cane bundles? Further up the mountains where they grew better and juicier sweet sugar canes, they had long replaced this noble tradition with the bottled fizzy drinks. Yeah, but it was not something to compose a song over. Perhaps when the last of these cane growers died, he would compose one.

'Those who don't plant sugar cane, - may your teeth be broken.' The person bearing the bundle jested a reply to Greenie.

'Yes, *Apo* Greenie, we are not planting gardens nowadays, its *kandis*' that we plant, and our food gardens are running away from us. There will be a time when we will buy sugar cane from our neighbours.'

'Yes, all these men and women, their young bones, just wilting away at the *kandis*, we will all die of hunger. Men don't realise that a man is valued by how many sugarcanes he can cut, how many bananas he can bring, how many pigs he can bring and contribute for our troubles and problems; these are values that make a man a man in the village. Instead, we are going down the road where our men will be seen as wimps and village layabouts.'

The conversation was interrupted when Aishi started a song that had all in the house joining in. The ladies' high pitch made the refrain soar up through the thatches of the *kunai* roof. When it ended, the silence left a desire for more of the high pitch tones of the ladies.

'*Oho! Seliné ne ve*, you ladies give these songs life. Sing that stanza again for us please.'

'So, so. …there you go', one of them replied. 'We want to bring another lady to become one of us to this village and we happily join in the process. While we start and there will be some of us who will hide into our own shells for whatever reasons, tonight, let us be merry and show our whole heartedness in this gathering and work.'

'Hear! Hear', another said and burst into the refrain.

A loud voice outside the house announced a presence. '*Seliné ne ve*, those good voices from the good flowers of other villages, all you girls, we wanted such voices, and we married well. Its sweet listening from outside. I stand in the rain and cold outside and your voices warmed my bones and my stomach. Please sing some more.'

'*Seghané ve* for you praising our women. Thank you, *Veramino, Goodman*; your bones standing outside in the rain and cold will not add value to our singing songs of praise. Please join and bring all your voices into the house.'

The door opened to welcome more villagers.

Sisi-Vena brought more cups and a bag of groceries, most probably sugar, coffee, and tea. Her daughter followed with their big pot. Another followed with two canisters full of water.

There were a lot of greetings which were silenced by another song. Aishi sung the first stanza to lead into the song. It was a new song that he sung, and he paused for a while.

'Let me explain that song. I think I did explain this song when I sung it before but let me tell you all. I was in Port Moresby with Pele when there was this helicopter robbery over in the big bank there. There was this helicopter that was going *wiggi-wiggi* and going in circles all over the place at Paga Hill. The robbers had landed on the roof of the bank and were *hands-upping* all the people there. My two daughters, that is Pele's daughter; were selling ice block and they took their eskies and ran here and there, running away from gunfire; so, I composed this song for them. The refrain describes the horrors on their faces going up that Paga Hill, thinking of the peace in their own village Mitega Hill. Their Mitega Hill oozes no such trouble. The girls should have been singing and frolicking in peace and tranquillity here. Yeah, they have their own hill here where it is all laughter and fun and where they would have all the fun of teasing an old man to spear them. They should not get shot at with machine guns.'

'So, let me sing the first stanza and refrain, then you all can join me in when I start the second stanza.'

'*Seghané, Seghané ve*', a chorus exploded when the song ended. 'You have coloured their situation very much in such a colourful song. It is only you who can compose such song with such complimentary verses.'

'Aishi, it warms my heart that you can record such experiences in song. We can retell that story and I am paying you for the right to sing that song. Please sing that song again for me to record it in my heart.'

Pele's bubu pulled out two two-kina notes. 'I buy that song now with these four kina.' He laid out the money notes as a token of payment.

'We can repeat that song during the night and put it to our memory to sing forever. Thank you. Somebody, start another song.'

Aishi looked crossly at his nephew.

'Listen, young man, I am the one who is doing the songs now. Don't tell another person to start their songs. I took over from Greenie just then. It is only two songs and you want to disrupt me and my song leadership.'

With that he started another song, a song where a woman shunned him because he was earlier seen talking to the sister of the woman, the more beautiful one of them. The refrain talked about the beauty of the person and not her face. The women sang with smiles on their faces joining with their alto crescendo again rippling through the roof as more people streamed in. Aishi was selecting good songs to sing tonight. It was going to be a good night.

More praises rang out from someone near to the door thanking another person bringing in more sugar cane bundles.

Mama Heloiseh made more cups of tea and passed that around. It was sweet and she had copied the ingenious *Morobe Waria* method of burning sugar. The big scooping spoon was black from the sugar molluscs that she made. It used less sugar, and the tea was sweet.

The heat coming from the Coleman lamp was beginning to be felt. It was fortunate also that she was heating water from one of the recent comforts in life that her husband had installed for her - a portable gas stove! She had brought it along with her, and it ensured she could make tea for those who mattered in quick time. The rest of the village would wait for the big saucepan that was sitting in the hearth in the middle of the house. The heat and smoke from this fire was making the house intolerable in quick time.

Papa Ave had placed a small coffee table on one side of the pitpit bed and had it covered with a new tablecloth. On it was a new thick exercise book and two cheap biros.

Mama Heloiseh looked throughout the house and seeing nearly all the family were there, nodded to her husband. When the last of the refrain to the song was sung, he held up his hand.

'Thank you, *Seliné ne ve*; my fathers, brothers, sisters, we did a *mumu* today and you all ate the *kaukaus* with the vegetables and the innards of the pig. We asked you all to come over here to talk about bringing to our home a wife for one of our sons. Like all things, the family must talk first before we bring it out to the public in the village.'

'What other stories you would have heard, you put that to one side; it is not the night to talk about these gossips. The reason for the food and songs and this gathering is you may have heard that La'ano wants to bring a wife for his son and we, as necessitated by custom are to help to make sure that happens. La'ano is threatening to go back to her village on account of her husband fighting her and that is her wish and something to talk about later when that happens. We discourage her about that thinking and it is not for any of you to be thinking about it. Instead, we are gathered here to assist her bring home our new daughter-in-law.'

'Women have never gone back to their village once they have come into this village. La'ano dares to try that. You all know that women have gone back to their village and have crawled back, even those that tried to find new husbands have always returned.'

'Yeah, all you men making *puripuri* and *murramurra* magic that casts spells over us women to make us slaves of you men of this village.' A woman interrupted in the laconic voice.

'Eh, which woman dare interrupt me? We make *puripuri* and *murramurras*, wait, the next one we make will ensure that you are like that bird, the *Selemene* that does not have a nest of its own but drifts from one old nest built by some other bird to another old nest by another bird. You won't return but drift from man to man forever until you go mental.'

'*Egghe,* stop making this *tolumo togessa* too serious. It should be a night of fun.' Mama Heloiseh spoke for the women who were taken aback by that response.

'Sorry, sorry, my good wives, let me take back that.'

'My brothers, your good wives are singing well, and their nice voices gives me hope. I think the knowledge that night is going to be a success has gone to my head. Goodman, whose house is three houses away have already been shouting out your praises and just on that praise alone, I have good vibes that our gathering tonight will be a successful one.'

'You all know that this first night is for the family. Our family *will size ourselves up*. The rest of the village we will give them space tomorrow and onwards. So, tonight if other villagers are here, please join us only in the singing and watch this family first try to do its contributions.'

'Now to my family, as a practise I will call each of you men as head of `your household and later we will check with our girls and *ghettos*. You don't have to be ashamed. If you have nothing to contribute, say so. Don't pain yourself to commit yourself when you cannot meet it. We will contribute money, pigs, gardens, time, and labour. The first two are a matter of what you have and gardens and time, a must. The last is compulsory and it is important - this is a time of intense labour, and the family must take a lead in all these activities.'

'Aishi, my good father, sing us a song while I take a drink.'

'Mitaghole veguwo ahalame ilaieh

Gholoueh apa maule ahalame ilai eh

Gholoueh apa maule ahalame ilai eh

Gholoue apa maule.'

It was the *sipaki* song but a good song as even the tiniest of child was soon singing it. They sang the four stanzas with such rancour that as they sang a repeat of it, they made such a loud noise that the cinders hanging from the roof reverberated and broke free to fall brackish dust on all of them.

'There, there, *egghe*, your singing has woken up the spirits and they join us in the singing. Cinders don't fall in big numbers like that. It warms my heart.'

Papa Ave made a bed with a new laplap. He pulled up beside a dirty suitcase that had seen better days.

Another song was started but this time, it was a *Homasi song*, a worship song that sounded like a *dirge*.

Papa Ave opened a dirty suitcase that had been there besides the centre posts and took out a long and night black plume of a Bird of Paradise. He then stuck it into a banana stem and put it out on the *laplap*. Next, he got a necklace of *ghilli-ghilli* shells and laid it in front of the plumes. He pulled out from the bag a *half-moon kina nopeya breastplate* and placed it below the necklace. He looked at Aishi who through the song nodded his approval.

Papa Ave then found two *anama* - arm bands and placed them on the side. Once he had done that, he stood up and reached into the rafters and pulled out a fresh new *nakani* cane. He took pains to clean it and place it over the shells. He looked up and Aishi broke off the *Homasi song* to start another short boisterous song that had everyone joining in.

When the song stopped, he held out his hands up to silence everyone.

'Thank you, Aishi, my good father; what you see in front of you and for you - young ones, this is the bride price that was paid for Te'enike; my sister who is married to that Gahuku man. They put two birds of Paradise plumes, one *Lahone* and one *Musso*. The *Musso*, you see it there. I think uncle Jouwo took the *Lahone*; for the young ones, *Musso* is the black bird with the long tail plumes that you see plentiful of - on the heads of those partaking in the *Simbu singsings*. There are plenty of these birds in the forests surrounding their place. Our mountains are full of *Lahones*.'

'They laid out a head *ghilli-ghilli* amulet and the *nopeya ghatane lulu;* what you call now as the *kina shell* with some *bilas* things; four arms bands - two *anamas* especially for the arms and the other two *hakijes* for the legs that are worn around the calf muscles. The groom's people unfortunately did not have a *geheko,* so they did not put it up as part of the bride price. These two *anama* - arm bands were my share, and the two *hakije* - leg bands went to Pilipo. I don't know what he did with it. These are very old, made from *ghahu* tree fibres and last for a long time if the rats don't get to it.'

'If this was the old times, I would have been a rich man as this *nopeya* or *kina shell* you see here would have bought me three huge boar pigs with tusks fully grown.'

'Te'enike brought us ten live pigs on ropes and a similar number of pigs came dead on *iye kakas* or pig stretchers.'

'Our aim here is to try to come up with something like what our *tambus* did with the bride price for Te'enike. The *kina shell* we must replace obviously with money, the *bilas* things with modern clothes and *bilums* but the pigs, Bird of Paradise feathers remain the same. The rituals too remain the same and we will try to observe these during the coming days.'

'So, what you have is a picture of what we should achieve in the coming days.'

'I have placed the *nakani stick* on the bed and that the gathering tonight and those in the coming days is official now. I now say that I will be the *maus-mahn* for the family and take the lead going forward.'

'Now let me continue and say this. What you give and what you pledge will not be changed. You can improve on it though. I stated out my example. I don't have anything now. If I however in the next three days happen to find something to improve on what I said, then that is something that I can come here and state for all of us. If I have contributed something, I cannot come and get it back. So, by the end of this night if I have contributed ten Kina, come tomorrow, because I want to go to town, I cannot come in and ask for my ten Kina back.'

Greenie interrupted with, 'That is something that is never done so don't think about it. You will be showing your hands - good by contributing and will bring worms to the same hand if you come to take away what little you have given. It is also a way of saying you are a poor *ghohove* person in our society when we should not have one. I remember that it has been always our way to contribute small and big in our troubles and together with the little we contribute, it gets to help our cause.'

'Thank you, papa Greenie, for those sage words. I think we all agree that at the end of the night, what we contribute will be counted and packed away among the women's things so once these monies have *been jumped over*, we will not risk it to ask for any part of our contributions back.'

'Now I am doing all the talking; La'ano, thank you, good woman, our *big mama*, I am giving you space as the sponsor of this idea to bring on a bride for the boy to say something.'

'*Apo*, I have done a lot of talking in the last couple of days. I don't want to say anything more. I think I'll wait till the end of the family contribution and then I might say something. However, it is for you men to take control of this. I will remain as the mother of the house and make sure that everyone does not leave the house on an empty stomach.'

'Thank you, Mama La'ano. And you, Mama Heloiseh, I give space to you other mamas to talk to the family.'

'No, me too! I have nothing to say. Only that I would like to ask each family to come with sugar and tea. Some, we can use as a family, the rest I want to save for when the rest of the villagers come for their time of making contributions.'

'And one more thing before I forget.' Mama Heloiseh wanted to correct her husband. 'You mentioned something just then that I don't like. You cannot be saying that the monies must be jumped over. I understand you want to secure the money before someone hands-up us but whoever wants to hands-up us will do so whether we hide it under our undergarments or not. There is a serious possibility that we will invoke a curse by protecting it in the manner suggested but it also may curse the work we want to do, There is the added curse that it may follow us when we take same out for 'the walk'.

'Mama, thank you. My thinking is short after the success that we have in this start to the collection, and I was not thinking correctly. I will be careful with my words from now on.'

La'ano looked to her. She thought they had conversation about her calling for assistance, but La'ano was going to buy the sugar, tea, and coffee in bulk. Mama Heloiseh knew of that, but she felt that some of the women were too greedy and were not contributing to family obligations. This was the time when women of the family came to the fore.

'Meri Simbu, you have something to say.' Ambaii Urr looked at the ground in front of her. She wanted to say something but held it back. She nodded a no instead. 'Okay thank you. Sisi? You want to say something.'

'Is the *tolumo* open? Do we start contributing?'

'*Apo*, all you nice ones ya, sorry, let me apologise. I nearly forgot one thing that we must do first before we start with the contributions. After Greenie talks, we can start about when contributions can happen. I will first ask for Greenie to summon up our forebear's blessings.'

'Those of you wanting tea or something from the kitchen, please send that request silently without sound or noise. When Greenie finishes, perhaps the pork meat can be distributed. This village is renowned for its inability to put bride prices and what we are going to start now is going to shake up the village and break new grounds.'

'Greenie is the elder in the family. He will say and do somethings, then we will proceed.'

'Greenie *Apo ya!* Now you take over.'

Greenie passed Papa Ave some sticks that he had been twiddling with. Papa Ave received the sticks and without a word, broke them further into smaller pieces and handed them to a child near the fireplace to throw into the fire hearth.

The child threw them in and immediately there was a sizzle and sparks to produce bright blue flames and yellow smoke. Everyone's eyes ogled in awe at the sight.

$$6$$

IYE NAKAVOSA - STICKS AND PIGS

For most of the young people seeing a stick produce yellow smoke was a phenomenon as they had never seen a stick produce coloured smoke.

'The omens look good. We have got the good luck yellow smoke and blue flame. This outing that we want to start is on a good start.'

'Aishi, sing us some *Homasi* songs.'

The singing was an indication that the ceremonies were ended. As the women took the stanza of the *Homasi song* to a high pitch, Greenie wiped a tear. The *Homasi* always made him teary.

It was an old, old song that Aishi started, and he knew by the end of the night, Aishi would sing the whole gamut of these songs. Aishi was the last of those who knew and sung these songs and it was worrying. If Aishi were to demise at any time now, these songs were to be lost forever. The beauty about these songs were that they were sung in a faster tempo, but it was in a dead language that most of them did not understand. The handful who understood the prose and words were so busy singing the songs that they forgot to teach the language to the younger generation. They did explain the words to the songs, but they were immediately lost when the next song was sung.

Aishi strung the songs one after the other. They continued as if they were singing one song, and it went forever. After a marathon of twenty different songs sung in the same breath, the voices petered out from cracked voices and exhaustion.

Aishi was exasperated that the villagers could not stay in song with him, but he too stopped after the long stanza.

'*Seliné ne ve*, this is my house,' Papa Ave voiced out in a loud voice after the pause in the singing. This was the start to the contributions.

...'and I asked that the gathering will be at my house as I am Josiah Mamu's father. Family, I will take the lead and be the *maus-mahn* to all these gathering nights. I should be the first one to start the contributions but at this stage, I am a walking, talking *rabismahn*. I don't have any pigs, money, or gardens. If it were my choice, I would not have even suggested this *lulu tolumo* idea.'

'But *big mama* - La'ano is not waiting for us - fathers, to take the lead and I agree with her. If we, the brothers, and fathers had it our way, we would not even have had started this night. We are like the rest of the village, agreeing by our no-care-for-bride-price for our sons to live in *dinau marits*.'

'Josiah's mother, thank you; we will let you take ownership and I and my brothers will be with you all the way. La'ano is taking ownership, and she is now calling the shots. She is starting the ball rolling by calling in on all her pig debts. She has since day one, on coming to this village in marriage, had been killing pigs for just about everyone. You see this wrap of split sticks; they represent the number of pigs, and each stick has a name to it. Those of you who owe her a pig or two, start checking your *hauspik*. You will have to pull one in.'

'She knows she is getting the pig support from the village. She also says she wants to clean out her *hauspik* so the pigs for the inner circle i.e., the one for *the feet of the bride* and the *stomach-pig* for the bride's mother, she has that covered.'

'Now pigs only don't determine a woman coming in marriage here. The money bit is important, and her contributions is going to determine how much we can match her. She thankfully says she is putting out *two mulises* that will be the main core to the bride wealth.'

The house went quiet. It was not a normal sum that a parent was expected to come up with. It was substantially quite a lot.

Then a meek voice asked, 'Dah, what is a *mulise*?'

Papa Ave broke into a laughter.

'*Seghané*, my child, you have been to a white man's school who taught you some numbers that made you forget that we in the village do have some numbers too. But they don't run like the one, twos and threes.'

'We count on our fingers to ten. Then it gets a bit funny. When a person says he has *a stick*, it means he has ten of something. When a person says he has twenty of something, he has a *wrap*. *One wrap* is all our fingers and toes. We have twenty digits so that becomes *one wrap*. If he says he has *one wing*, it means he has a fifty of something. Obviously *two wings* will be one hundred of that thing. We then call that hundred, a *top of a mountain* or a peak in the *Tok Ples*. When you have two of those tops or mountains, it is called *a bilum* - two hundred of that something. When you have five *bilum*s it becomes *a pile* or a *mulise* of something; the word means the same thing as *heap*, which is a thousand of that thing.'

'Eh, stop wasting our time teaching children. His parents should be teaching him.'

'Some of you parents don't know what I am saying. You too have lost it so listen to me and you might learn something of our traditional numbering system.'

The young kid beamed a big smile. He did not understand the counting but the least he learned was that *bilums* and *mulises* were a lot of money. He would take to his parents to teach him the rest.

Someone prompted Greenie to start a song and he knew when to start but the song stuck in his throat. He was shocked by the amount that La'ano was putting out. That sum alone was, sufficient as the bride wealth. He looked back at the presentation being laid put out by Papa Ave.

'My apologies. Yes, the *tolumo* or contributing time is open now. La'ano is putting up two *mulises* to start the contributions.'

He paused for that to sink in. It was a record of sorts for the village, that the parents of the groom came up with such money.

Papa Ave rearranged La'ano's money on the coffee table so that all could see the pile of notes – good money. He looked at Greenie with a glint in his eyes.

Greenie spoke for those in the house. '*Seghané, Ave-ghama*, La'ano, Hoveyau, good people, we are thinking that what we are seeing tonight was not going to ever happen, but it is happening. That's kudos to you all.'

Papa Ave picked up from where he left off.

'*Seliné ne ve*, if the sticks did not catch fire and produce those yellow smoke, I would have been worried, and Greenie was good. He has called on our old relatives and their ghosts to look on with favour on this program. My good family, we must not disappoint these family ghosts. We should do our best to make this event of bringing on a wife for Josiah a memorable one.'

'La'ano, *Big mama*, we don't call you a *big mama* for nothing. You have lived up to your name. *Seghané ve*. Now, good people, not only has *big mama* come up with the cash, but she also has six pigs altogether for this occasion. Two dead pigs for the bride's parents and the pig that goes with the bride price. She is putting up two more pigs for the live pig stakes; one for the village *tolumo togessa* at the end which will close the contributions and pledges and send out the bride wealth for the first of its *bridal walks*. This last pig is earmarked as the pig *for the legs*. It will feed those taking the bride wealth around for the walk and for us to energise and wish them success on these walks.'

'How much should we put up for the bride in cash and pigs is something that we decide at the end of the *tolumo togessa* session which will include all the collections from everyone, that is, in about the tenth day from today. La'ano our *Big Mama* has started the contributions rolling. It is now time for us to think back of our *dinaus* and we decide that those who owe us, we talk to these people and ask them to come good on their *dinaus.*'

A stink bomb erupted next to Papa Ave from a sleeping child. The children too were in the house sleeping in between and amongst the adults; with a lot of them in their own world, adultering the smoky night air with their farting.

'*Egghe,* stupid children, ask them not to *kapupu* too much or we adults too will all be farting in here. Do you parents ever tell or force your children to drink cold water? Now, where was I?'

Papa Ave stretched and yawned; the night was getting longer. He indicated to Mama Heloiseh if she could hand out the sugar canes now as people needed to get some sugar into their system. He himself though wanted a cup of piping hot sweet black coffee.

It would be an effort to get the water boiled.

It was hot and stuffy in the house as it was from all the heat that the Coleman lamps and there were two in the house generated, and from all the bodies.

A fire would make it just too hot.

The morning cold and chilly air was trying its best to get in through the eaves of the house. This house was built with the notion that there would be no fires made inside the house and it was built to retain whatever warmth the house generated. Now that fire was made, a little bit was creating much more heat.

'Here, cut these canes further and share them. That song has really exhausted us. Aishi, my father, I believe in that song and all those *masalais* will not look at us in a bad way, thank you.'

Mama Heloiseh started distributing the pig meat with pieces of *kaukau* and a morsel of vegetable on plates and banana leaves.

Aishi was wanting water after the *long piece of evocation* he sang, and he asked Greenie to take over as lead singer.

'*Egghe*, why is the *Homasi song* going to sleep when we are just starting', a few dissenters grumbled when Greenie started his own brand of songs. But they then joined in the song. The villagers lost some girth and pace which brought on lot of animated conversation in between songs. Greenie felt it. It could possibly derail the night.

Papa Ave did not like that as more and more people stopped singing, the volume of the singing dropped. He cleared his voice to take control when the last stanza of the song stopped.

Greenie stood up and made a show of getting out La'ano's *bilas* of breast plate ornamental of sticks from the centre post and with a revered action that demanded attention from all in the house. Most of those inside the house knew what the breast plate of tied sticks meant.

It was a tally of pigs that someone would have raised and killed in their lifetime. This breastplate was the record that the keeper has of pigs that were given out or slaughtered but as a debt. The longer the breastplate, it indicated the owner of it was a good and successful pig farmer and that they were generous with it. It was steeped in authority of a generous person. But a formal *big mama* title was never bestowed on La'ano. Everybody knew the unspoken; Hoveyau was the reason why La'ano was never out front and centre.

Greenie handed Papa Ave the bundle of roped sticks.

'Now listen, when La'ano came as a bride here, she started killing pigs for people in the family and the village. She kept a breast plate tally of sticks.'

He held up the stick score tally for all in the house to see.

'These are the number of pigs that we collectively as a village owe her.'

'It is custom that we don't go around telling people in the face that they need to repay debts that we have against people. We know that we keep our own records of sticks that tell us who we killed pigs for and those that were killed for us by other people. If one of these strands of stick has your name on it, this is your time to own up. She is not going to call out the sticks in public. You can, in the next couple of nights, tell us that you are contributing a pig in order for us to remove the strand of stick that has your etched on it. During the week, if you are not sure, come and see me to discuss it.'

'Now the bed is made, and the formalities are done. You all have contributed well to sing beautiful benediction and our *masalais* feel good. The *nakani stick* is laid out and will stay out until it is time for *the walk* to look for a prospective new bride.'

'Tonight, this first night, we the family will check ourselves out first. We will do both money and pig contributions. We check ourselves and when we have the bone of the bride wealth, we will then invite the rest of the village. For the family, it is three nights starting now and from the fourth night the rest of the villagers will be called in.'

'The new moon has started, when the moon dies, we want to think about taking this bride wealth out for *its first walk*.' He paused for the timetable to register in the minds of the gathered family.

'So, we start with the family, the first family will be the Solepano family and in seniority are Hoveyau who is the eldest, followed by Pilipo, then Goi and me last.'

'I am *maus-mahn* for the family and while I will try to stick to seniority, it does not matter. I will call whoever is near to me or pops up in my mind.'

'Good man, *Apo* ya, Greenie, let us start the ball rolling.'

'I repeat, it is La'ano who is the one with the idea to bring her son a woman, and she is putting up two *mulises* and one pig for the parents of the bride and two for the lead '*kaka.*' For the young generation, I again repeat that the *mulise* is a thousand kina and the *kaka* are the beds or stretchers that is used carry the slaughtered pigs.'

Papa Ave set out four sticks – new, carved out bamboo splinters that were to be tied on the bride wealth plate - on the bed in three neat rows. This was to record the pig contributions that were to be committed, pledged, and brought to the bride wealth contributions.

'I will start by calling family after family. There is no need to ask more from Hoveyau and La'ano. Mama Heloiseh, you say, you have something to say.'

'Eh you're the man, it is a man thing; about your son, why ask me.'

'*Apo*, this is not something to be angry about. I am chairman and cannot be chairman and contributing; so, my *Apo*, you will speak for us. It is family contributions so you, mothers - if you say something, it will be our collective family voice. So, Mama Heloiseh, *Apo*, what you say will be our voice – yours and mine.'

'*Apo*, that is a bit irregular. You have the money; you want me to call that out.'

A bemused smile crept across Ave's face acknowledging that she was going to speak for her household.

Mama Heloiseh swallowed some hard-bitter bile. She would talk about money that she did not have on her. Besides it was such an insignificant amount after La'ano had put out hers. Also, it was irregular for a woman to mention out in public, her, or her family's wealth. She bit her lips and mumbled out something incoherent. Those nearest to her could only make out her voice.

'Okay, we are coming with two pigs, one live one and one dead one. Money is something that we are in short supply now. I think I heard our father say that he has something like *two wings* or something.'

'*Apo*', Papa Ave echoed her wife's words. 'One *wing* is fifty and when I have two, I would have two fifties and so it will be one hundred kina.'

'*Seghané,* thank you, Mama Heloiseh', as clapping happened that soon spread throughout the house.

Papa Ave took out the money that he had in his pocket. He counted out the two notes that added up to a hundred kina for all to see. He then put them down on the bed made for the contributions. He also added two stick, one twig from a casuarina tree and a bamboo chip.

The twig was going to mark out the *dead pigs* and the bamboo chip for the *live pigs*. The live pigs did not matter in order, but the dead pigs needed some consideration as some of them were to fulfil some functions and the size of these pigs mattered. He needed to tactfully ask the appropriate questions.'

'The pig that Mama Heloiseh is suggesting that goes to the *dead pig pile* is the pig that will welcome the new bride when she is delivered and will decorate the *feet of the new bride.*'

'Eh, I think you are speaking out of turn. Let the contributions come in then we can decide where each pig will go.' a voice from the men behind Papa Ave was heard.

'Thank you for that but I feel the family should fill in the *heavy parts* of the work here and the village should fill in the parts where we cannot fill them.'

'I think we can decide what pig will do what a little later. Perhaps tomorrow. Sorry for interrupting; please, Chairman, go ahead.'

'Okay, Goi and Ambaii Urr! Are they here?'

Goi was not in the house. Ambaii Urr spoke for them.

'Pigs are one thing that we women care for but nowadays we hardly look after them. I have only one pig that I will give as a live pig when the bride's people come to undo the pig's rope. As for the family contribution, our father has them, but he had a visitor, and they were talking when I left the house. Can you move on?'

'You should have said that first and not tell us about the pig. You will have to repeat that when Goi gets here. By the way, who is he talking to?'

'Oh, that joker, Satulie, they are always telling stories. But I think this time it is serious. Our father was giving advice to Satulie about the *ghetto* at the school. Satulie has been making inroads to the school wooing that *ghetto.*'

The house broke into a group laugh. The young ones knew which *ghetto* Satulie was wooing.

'What *ghetto*? All those female teachers at the school are married, are they not?'

'No! Not one of the teachers. There is one elderly lady staying with the Manus teacher. They say the lady left her husband and has come to live with his teacher brother.'

'Oh, that *hii yaga hey* one. Since when was she a *ghetto* and you think she will fall for our green carpenter?'

A gurgle of more laughter followed by heehaws erupted throughout the house. Satulie was a bachelor, advanced in his years and still green and still without a wife. He also stuttered a lot and that was the reason why girls would not have had any conversation with him. Even in the village, he kept well away from everyone unless he was drunk.

'*Egghe*, that carpenter is always missing the iron nails for his own fingernails. You see his hands. They are all flat from all the missed hammering. So, all that maintenance work he was doing for the school was to get nearer to the *ghetto*.'

'Ambaii Urr, send a child to get your husband otherwise he will be chasing that *ghetto* himself if Satulie does not.'

'Eh, where do you think he will bring this woman to? We will fight her and tear her up like paper.'

'*Sorre, sorre*, this is not a night for talking about *poromeris*.' He called out the ladies with a grin.

'Now, where was I? Yes, it is the family contribution night, and we want to size it up for the village. While we wait for Goi; now who is next? The four will be his fathers and now all you, others. Inside the family, we are ten altogether. There is the four of us and you six others.'

'We should wait till Goi is here first.'

Pilipo without being asked, spoke next.

'You know that Josiah grew up in my house. I thought Sisi-Vena was his mother. We should be the ones calling the shots here, but *Big Mama* La'ano has her own agenda. We are a bit miffed that she did not consult us first, but we think we understand why she wants to go back to her village. It was a long time coming.'

Sisi-Vena interrupted him and grabbed his speech. She continued in saying.

'Us, four sisters are in the same boat. We are married to men who *don't know what a spade looks like,* nor do they *know what a bush knife does.* Our husbands think they are the *itehetu Atamus* of the village and walk around like they are ramrod *yomba posts* in the *hauslain* at all the gatherings and *kandis*. They make us poor *Eva* women and we struggle like all the other women in the village.'

'My husband and I are Josiah's de facto parents. He is the eldest of our boys and rightly, we are coming with three pigs; one to kill as a dead pig and two as live pigs to go the stakes for our new in-laws to loosen. The *titivi* that we hold will be used to *feed our legs* when we start the journey to bring out these bride wealth - to go looking to find our son a wife. I will give back this conversation to our father so that he continues with what he was saying.'

La'ano was already cancelling out her debts to the family. She would pull out the sticks from her string of sticks. She would at the end of this start a new debt to her and Josiah by one pig. She had in her time killed several pigs for Mama Sisi-Vena's children when they had parties.

Pilipo took back the conversation from his wife but instead of speaking, gave a wrap of something to his brother Ave. He did not say anything more to accompany the gesture.

'*Seghané ve*, Sisi-Vena, you too have a *big bilum* that we the family look to. You feed the pigs and the family from that *big bilum* well. We appreciate that you are contributing a lot of pigs. Now I am given something here by your husband. Let me see what it is.'

Papa Ave unravelled the package. He gave a gasp at the sight of such a large amount.

'Mama Sisi-Vena, *Seghané ve*. You are a woman of means. You have again stunned us from your big *bilum*. Now you further shore up our praise and gratitude for coming up with *a wing to a mulise*.'

'*Egghe*, stop making life difficult for us. Use the modern counting system.' A voice interjected from the back.

'It is a lot of money. Again, for those of you not familiar with our counting system, *a wing* means half and a *mulise* is a thousand in modern counting. So, we have *half a mulise* i.e., this here what Pilipo and Sisi-Vena are contributing is five hundred kina.'

'Thank you for telling us that and stop being old fashioned for the sake of being old fashioned. The counting system is one, two, three, four, five etc. This counting by *fingers* and *toes, hands* and *legs* and *wings, mountains and piles* are the most stupid counting systems.'

'You even have the *sticks* and *wrappings*, gosh,' another piped in her disagreement.

'Don't disparage our counting system. It is okay, old fashioned but kept us well. We must remember a few things only rather than talk about things that are foreign to us. Our counting does not go beyond the thousands which is a *pile or a mulise.*'

'You think you are using the old counting system for the benefit of the children here, but they are going to school that teach them numbers beyond the thousand. They will soon forget what you are teaching them now.'

'I know, I know. It may be a futile attempt to teach the young people something that they will ultimately forget but let them remember that we traditionally did have a counting system.'

'Thank you, Pilipo and Sisi-Vena. The money is a huge amount of money. Thank you. Okay, for everyone's benefit, these two couple are contributing five hundred for the small man's wife and four pigs. He put the money in the pile and broke sticks to add to the pig pile amidst clapping and noise.'

A throat cleared and Goi indicated his presence. 'Ave, brother, I am sorry I am late. I had a visitor and had to have some conversation, but I see that the night has progressed. But here, Ambaii Urr and I are contributing *one mulise.* We have no pigs. In fact, most of them are small, *titivis* only and we will from time-to-time slaughter them to feed ourselves during these times. The next gathering for the village, we intend to kill one for that *tolumo* gathering.

La'ano stood up and did a jig and screamed *'ou-ou'* in sheer exaltation of gladness. Her happiness had got the better of her.

She was drunk in ecstatic gladness of knowing that she had done the impossible - to get four just about useless brothers to come up with a substantial amount of money – nearly two thousand was quite a lot to these villagers who rarely saw this amount of money except during the coffee season.

'*Seliné ne ve*, all you good brothers, I did not think you brothers would do that. I give you praise and my sisters, thank you all. May the gods of our fathers shine their eyes on your houses and gardens?'

'*Oui oui*' she crooned and several women joined her.

'Okay then, break into a song. Greenie, good man, where are you?' And Greenie on cue, started a song and the house soon was singing as one. It then followed onto a second song.

'Those who are wondering if Goi Siyoli and Ambaii Urr made any contributions; when he said, a *mulise*, he meant to say one thousand kina. They are going to use some of their *titivis* during the *tolumo togessa* period.'

'*Seliné ne ve,* that is a lot of money. For the pigs, we will need a lot of live pigs and I am hesitating to say yes to your idea of feeding us and the village for the gatherings. Even today's pork from La'ano could have been saved and used to beef up the number of live pigs that we would want our new in- laws to loosen from the stakes. We however thank her for making sure that our gathering in not on *kaukau* only. We would be hiccupping a lot then without the *abus*.'

'Meri Simbu, *Apo!* Good woman, thank you, you have brought us a lot of money and I'll say yes to your killing your *titivi* to feed us. Do you have a number that you want to give us?'

Ambaii Urr looked up to her husband. He gave her a blank stare, meaning she could have her say. She had already blurted out about the one pig for the slaughtering and her husband has added these others on. She needed to save face.

'Papa, I have mentioned my one pig earlier for the stakes that our in-laws will loosen. It is not a big pig. That is the one that I hold behind the house here in the *hauslain*. On top of that my *titivi* pigs are still small, just like the *Lupiye-Tapiye* that *big mama* La'ano slaughtered. I am backing up my sister La'ano with three other smaller ones. One will be slaughtered for the greater village *tolumo* gathering, another for the time when the bride wealth must leave this house and the last one for the time when we bring out the live pigs on stick stakes ready for the *iye nalawa wakase* when our new in- laws come to loosen and take away these pigs on their leashes.

'*Apo Seghané;* you ladies have this planned out. You put us men to shame. We men always want to go after new women and don't think who will look after the pigs for us. When one is taking care of pigs; that is our health and wealth and wellbeing. You menfolk should take that into consideration when you start thinking and smelling out new women and *ghettos.* You will be destroying your own health, wealth, and wellbeing. *Ehe'q* don't *play-play* with a woman who will look after pigs.'

La'ano could not hold back the happiness she had oozing through her body. She felt compelled to speak.

'Papa Ave, good man, I tried with two *mulises,* but Mama Heloiseh, Sisi-Vena, Meri Simbu, you girls have matched me, the mother of the boy. I cannot live with that. I am the mother of the groom, and my contributions must be the bone of this bride wealth. I am putting up another *mulise* to the ones I dragged out from the *sepeku* of my house. I will add another *mulise.*'

Papa Ave paused to look at her. Was she okay? Was she drunk? He looked out to Hoveyau who look bemused. All could see that Papa Ave was not consulted. Surely, she was not putting up another thousand kinas, was she? Where was she getting all that money from and how long has she being keeping it from them?

'Mama Josh, *big mama, Seghané,* thank you. I am glad that you are pulling out those hidden money to spend for your son. The first two *mulise* I saw you pull that out of hidden spot from the *sepeku.* Do I take it that the *sepeku* in your house is not what I think it is?'

'It warms my blood further. The people, Mamu's people will come with freshness in their blood and *come good* with their contributions they will come to support you properly. I eat my own words that I had long spoken that you could do nothing good with your liking for playing cards around the *kandis* circles. Tonight, you are showing me otherwise, a different colour of yourself. You are the only one of a kind that may have saved her wins from the *kandis*.'

La'ano looked on the bemused and confused face of her husband and the totally lost face of his brothers. She was enjoying it.

She threw down her *bilum* in front of Papa Ave.

'I am serious. Look, I don't have the money now but tomorrow, I will produce that *mulise*. I married the most useless of man in the village, but his brothers and their wives have come to his assistance, and they have gone beyond my expectation with their contributions. I am the mother of the boy. I pained and bore him when I thought I would not have any more babies. I want to bring on his wife and I am serious about it.'

'Papa Ave and all of you good people, I am going to spend the rest of the night singing your praises.'

Aishi broke into song, a short song that everyone found easy to join. The night had *spruiked* up.

Papa Ave looked to Greenie and when he found contact with his eyes, he nodded.

Greenie moved to the floor, took a deep breath and in exhaling, gave a loud rendering *ganine* whoop.

'*Mitega ghoi ha kupiii whee ii ha-ha. Seghané ve!!*'

The noise rattled the house and made the air in the house move. It reverberated through the inverse cone of the roof rafters, shaking the many hanging soot stalks. Tiny pieces broke off and cinder showers fell on the people below. One string of it fell and positioned itself between the piles of money.

Papa Ave stared at the fallen soot. It was uncanny, the way it fell into place in perfect alignment with the *nakani* besides the *pig score sticks*.

'Eh, Greenie, good man, *Seghané,* that was some *ganine*. Do you see what I see? This soot, you rattled it free with your *ganine* and it should break with the fall - into small pieces. Instead, it falls and without breaking into pieces, fits next to the *nakani* stick. This does not happen. It is not normal. Do I read something here?'

'Yes, that soot is strange. It comes from the very top of the house and to keep its form when it reached that bed is saying something. Do you think it is telling good story or a bad one?'

A murmur of sounds erupted all at once around the house as each one tried to interpret the situation before them.

Papa Ave spoke above all the voices but with reverence in his voice.

'The size of the soot is twice the size of the pig stick that is there however the length is the same as the stick. This, I would be thinking that the mother of this *togessa* will put up another pig, but I know, La'ano has brought all her pigs that she needed to bring. She has no more pigs but because she told us that she was making her two *mulises* to be three, the soot next to the *nakani stick* makes it two. I don't know - maybe something else.'

'My second shot at reading the soot I think means that we will do a good marriage – bringing on a good woman, a bride who will come with good pig rearing skills.'

'Now that the family have come, our sisters who are married out of the village may be coming tomorrow. We sent word to the three girls, and we wait to see if they will assist us. However, we welcome them even if they don't contribute anything. You all know it is our custom that when the men of the village go to front to greet people and visitors, it is our *tambus* that tend to the *mumu* and all the backroom chores that we men of the village will not attend to.'

'We don't want our sisters to feel embarrassed that they have nothing to contribute and shy away back in their village. They should bring their bodies and their husbands as contributions in kind because we will need them. We want them to come to assist us to do this work. So, send word out to them again if they don't come tomorrow.'

Te'enike Liivelave who had earlier arrived from her marital village nudged her uncle - Papa Ave and discreetly passed on her contributions trying to be as conspicuous as possible.

'This money?' He asked without looking behind. He had heard Te'enike call him out, but he wanted to be dramatic with her contributions.

'That is Te'enike Liivelave coming.' A person who sat across from them spoke up.

Papa Ave paused and looked around in front of him and around. He then spoke softly and with a firmness to his voice.

'No, no, she does not have to come like that. Isn't she a married woman? This money cannot come by itself. It must have a story to it.'

Te'enike Liivelave bowed her head shamefully. She spoke in near whispers to her uncle.

'*Shee-eeh*, that is my contribution. There is nothing more to it.'

'My daughter, don't you *sheee-eeh* me. You must know, Te'enike, my girl, we, your fathers don't know about your movements. Only yesterday you were a small girl in this village. Now you say you are a married woman. Now how did that happen? If you want to be married, show your seriousness. This gathering is your gathering. I don't see anyone beside you. The man that you claim to be your husband, is he here?'

A dead pan silence.

'If a man claims to be your husband, he must be interested in all things that affect your life, including what happens to your family back in your maiden village. This man that you claim to be your husband cannot *play-play* with you and leave you to your own when you have situations like this happens amongst your brothers and fathers.'

Te'enike Liivelave hung her head down. She had a year ago moved in with her beau and was sort of living a *giaman marit* relationship. The village had no terminology for this type of defacto relationship and for all intent and purposes she was a married woman. Her husband was supposed to accompany her to her village when there were big gatherings like this one. But it was accepted that young men do sometimes find it difficult to make the transition into married life and to learn the many intricate roles that married people play in a society like theirs. This transition works slowly and sometimes comes in a hard and brutal way.

Nonetheless, Papa Ave had to make his statements.

'You are just a girl wanting to be a woman. It is your husband that should be putting his family contribution. Any contributions that he makes in times like this should be seen as part of his down payment towards the gathering of his bride wealth for your bride price.'

'You must also know that when we want to share food and call out to thank you to all those who assisted us, it is your husband that we want to praise and say thank you to. We call out your husband and his name in public and it is always the man who must front up to get the kudos and food. When he goes back to his village, he will give praise to you and say he does not return from your village with an empty hand.'

'Now this goes for all our girls who are married out of this village and even those who have returned and have brought their husbands to live amongst us in this village. Let your husbands come talk to us. You shouldn't be hiding at our backs to give us your contributions.'

'We will not be part of your agenda to make *a pipia* of your husband.'

'*Ehe'q*, don't you girls practise this *giaman marit* thing. It does not work. When you move in with a man, you are *tru-tru* married. Full stop. There is no *giaman* to it. When you become pregnant, that pregnancy is not *giaman*, is it.'

'Think and act like a woman and your husband should also do the same and not think like the boy he was yesterday.'

'Now what do I do with this money?' Papa Ave asked, looking to the gathering for guidance.

Someone piped up from the back. 'I am thinking that you should give it back to her so that she can come back with her other sisters' tomorrow night. We have marked out tomorrow for them to come with our *tambus*. We should recognise her for being a married woman by then.'

Another retorted. 'She has already given you, her contributions. Why do you dare to want to shame her now for doing the right thing? The fact that she had come early should give you men cause to be happy for her. Instead, you want to take issue with her husband. Some of you men become sluggish when we women suggest you come to our village. It is the same with this young husband. Give him a break.'

Ambaii Urr spoke out her support. 'Gosh, man, you look for statements to make. This is her first contributions ever as a woman and you want to make a school out of her. Find some other woman to be your stooge. Give her back that money and tomorrow she will gamble away all of it.'

'Eh, thank you for your support. Te'enike, you have mothers who support you. I think Ambaii Urr and the other speak for all the mamas in the house.'

'Why don't you hold that money in reserve? Don't mention the figure to us yet. Tomorrow, when her sisters and *tambus* have their night, you can then mention her and the amount.' Mama Heloise spoke up.

A general murmur of consensus broke out in the house.

'Thank you, thank you to you all. I concur with all your murmurings.'

Papa Ave quickly counted and folded the money Te'enike Liivelave contributed. He put that aside separately. It was clear to all that it was a good sum - something near to around a *bilum, - two hundred.*

A song started but then faded out as attention was drawn to the immediate cousins who started their contributions. In between songs, stories, and jokes but before early dawn, they had contributed another substantial amount in cash and pledged seven pigs.

All together they now had seventeen pigs that were pledged. Josiah was going to start his marriage heavily laden in pig debts at the rate the people were committing themselves. Despite it, La'ano could hardly contain her happiness.

Eight of these pig pledges were made by the family and they were free pledges, pigs that Josiah would not be expected to return. These were pledged because those offering them were trying to make a name for themselves. They were a form of status building from people who were competing for status in the village to show they would have the ability to raise and kill pigs.

La'ano further crossed out two sticks as debts that would be settled. She then took out six new splinters of the bamboo shiver that she would add to the breast plate of stick as new debts – debts that she will pass on to her son and new daughter-in-law.

As soon as dawn crept into the sleeping village, La'ano cleared her aching eyes. In her jubilation, she had mentioned her reserve. She was going to make good on that. She took out her three bottle tops from her treasure bag and went to Unca Holoe's house.

The morning mist was rising from the ground when she broached Holoe's house. She paused when three children called out to her from the outhouse where a fire was briskly burning. The children had a pot on the wire stand with a briskly burning fire underneath and several *kaukaus* on the roast. They were bickering over who was to get yesterday pot of rice.

'Eh, good children, where are your parents and you are roasting *kaukau* for yourselves.' She put down her *bilum* bag and pulled out a banana leaf wrap that she proffered to them. It was a meaty portion of pork. The children looked at her and out towards the door of their father's house. He had his own house and a sort of office, and the children slept with their mother in the big house. Unca Holoe's did not take pork - he was an Adventist, but his wife and children did not bother with his affiliation. They looked with relish at the appetising pork with anticipated growling in the stomach.

The eldest called out to their father. 'Daddy, Mister Holoe? Visitor!!'

'Whoa, who's that?' He called from inside the house. His wife stood in the doorway of her own house to see who it was. She shouted out her greetings to her.

'*Egghe, Apo ya*, good morning. We heard all that singing and thought all the family would be sleeping in. Now say tell me, how was the night? By the tenure of the sound of noises and the many *ganines* that kept on going all through the night, it must have been a success.'

La'ano did not reply. She put out a sheepish smile. She did not want to boast about the night as it was a night of her calling. The smile said it all.

Unca Holoe came out of his house.

'Morning to the Mrs Hoveyau. *Seghané,* oh you brought some meat for the children. You must know that I don't take pork, but the children and their mother want to differ from me. They eat anything and will gladly eat dog meat too.'

'Dad', the children chorused. 'We won't eat any dog meat. That we promise you.'

'You children wait until *Maunten Mahn* does his special. People don't ask after what type of meat would be in the bamboo. It was always *an aromatic bamboo* that he cooks. He cooks it so well with as much herbs as he can find. After these, any greedy person will devour the cooked meat greedily. I've seen people even roll their tongue up on the bamboo casing. Only after the person has lapped it up, then he will tell them it was dog meat. Some people have tried to throw up when the food is deep down in the stomachs but sorry, it has already gone into a place of no return. You ask your uncle Patole. He will tell you that he now likes dog meat. If you guys want to eat any and every meat, you watch out, you may end up like Patole.

'Yuck.'

'That should not stop you children from enjoying that pork that Mrs Hoveyau gave you. You should cut it into small pieces and heat it up on the fire.'

'Sorry, Mrs Hoveyau, I should have come last night to the gathering, but I had all these body aches from carting that coffee from the garden to the house. I thought I would shower and then come in, but I slept for a while and then when I woke up it was when the cold morning air was slipping in through the eaves of the house. I will come over tonight though.'

'No, you don't need to come as that is the time for the sisters and their husbands.'

'Okay, but I'll come in to say hi to the *tambus* then only.'

'I am going into town and say, is there anything you want.'

La'ano looked at the ground shyly. 'You know, last night I was drunk with jubilations. I was clever and stupid at the same time. I opened my big mouth and it just spilled out that I was putting up another *mulise, a pile of money* to what I had previously put up. I now must do something to save face and I am wondering if ….'

'You don't have to worry me too much. It is your money, and I am only doing a safe keeping job for you. It is for situations like these that I'd be more than willing to undo them and bring them to you.' Unca Holoe smiled to allay the fear that La'ano was having.

'Now we have three bottle tops left. Do you want me to undo one more top or what do you want me to do?'

The butterflies were starting to grow in her when she took out all the bottle tops and handed them over to him without further words. She was now fretful that she was digging into money that she had reserved for herself. If she left for her village, she was going empty.

'You are the only woman that gave me money for safekeeping and forgot about it. The other women in the village would bring me money in the morning and in the afternoon ask for it back. I was always wondering if you had forgotten it all but when you asked to buy your son his wife from the money that you gave me, I was pleased for you and for your investment. I have no problems. You remember you have already paid me for keeping your money. When you gave me those money early on, you gave me an extra five hundred kina. I have made interest on it too and I need to thank you for that.'

'Now I am a bit concerned that you are going to deplete your savings all in one go. That is advice that I am going to give and if you want to take the rest of the money, I will ask you to pay me for closing your account.'

La'ano brushed aside the ground in front of her with a twig overtly embarassed. She heard Masta Holoe, but she worried none about having to pay him. She was going to benefit big time from his cleverness, and she was not going to dispute or cringe over it.

She was a bit fretful that she was going to go to her village empty, with nothing. She rued that custom dictated that she came with nothing to this village, she returns with nothing back to her village.

Some people write dastardly customs. It was a male society where inheritance was passed from father to son and the daughters missed out big time. She would return to her village and not own any land. If she were to make a garden, it was going to be at the invitation of her brother's wives.

'Okay, let us look at how much your one top will change into. If it is not enough, you can turn in the other two. Right now, you need to give me one top only and you can hold onto the other two. We will take out the first top. Mama Josh, I will bring the money over. I did put your first, second and third lot of money into the same type of IDB account and both will have some baby money - interest. The fourth and last lot of money were invested well after the banks were giving good baby money and it may not have grown too well.'

What! La'ano cocked her ear to hear better of what Masta Holoe was saying. Did he say she had some more money with him? She could feel her body quivering with excitement now that there was some more money that she thought she did not have. She tried to remember if she gave him more money to keep for her.

The passage of time was such that she could not remember how much money she gave over to him. She could remember that there were some occasions where she had come over to him to get back some of the money that she gave over to him previously.

She was sure that she meticulously kept *rip top lids* from the *San Miguel beer* bottles. Each rip top was two hundred kina and she had strung these on a string. She was not too sure now as there was one time when the children were playing games with rip top bottle tops.

She was sure that they had removed a string from the several she had kept under the bed but then she was not too sure if this came from the records of money that she gave over to Unca Holoe or from the cash that she hid under the *yakise* post of the house.

It was only later in life that she had taken the rip tops for proper lids and had replaced ten of the rip tops with one lid.

Now the uncle was saying she had one more lid.

'*Apo*, you say I have four tops. One must be still in the bag at the house. Okay, I'll let this one out of my *bilum* as one that I have taken back from you. *Seghané,* thank you.'

Unca Holoe went into his house and from his metal trunk brought out his old diary. He took out the four IDB receipts for La'ano. He studied them, took one out and returned the others to the diary. He then wrote a short note and brought out his old stamp pad that La'ano affix her thumb print on the note.

This was not necessary, but Holoe did it to clear himself of any wrongdoing though he reported to no one, and no one audited his semi banking for the village. The village had unfettered trust in him and gave him their money to keep. He had made it his habit to bank any money that he had in custody every second Monday. Any amount over five hundred kina he created an IBD account. He was always a single signatory.

During the days when banks visited schools to get children to open accounts, Holoe made an agreement with the bank where he could do banking for the village. They allowed him to open trusts accounts to each villager who gave him money. When he thought a person was of a good character and would not unnecessarily deplete the account, he gave the bank book to them to keep and bring to him to sign the banking slips. Those who wanted their own accounts, he helped them open them up and those that did not want, he paid into his own account with the proviso that they can ask for their money back only when a big event took place in their lives.

Unca Holoe looked at La'ano.

'All four of your accounts are long time accounts. This oldest and first account is thirty years old, and it looks like there will be some good baby money. You may not need to ask me to undo the other tops if I undo this one.'

'Oh, thank you. I did not know that you were doing that. We were thinking that you kept the money around the house in some out of sight places.'

'You want the young boys to break into my house every so often. I don't keep money in the house. When people give me money, I take it to the bank straight away.'

'Your one *mulise* - a thousand kina and a bit more of it, may have grown into two or three *mulises*, even more now. I don't know. It may take a day or two to close the account and get you all that money. You remember this is the first one that you gave me when you just came in after your marriage here. Your three children were not born then and now they are adults.'

All of these did not register with her. She heard him say ... grew into two or three ... ... gosh, bless him, she uttered her blessings. Her heart was beating hard. There was excitement growing in her that she was having more than enough money to pull off bringing her son a wife. La'ano was just grateful that Unca Holoe has kept these monies and had not used it up like some of the village men would have done to monies they were given to keep.

Late in the evening, Unca Holoe returned with a smile that was a mile wide. He called La'ano over to his house and sat her down. He took out his bag and set down some money, plenty of it; in front of her. He took one set from it and placed it away from the rest.

'You had given me money on seven different occasions. The first three you had forgotten about it. The next two, you came back asking for them soon after. The first one was when your brothers wanted *het pei* for your children. That we took those two *full bilum* - four hundred and gave it to them.'

'Yes, we did, and I have been grateful for that as that *Itehetu Atamu* is one useless guy. He still is and I wonder why I have been here for so long. But it makes my heart rejoice that I know that you have been so good for this village. Masta Holoe, you are a real blessing to the village and to me.'

'This is your original money', Unca Holoe pointed to the plastic holding a wrapped high denomination note. 'All *one thousand five hundred* of it. Now this second pile is the baby money that the bank gave to you. Since you did not touch it, all this time, it has added more and more to it, so the baby monies are this big and has gone past the *mama money.*'

'Now you tell me how much that is as I am too scared to know what it is.'

'You are one lucky woman. When I opened and put that money and this was one thousand five hundred kina, I asked that interest, that is the baby be paid at five percent and in thirty-three years you have left it at the bank, the baby money is four times more than the *mama money,* so you have nearly six more *mulises.* What you have in all these piles of money altogether is seven *mulises* altogether and a bit more with these little changes.'

La'ano's ear popped open.

A ripple of sheer joy cascaded through her body. She wanted to sing and dance and do the *gamakilise* here and then, but she was alone. Mrs Holoe was cooking at the back, and she was never interested in the banking chores of her husband, so she missed the exhilarating joy shown by La'ano.

She quickly worked through her mind what she could do with all the money that she was told that she had. She tried to work out what she would want now for the ceremonies. In the end she decided she was going to make this bride price ceremony as good as it could be.

The children saw La'ano's muted exhibition of joy and could tell that she was wanting to do the zig zag dance. They had seen so many people come asking their parents for money and have left with various shades of colouration on their faces. La'ano's was the most shining face they had seen over their years in front of their houses, and they knew she must have good news.

When their mother came around to getting her second cup of afternoon tea, the children quietly whispered that La'ano must have a windfall from her demeanour and colour. Mummy Holoe asked her husband but as always, he brushed aside the question and did not advance any hints on how much he got for La'ano.

So much for her gossip mill. La'ano was at a loss. She had earlier wanted to get cash in her two bottle tops too but the money that she gave over in her first year of marriage was paying good dividends now. There was no need to cash in the other tops now.

It has been the year when the coffee prices had skyrocketed because of some sick to the coffee in some far away place. She had sold a half bag of coffee that she harvested from the small plot her husband had inherited from his father. She used half the proceeds and hid the other half. To these she added other money to make the first one thousand and the next five hundred. She remembered the night where new coffee money was plenty and a lot of *kandis* groups were gambling for big cash. She had also won a substantial money at the *kandis*. She put these moneys to those that she had hoarded, kept them safe with her life and then Unca Holoe and his keeping money safe scheme happened upon her.

She was going to cash in the next one top but from what he was saying, she would be better off leaving the other two tops with him a bit longer. At least one of the tops can be used to buy her a coffin when she dies.

Elated, she picked up her bag to take her exit. She paused and pulled a small wad of notes out.

'Unca Holoe, when I gave you the money, I did not know that it would make baby monies or at these amounts. Now I am trying to get my one *top* you give more back, more than what I gave you. I cannot thank you enough.'

7

YAHAMETA GHEHENE – POISONED MONEY

'I also cannot walk out of this house without sharing some of the baby money with you.' La'ano said through tears.

'No, no you keep that money. You have a situation on your hands, and you will need all of that. You are the mother of the *togessa* and *tolumo* gatherings. You and your family will have to be very generous with tea, coffee, sugar even sugar canes or there will be plenty of *tok baksait* by those who come to see you make blunders and will tear you down in gossips later. They will not come with food to assist you but will have plenty of *tok baksait* and gossip.' Holoe stood with a grin.

'If you insist, then consider what you want to give to me as my contribution towards the cause. You can mention my name but don't mention the amount. You must know that the village will be coming to your house, and you will have to provide everything from tea, coffee, sugar, even sugarcane. This people will come with an air of expectation that they will be fed at your house. You will be expected to take part of the contributions to buy these to feed them while they come to sing the nights with you and the family.'

'Also don't expect me to be gracing your house anytime soon. I will come for one night only and then will bring my own contributions.'

La'ano's eyes streamed happy waters. Whoever gave this man such wisdom, may he be blessed. He was godsend to be in the village at this time for her. She walked away happy but with a heavy heart.

La'ano was all bouncy as the second night crept in around her. Her *bilum* was now a prized possession. It held one part of the money that she picked up from Unca Holoe. She had quickly divided the money into five piles and had discreetly hidden them away in strategic places in the garden, the *hauspik* and in her house.

The presence of the money in her *bilum* gave her more reason to prance about and mention in spite sometimes against other women in the village.

Hoveyau' brother Goi held court this second night and chaired the *Tolumo togessa.*

La'ano was all a bubble of joy, but she quietly passed over the *mulise* that she had pledged the night before.

Goi gawked at her slightly, taken aback in disbelief the crisp notes that she gave over.

'Me, I am a woman of means.'

There was some arrogance in La'ano's mannerism, but she voiced it in a low tone. The few sitting near to Goi did not get her boast.

Everyone craned their necks and opened their eyes wide surprised as Goi spread out the money on the bed made out in front of him that was central for the gathering. The fresh new bills competed for colour with the white flour bag.

'I saved that money from the first day I came into this village as a young woman.'

Hoveyau's ears stood up. He was always uneasy about his wife's inability to make a good garden. She was always lazing about the village, and it took a great effort to make her leave the *kandis* to go to the garden. She would take a spade and if there ever was a *kandis* in progress, the spade would spend as much time as her besides the *kandis*. It was also the same with *bilums*, bush knives or planting materials for the garden so how and where, when did she get these saving savvy. The implements have very little time working in the garden.

On average she would in totality spend two days out of seven in the garden and five in the village. She gambled at these *kandis* and there were times when he wondered what if she ran out of money. He had gone into ingenious ways to spy on her on these early days but then gave up when she always came up squeaky clean and more baffling was, she always had some money; not plentiful but enough to earn them some repute in the village. And she kept a house of good pigs which again earned her more kudos and respect.

Maybe! Women: they were a specie you could not trust.

Now she trumps over her extra thousand. He was feeling unease.

He had been relieved when she dug up the first thousand from the holey corner of her part of his house, but these fresh crisp notes meant money from somewhere that he did not know existed.

Was there another man involved? He tried going through his mind names of possible suitors. He knew that he had not been doing his part in their marital relations. There were no one else in the family, where they had plutonic relations with others except for Unca Holoe and he was one that was friends to all and enemies to none. He was also the silent village tycoon and the only one in the village who was bank savvy, and everyone looked up to him. He would have cordial relations with every woman in this village. The crispness of the notes would indicate his involvement, but the huge amounts baffled him. His wife would lack the ability to hoard all these monies given the amount of time spent at the *kandis* and her half-a-garden.

'Why don't you stop strutting like 'a loaded cocky rooster', he made the utterance into his breath that still could not hide the anger and jealousness.

If La'ano heard it, she let it pass. She was going to live in her glory for the moment.

Mama Heloiseh came in and gawked in silence at the amount of money and the freshness of the notes.

'These new notes, where did these come from?' She whispered in a hush voice all the while trying to stifle her excitement.

'All you women, when we thought that money was hard to find, you come up with all colours of money. We can only thank you girls.' Greenie was all praise for the girl population.

'They may be bringing it from the sale of their bodies', Hoveyau drew it out in a slow drawl. 'Don't give them praise yet.'

'What, what are you men saying? You who *don't know what a spade looks like* and whom, you, even the bush knife cannot say *'daddy'* to you. Don't talk about women's money even if she brings to these contributions like these. Where the money comes from, be it from the garden sale, from the *kandis* or from her *'thing'*, don't you men make noises over it. It is all done and produced in your name.'

'Don't tell me that our women are sleeping with other men just to ensure our names get the appropriate praises.' a man who came into house said without looking up.

The women in the house screamed in unison at the man who uttered the sentence.

He wouldn't dare to curse in a reply to the angry women.

It was electric inside the house.

'*Egghe egghe*, I knew that it was going to head in that direction. Please, please, my good family, we can discuss that in a couple of weeks after we have our new wife here. Also, when we *'make fire' to give school to* the young bride, I think we should talk about that so the new bride will watch her steps over these ideas that are out there. Now if there is some woman doing that, she needs to stop.' An elderly woman competing for a time to speak voiced her concern loudly through the murmuring dissent in the house.

'Now if all you people of now, if you will stop wasting your time at the *kandis,* this ugly thing that people readily talk with no shame will not happen. This thing about men pulling other men's wives has always been in our society since time immemorial and men have been speared for it. You, today's men now, enjoy the money that the women bring to you so you either keep your eyes closed or you just agree for such to happen. We hear that this was happening in the towns where because the women don't have a garden, they put their *own 'garden'* on the market. It is a shame if this is happening in the village when we have all these bushlands wasting away. It is regrettable that you men have all these young bones that you waste doing nothing, so you now must let your women bring disreputable money.'

'Yeah, we hear that you – our dear village women too are doing it just for your soap money', another piped in.

'*Egghe, Egghe!* Soap costs just twenty toea[1]! Is that how cheap, this has become?'

'Eh, stop all these *rabis* talks. You think you men and women are doing a good thing and you continue in such activity. Just watch one of you being caught. I think that history will repeat itself with the story of the work that old Sukuluho did.'

'Okay what did this Sukuluho do?' a young boy enquired loudly.

'Greenie, can you tell these young boys what the old man did to the woman who was caught in adultery. I should think that would have been a running lesson in the village to remind us that such activity of pulling another man's wife is taboo.'

'That is true, we should also make it a rule that a man caught in adultery should be castrated.'

The house roared in laughter at that suggestion from a woman.

The fun, banter and singing continued through the night as the rest of the family brought in their contributions and pledges of pigs.

Hoveyau sat furlong, his mind becoming poisoned and wondering how a woman could suddenly flout a vast sum of money.

The body odours and smoke mingled to create a nausea smell in the house. La'ano burnt the first of the lemon bushes that she had for this fourth night. The scent waffled through in competition with the

---

1 ~cents

smell that was already there from the previous nights. The smell of the cooked pork did not help.

Tonight, was the night marked out for the rest of the village and other clansmen with their families to make their contributions? The house was filled up with little room for standing. The house was hot, and it did not help with the smell of sweat, bad tobacco smell and body odour.

It was turning fast to be a sour night.

It began disappointingly. The first person who contributed, put out four kinas only. He felt it entitled him to speak longtime and he made a rambling nothing speech.

Others from his group wanted to be gone and were agitated. When he was abruptly told to stop, he raised his voice back in anger. As the elder in his family, he was supposed to lead with his contributions and his contributions was supposed to be a good double- or triple-digit sum. Instead on his measly sum his rambling did not go down well with both his family and the rest of the people. Being an elder did not automatically give him the licence to ramble.

La'ano could feel the sourness and was disappointed. The last time she had contributed something towards the problem of this person was just three weeks ago. She was the only one who contribute the full sum of fifty kina when his wife took him to the village moot court for swearing bad words at her.

She also could relate to the previous times she had contributed to his causes, all good amounts and usually two-digit sums. She would partake in a lot of their activities, and she had done some good contributions for this family as they shared the same bushland.

Now his measly sum might lead the family to not come good. She tried to fade out from her memory what contribution she had done for him and his family.

Papa Ave wanted to speak out, but this was not his night. The night and the next three was for the rest of the village and they had chosen another person to be chairman of the night to call and direct the night.

The chairman of the night, Goi, looked a bit crooked, and he quietly probed the person to look for some more money as four kina was not enough. The chairman was the one who had sat at the leader's court when a hundred kina was collected for this person's court case. This gathering now was at the behest of the very same lady that contributed fifty kina to his cause. He bit his lips. He was going to be diplomatic.

'You, this man, these four kinas is not enough. I will keep it at my feet here. You look up some more and add it on. When you do, I will move it to the big pile. We are contributing to buy a wife, and this is money that we must give over to our *poromahns*. We give them something small; they will ridicule us. When we want to buy a man his wife, it is serious business. You must bring money that you say you don't have, money that you would have hidden somewhere in the *sepeku* of your house, to this contribution.'

'Now, let me say this, our good mama, La'ano has done well to put out better part of the bride wealth but that is not to say we as a village will not contribute. She has made *our blood boil gladness*. Each family must keep that spirit going and all of us must feel good afterwards. It was incumbent on us as a village to contribute to all bride prices for all our wives, something that we have a bad record of as most of our wives are *dinau wives* with their bride prices still outstanding.'

'We have them outstanding because the very people who are going to say – 'I will put bride price' are not taking ownership of it or are not coming good at the contributions.

'And these very people having difficulties coming up with some good amounts to contribute are becoming like a *cuscus* hiding way up in the top reaches of the tree. You want to stay as far as possible up in the top of trees and as far away from the village and not do your part.'

'*Ehe'q!* Don't think nobody is watching you? We have *small eyes*, and we keep you in our view and see your actions and when your turn comes, we too will become a *cuscus* at your time.'

'These types of gatherings are times for contributions that you make *good of*, remembering all the other times of your life when a person would have come to your assistance. He may have come with small or insignificant assistance, you may want to put at your leg, but remember this assistance helped. If you do the same now, it will help us. If you want to come small with money, perhaps I might suggest a pig to beef this up.'

'This man, what do you think?' He finally asked the four-kina man.

The question was left hanging when another family unit interrupted and forced in their contributions. It was a good money - *One bilum.*

8

FOKOFIS AND GHETTOS

This contribution of two hundred kina was timely as the people in the house were nearly going into shut-eye mode. They perked up and with it the noise also. The singing too that was going flat, perked up.

The night wore on slowly and the contributions from them grew slowly. The night was interspaced by songs, and stories and jokes. There were lots of ribald jokes and anecdotes. There were talks of promiscuity in the village and one or two women made the beeline for the door and night feeling uncomfortable.

La'ano made tea for those gathered knowing that the subject of promiscuity by women in the village was there in the air. It was all talk until someone was caught. If they were caught in the adulterous act then there were fisticuffs, fist fights, and the occasional spearing of another man. Then the making of the peace *mumu* when one party makes reparation to the children for the *act of giving them the end of the fingernails*. The thought of being caught sent another reminder and a thrilling shiver up the back of her spine. She needed some excitement and perhaps to do her own fisticuffs, fights - perhaps the spearing and then do reparation for giving her children *the end of her fingernails*.

She listened to the veil threats issued against the women - always against the women. She tried to review parts of her own marital life. She kept a lot of secrets including sidesteps on her husband. Many men had let in the occasional gaffs and hints to her to leave her husband and to shack up with them. They knew of the laziness of the walking bones, but she stuck to him despite her occasional splaying out of the melodrama of her own two-timing shenanigans. She felt that these other married women kept old beaus alive in their lives.

Okay, when she was still a young married teen going back on visits to her own village, she had found the occasion to cavort in some discrete liaisons. It also included some liaisons with old beaus. These meetings had since petered out as she matured in her marriage and found the ability to live albeit decently on her own. Now these people are talking about shenanigans; the hairs on her hands stood upright. She shivered and tried to concentrate on her hospitality.

Her thoughts were interrupted by clapping for Mongi and her entourage. She came with all loud brusque voice and humour. Her girly big voice reverberated around the round house. She was the eccentric of the village who looked like a man, dressed up like a man, drank like a man and passed like a man. She was the *mama ghetto* of the village and was the known loose woman aka *pamuk meri*. Her house was filled with all the *ghettos* of the village and there was always the running argument that all who associated with her and slept around in her house were mostly *pamuk meris*. Whatever they were they did their *pamuking* outside of the village but the village whilst being intolerant of them treated them all like queens.

'We, these *ghettos*, are the *pamuk ones*,' it was Mongi now with her impromptu speech trying to find space in the village where the males of the society had all the power in the village.

'Hey! Hey, listen, shut up and listen, a woman wants to speak. The *ghettos* want to contribute so give them space.'

This was met by general sneers from those in the house, especially from the married ones.

'We are the pariahs of the village, and we are scorned plenty of times. Through it all, though, Josiah is our man to go to when we find our going abouts a tad too difficult. Josh has rescued us time and time again and each one of us girls felt we had to give back something in return. We *coins-coins* together and the result is that we as a group as … as the *ghetto meris* are putting this small amount of money. There are seven of us who are … … are….'

The smirking and stunned crowd craned their neck to see the seven *ghettos* in the flickering light and what amount they proffered as their contributions - something that usually does not happen.

'Get out from the light's way. We want to see all those *ghettos* unless you too are going to contribute like these girls too, oh.' The comment in reprimand to the person blocking the rays from the Coleman lamp that was lighting up the house.

'*Apo, ya,* this two *bilum* and a *wing* is quite a lot of money. Goi who had stepped in to relieve the chairman to do the chairing voiced out. He accepted the money but placed it down beside him and not in where all the other money was piled on.

'Our good *ghettos* have come good and you, mama of the *ghettos,* don't have to mention where this money came from or by what means you raised this amount of money. You don't have to tell us what you do with yourselves - *from your skins.* We the men recognise that you have no gardens and you will always be servile to your brothers and their wives.'

'We know what you do and if these monies are from your business - *from your skins*, you know, there will be issues of it later *covering our skins.* That is not to say we refuse your contributions. We will take it and hold it. I am going to ask these moneys to be held by Mamu's mother La'ano to buy sugar, tea, and coffee for the gathering. I am going to ask you *ghettos* not to be dismayed with the moving of this money to the side. I have placed it over this side, away from the big pile. It will be used for the same cause and there are three more nights for us together.'

'U-uh,' Hoveyau blew hard into his throat to interrupt. '…that money, that *ghetto* money, my brother, is good money. Leave it in the pile. All these monies, all these in the pile, we don't know where they came from. Some were brought here by legitimate means. Others we don't know. Some of the men may have stolen it by a raid on the *Sainamahn's* store. Some of us were given money by our wives to contribute but we don't know where they got the money from; perhaps they got if by unlawful means.'

'*Wheeah!* What are you saying?' La'ano raised her voice. 'You, the fence post at the *kandis*, what are you saying? You imply that we are all *pamuk meris*. You say that about women who are married to you in your village! *Whee!* Come on, say it out loud and straight. You imply that we women are all loose women. You make it out that I flout all these monies by being a *pamuk*. You see all the men that come chasing me like flies, so that is why you say that.'

She pulled out up a branch, a yar tree branch that she wanted to hew out a wooden thong from the rafters of the house. She tried to walk onto the bed, all the time throwing barbed words at her husband. She wanted to clobber her husband.

'The lazy bones, you waste your big bones and precarious life away at the *kandis* and you want to say something.'

'*Egghe, egghe,* now who is that trying to bring chaos to our chairmanship?' Papa Ave breached the door and tried to bring order into the house. Papa Ave's presence brought new zeal into the house and the women now increased their loud animated noise even more in support of La'ano.

'He is doubting where I got all these monies from. Useless man, the big lazy bones, he dares to question where I … all these monies come from. He makes disparaging comments about all the contributions are from women including me claiming we are contributing from our efforts out there *pamuking*. Ha, he wishes that what I laid out were monies from my *kapis*.'

'Tell your brother, his eyes are very *heavily closed*; he is blind. He who has a *short-hand*, a man who even the spade cannot say '*daddy to*'; should not question us women. He questions and wants to know if the money comes from our working our genitalia; so, what? It will be so if you men don't know your manly duties and find money or be involved in productive activity that will bring money into the family and village.'

'Papa Ave, your brother there, he sits like a *ghahali'q* scabies sick dog and throws barbed words that makes my stomach churn. He wants clean money; he and all you men should throw down clean money and we women and girls will do the same. When money don't say '*daddy to* you', you don't chase it away by throwing barbed statements, a *ghahali'q* - a sick dog will speak like one.'

'What! You call me a *ghahali'q*; did I mention you. I was making a general statement, a stupid woman like you….' Hoveyau stood up. He could not stomach the rebuke.

'Now you label me a what! Whee, you call me stupid!' La'ano hoisted the branch she had over her head.

'Mama, mama, tone down your voice,' Mama Heloiseh walked in front of the foaming La'ano and stood with her. 'Easy now, *Apo*, you have said your bit. Our *ghettos* are scared.'

'Don't stop me. This man has been taunting me all my life here with him. He thinks I am a whore. He has nothing to show here, and he throws words that stink and cut to the bones. If a man cannot make a garden and keep pigs, he ought to say nothing. It is okay if women bring food to the table from selling their *'prized possession'* and …and …bones that have nothing to show, should put up or leave.'

La'ano was frothing from the mouth. She was riled up bad and was looking for a fight in the house.

Hoveyau looked spent as he huddled back down to the back of the crowd in the house. The strong words from his wife drained all the energy out of him. It was known that he spent his days in the village and wondering from each *kandis* group to *kandis* group watching people gamble their money. If one was good to share with him some of their wins, he spent it again within one of the *kandis*. The occasional foray to the garden and *hauspik* was when there were no *kandis* and he was very hungry. Those occasions were few, just about as much as the fingers on his hands where he had cooked and eaten what was put out for the pigs. That was how poor he was now, and his wife was gloating over him. He swallowed bitter bile.

And Greenie started a song, a *Homasi song*.

As the second stanza petered out, Papa Ave spoke out.

'Sorry to the chairman, let me say something.'

'Eh, these types of arguments and fights always happens during times like these, and it is normal, so my good family, we will still have plenty of fights before our new wife joins us. It is good that for now, no blood is spilled yet, but you people, mark my words, there will be blood spilt before the end of this bringing on a new wife. Now everybody clap your hands and we let peace and harmony rule the night for now.'

There was no clapping. Just a stunned pause as everyone looked towards La'ano and Mama Heloiseh huddled over to the side. Mama Heloiseh now had the timber that La'ano had brandished around her.

'Our *ghettos* now where are you. Let me see you all.' Papa Ave broke the tension.

The *ghettos* who had timidly shied away into small spaces they made to make themselves inconspicuous slowly moved out to make their appearances again.

'All you, my good *Apo* ya, you are the nice ones, the flowers of the village, you are alive, and this village is alive. Men from our neighbouring villages become alive when they pass through the area. They claim you girls have the spruik and they go one step up in your company. These men ogle for and enjoy your camaraderie.'

'I do say thank you, your two fathers here had decided to keep your contributions to the side which has caused some consternation from you. It was your right to be angry with us. Your mothers have been very supportive of you. I will speak for and with the chairman of the night, and unfortunately must decide to either accept your fathers' ruling or decide otherwise.'

'That money that you contributed is five hundred kinas, a big sum of money, again let me thank you all. Let me say this to everyone here. That money is not going to spring out from that pile in the middle and sing out saying look at me, I am a coloured money. It is never going to say I am a *pamuk* money.'

'It will never do so, thank you, *Seliné ne ve* to you *ghettos*. The chairman and I have now agreed that we will be for moving your contributions into the main gathering.'

'As for *something bad covering us*, we will do the *seme'ne mumu* and break that curse if it ever falls on us.' He poked Greenie in the side.

On cue, Greenie's whooping *ganine* screamed through the house. *'Mita Ghoiha Ku piii!!!'*

Those sleeping woke up and rubbed their eyes. They had earlier joined those whose blood had quelled to sleep. They jolted awake as the *ganine* injected much needed adrenaline into their veins.

Ou!! Ou!! The accompanying women's chorus was from one woman and as it ended, the rest of the women including the youngest girl shouted in a unionised cacophony of noises joining the general *gamakilise* of the men which literally, lifted the roof of the house.

Everyone sang their loudest to the second stanza to the *Homasi* song. The whole house was oozing noise.

The *ghettos* took their exit. Outside the houses, they started their own song that reverberated up the length of the village. They were raucous in defiance to the men who wanted to refuse their contributions as 'dirty money.'

They threw out into the village night, words they could not speak back to the men inside. They sang songs that they tarnished to show they despised the men of the village. They yelled and sang out unspoken words that they knew were voiced in whispers inside up through the village to the main road.

'There now, your *ghettos* are trying to raise some more funds for you people from *their good things*,' and a good belly ache laughter broke throughout the house.

This fourth night for the village contributions had been fruitful. The bride wealth was looking good.

On the fifth day she nearly let the day for this small ceremony slip by. La'ano woke up quickly from her morning nap. The late night had nearly derailed the day.

She was still reeling from the imputations that Hoveyau threw last night.

She hurried out to the *hauspik*.

She went by the garden to dig up a particular *kaukau* that she had replanted for this purpose. From the *marretta* patch, she picked up the *muho* plant and looked around the end of the garden for the *pig-grass*. This time though her search for this grass took longer as her neighbour had built a bushfire that got out of hand and burnt part of *kunai grasses* on her side of the fence which also singed most of the green grass. She was about to give up on the idea of the ceremony when she finally found it.

The *muho* plant is an herb that grew profusely amongst *karuka* trees up in the mountains and were introduced to the lowlands where it struggled to grow. The plants were now planted amongst the foot of the *marretta* plants.

She cleared out the whining pigs from the house and built a fire. She was going to do the pig rearing ritual and feed these pigs the results. She took a few *kaukaus* to roast. She added a few more for herself. When the *kaukau* were on the fire, she rubbed the pigs and sprinkled ashes over their manes.

She returned to the kaukau on the fire, took great care to roast it to perfection. She then scrubbed the black soot off the *kaukau* and shoved them into the ashes to further roast them. She then pulled her *bilum* to her head on the bed as a pillow and drifted off to sleep.

She woke up with a start.

La'ano raced around to brush off the ashes and the burnt skins to the cooked *kaukau*. It was the special one that she had dug. It was perfectly shaped like a grub, big on one side and tapering away at the other end.

She took out the *muho* leaves from her *bilum*. Her grandfather had told her that these leaves had some magical qualities about them. He had shown her how to prepare *kaukau* and the leaves with the *'pig-grass'*, a three-piece combination that did three things to the pigs.

Firstly, the combined feed helped to calm down the pigs and keep them docile and tame. They would mostly stay around or near the *hauspik*.

Secondly it ensured that the meats from these pigs when slaughtered were going to be plentiful.

And thirdly, the pig would taste better so that even a person having a morsel from it would remember the taste.

Then there was the sacred rhyme that her mother would say when feeding the pigs. She did this very time just before the season for planting *assbeans*. She remembered the tune and hummed it along as she gave morsels of the *kaukau* to each pig. She did not know the actual words. They were from an ancient language.

It however was a tune that the people rhymed to keep time - to mark each setting sun over the mountain ranges. The range was between the Korepas and the Kofena mountains. It started at the Korepas end which was the end of rains on the return run. As it travelled back up, that was the time for planting taro and yams. The time for planting *assbeans* was when the sun fell in the last big dip over the Kofena end. It was also the time to do the pig rearing rituals. The return leg was the time for small rains when the leaves to the *assbean* bloomed. Most rituals were done about this time and this business to bring on a wife was good timing. Midway was when the dry season came on it was not a good time for partying. Food became scarce around these times and was not a good time to hosts feasts.

La'ano had proposed this thing to bring on a wife for his son without consulting this rhyme in the setting suns to see when it was the best time. The weather may spoil the whole thing for them. She needed to consult the oracles.

'Good pigs, don't you dare go into somebody's garden today. Please remain near to the house.'

She cut up the *kaukau* into smaller pieces and fed each pig a piece. She rubbed their manes and ran her hands down their cheeks saying piggy words to them.

Finally, she hit each one on their rumps and released them. The pigs still on their leashes moved into the bushes to root for the late worm.

La'ano cleaned the house. She removed all the grass for the last week and swore out loud when she found that there were a lot of droppings among them. She realised that one of the pigs must have diarrhoea. She would have to do a pot of *ghohuno* leaves which was a sure remedy. She must find the time in afternoon or tomorrow to get some leaves that she can cook for them.

She then went outside to change the leash on the feet of the pigs. The first one acceded and gave its feet over to La'ano to change. She thanked the complying pig and moved to the next one. This one was a bit of trouble. It must have smelled a big worm and refused its feet.

It was then she heard a faint whistled shoot through the air. It was from over the next ridge, and it sent a tingling sensation through her. It sent her heart fluttering and as she paused, the second shrill whistle rang out again.

She waited for a while, her adrenaline now at its peak. She went into the house and brought out some burning sticks to set fire to the rubbish that she had cleared from the house. Thick white smoke bellowed out from the grass. She looked up and when enough smoke cloud had gone up, she quickly shut down the fire.

It was their prearranged signal; they had decided so many years ago and put in practise every now and then. She made this smoke firebomb to indicate she was willing - whenever she heard the whistle. It had been a long while.

She had to while the hours away hoping for an opportune time to sneak into their rendezvous spot.

She pulled out a spade from the house and worked around the house covering the areas that the pigs had dug up. She cleared the drains around the house to ensure the passages were not clogged up to let rainwater into the house. She then attacked the fresh growth of weeds with such vigour that soon she was sweating profusely.

It had been some hours ago since the whistle had sounded.

It also has been a long time in between rendezvous since that time her desires were thwarted. She craved to leave now to go to the creek to bathe, but she knew the bushes and the animals talked. She had to be careful. Working up a sweat was good reason to have a bath.

She then remembered with dismay that she had asked one of the *ghettos* to accompany her into town to buy a new teapot. Her old pot last night had sprung a leak that led to some of the crowd not getting a cup of tea. She was going to buy a big replacement pot and the *ghetto* will soon call on her to hurry.

But the whistle woke up a yearning in her. The last time she hugged up a firm body of a man was a long time ago and it was not her husband's Hoveyau. Hoveyau slept in his own bed.

After a night of veiled accusation against her for bringing money from her suspected infidelity, it had made her angry. She was going to take it out on him. The wimp… well… the whistle.

She stoked up the fire with fresh green grass to create more smoke - she was willing for a meet. These smokes whiffled through the screen of *pitpit*. He should see that.

She stood and viewed her handiwork making sure that it was not going to burst into flames.

She fished around for the piece of soap that she kept up in the rafter storage.

She tried to count the many clandestine rendezvous that she had had with him. She had tried to fight the fear of being caught with him but knowing the consequences of such meetings, she still craved for these moments. They brought excitement into her life.

The whistler was one of the many men who courted on her when she was a young girl. He was deemed one of her boyfriends, except the bride price came from another person - Hoveyau, if not she would have come in marriage to him.

Her uncle was the one that was adamant. He had forced all to accept the bride wealth even though he was told that La'ano did not know the groom at all.

They were told she was going to marrying into good stock, an old family – an *itehetu* that had plenty of land except that they missed out on telling all that this old family was the laziest in the village. Their vast lands laid bare.

She should have seen the laziness in the first instance but the aura of being a newly married woman masked it all.

The practise was that after a bride wealth was brought to the groom's village, a girl was supposed to stay away from any contact with any young male person in her new village. It was known that there had been some pregnant brides that had derailed the whole process, and the return and repayment of the bride wealth was a cause for consternation.

There would be no formal contact between bride and groom until the *tóhamo ceremony* and that could take as long as two years depending on whether the parents-in-law thought it was the appropriate time. This ceremony was also a taxing time where there was more outlay of pigs and garden food to which the young bride was supposed to work to contribute to it. Until the parents said yes, to indicate their approval of the young bride and to show they can host the *tóhamo ceremony*, only than the proper wedding will take place. It is only after this that the bride and groom could then come to live together as husband and wife.

The time between the delivery of the bride and the *tóhamo ceremony* was to test out the bride, whether she would learn the art of garden making and be involved in rearing pigs. If a bride could rear a pig and kill in a year, she would have passed with flying colours. To rear a good pig was the nexus to working hard in the garden, to have plenty to eat, a woman had to be prepared to work hard toiling the soil. These were all qualities that added to the worth of the bride cum woman.

Whilst that had been the normal way, La'ano had played on and hijacked the process in her own marriage. She had been making quite frequent trips back to her home and had occasioned these as opportunities to continue liaisons with some old beaus, one of them, the owner of the whistle.

These liaisons had the potential to derail her new marriage and it did. She had immediately sought out Hoveyau and forced herself upon him. She moved in with him without this ceremony. When it was done eventually, ceremony was low key and done during the *marretta* season where the village had harvested and *presented as a marretta gift* to her village people. There was a *mumu* then and amidst the giving of the *marretta* it was announced that they were now man and wife.

Her first miscarriage happened some months immediately. It was rumoured that she forced the *tóhamo ceremony* and then forcibly aborted that baby to hide her shenanigans.

Her own parents came from their village to build them their first house. Their garden was still the bridal garden, built and delivered to her by her own people immediately after she was installed.

Hoveyau's bag of lazy bones was evident then, but she accepted it as a time of the young man evolving into the marital hubris. She thought he would outgrow it soon as the reality of knowing that a young groom was turning from being a boy into a man sets in. For Hoveyau this boyishness never left him.

He rarely went to the garden nor to the *hauspik*. It was common knowledge that babies were made at the *hauspik* or at the garden hut. Hoveyau's aversion to these places meant that their attempt to do so in the village was beset with its own problems, one being that the house was shared with the village's growing children and the house was always full.

He slowly developed a lacklustre interest in all matter's procreation, and he also later virtually showed no interest in all thing's children. He showed however more interest in holding a conversation with everyone and all. He moved into standing and watching at the gambling *kandis* returning home late to crawl into bed.

This also compounded La'ano problems of keeping her pregnancies. One after the other she started having miscarriages and she too was starting to show a lacklustre interest. It was only after having sought out Gohens - the medicine man - that she eventually conceived with Ghitume Monopoliso, followed by several more miscarriages and another visit to Gohens for Te'enike Liivelave and then Mamu Josh was a surprise.

She toyed with the soap and looked down to the creek. This area of the bush belonged to them, and it was still virgin bushland. Nobody had ever made a garden and the bushes remained heavy-set as they were so from time immemorial. The *pitpit* here grew layer after layer where underneath the pigs frolicked for worms.

It was under these bushes she had previously marked out a spot for her illicit rendezvous. He crept in from one side, she from the other.

A young married woman, a lot of nights she woke up angry and frustrated. These led to her renewing old acquaintances by going back to visit with her parents and family. A discreet night at her family house or *hauspik* also meant a clandestine and amorous but risky outing. Despite the dangers she still had maintained a waning number of beaus and meetings.

With this whistler when she took the trips back to her maiden village, he followed and would come in the night where she would be bedded down. They were her best nights.

These yearning has led to more dangerous liaisons back with a lot more now happening here in her marital village under the very nose of her husband. The best illicit place was this spot besides the creek where there was suspense. The threat of being caught played a big part in this.

The whistler's land was on the other side of the creek so there was legitimate reason for him to be around in the area and there would be nothing amiss if they were seen within the vicinity of each other or even nearly together.

Today she was game enough for another outing.

The humiliation over the notion that she might have other means of accumulating such monies was more than she could bear. She was looking for straws in a strange way to justify her angst. She wanted to rebuff the angst of last night, the public voicing of doubt as to how she had more money.

The useless man was not contributing anything of substance towards getting a wife for his son. She reflected that he may not be his son, but it was too late to be worried about the paternity now. At least the nose of the son was her own.

The whistle again ran through the gully and the echo bounced off the cleared cliff face of the landslip and finally echoed back the small plea in the whistle. She imagined the man and it sent a shiver pulsating through her.

She put some urgency in her work, and she double checked the leashes to the pigs and hastily put out the fire. She picked her *bilum* up from the *kunai roof* of the house and started heading for the track to the creek.

'La'ano!'

Darn. She pulled up short in her tracks as her name floated down the gully to her.

'Whoa! Who is it?' She replied to the voice up on the side of the cliff.

It was her neighbour.

'Eh, good woman, Mama Heloiseh said you two were planning a trip into town. She is ready and asked if I could check up on you.'

Any anticipation that she had, fell flat.

The bile that was there rose and she spat it out.

'Oh! Thank you. I was trying to go to the creek to wash my face. Won't be long. If you can please let her know that I won't be long.'

She cursed her luck and hurried to the creek.

She was at a heightened alert as she bathed and was drying herself when a soft whistle whiffled through the *pitpit* stands rustling the bush around her.

She did not miss a beat but raised a pointed finger to cover her mouth. She indicated to the cliff that there were people up there.

She really wanted a quickie and was fuzzily pondering crawling through the *pitpit* strands to their spot. She pictured him already there, him all ramrod straight and firm and being comfortable. She knew him, his contours and …and ….

'Fiiii'ii iiiieee.'

An echo of an impatient whistle bounced along the gully from up the cliff.

It was another whistle from the village. Mama Heloiseh was always in a rush. She needed to get going everywhere in a rush.

La'ano knew she was always the tardy one in the family.

'I see her down in the creek.' Another person on the other ridge shouted across the ravine that the creek ran through – a precarious sign. The bushes and animals can talk.

It sent a shiver up her spine.

La'ano beat into a hasty run up from the creek to the *hauspik*. Someone else was watching. It was an ominous warning. They could be caught this time.

She retrieved her big *bilum* from inside the *hauspik*.

'Whoa!' she called up the ridge.

Her heart was running ahead of her. She caught up with it at the top and she paused to catch back her breath. She looked at the cluster of bamboo beside the path. They seemed to be mocking her.

She could smell the adrenaline from all the anticipation that ran through her, and her sweat pores were oozing in unsated desire.

La'ano looked at Mama Heloiseh's youngest daughter standing in the shade of the bamboo. She was all smiles.

La'ano wondered if she too was mocking her with that smile. She may have seen another head in the bush down besides the creek. Was she capable of making a judgement – that one plus one equals two - that the head besides the creek was not a chance encounter of two people?

'Mama Josh, I came down here a long time ago and Mama has been calling for me. I have been looking for bamboo shoots in your bamboo cluster while waiting for you. I got three young shoots here. I hope you will not be angry.'

'Oh, so that was what your smile was all about. You were trying to hide your stealing of my bamboo shoots. No, don't worry about that. Why, that bamboo cluster is as much as yours as any of your other cousins.'

La'ano blew a ton of hot air out of her chest. She was safe for now. She fanned herself with the *bilum*. It did not generate any new air. She felt exhausted.

'Okay, let us run along now.'

'Now tell me what your mother wants?'

'No, she just wanted me to ask you to hurry along.'

'I heard you shout to someone when I ran from the creek. Now who was it you were calling out to over there? '

'Oh, that was that new woman, Nomele, out there on the ridge. She was looking down into the ravine from her side of the ridge to say you were washing up.'

The hairs on the back of her neck stood up. Nomele was the wife of her... ... her... she did not want to go down the line of thinking she was having. Did the whistler know that his wife could look down into the gully?

A chill down her spine made cold sweat form in the groove of her back and she could feel it running into the base of her back. Her throat dried up and she felt like she needed a bucketful of water. She peered across the ravine. Nomele was tending her *kaukau* garden.

Nomele was the second wife.

The first wife of the whistler, Atuwato and La'ano did not see eye to eye. Atuwato made it her business to show some hate towards La'ano for whatever reasons she had. Atuwato knew that there had been some plutonic relationship between her husband and La'ano when they were young. She knew that La'ano's parents had requested that her husband's people put out bride wealth for La'ano.

Atuwato had not wanted to believe her husband and La'ano were continuing with any clandestine relationship.

Apparently, she would not have passed this information to this new second wife - Nomele. If Atuwato did, it would have caused Nomele to watch more closely at whatever activities happening down in that area around the creek. If she had watched carefully from the spot high above, she would have had a panoramic view, and she might have seen a bob of head or two in the bushes nearby.

Another information that few knew was that Atuwato as a young teen have had a crush for Hoveyau and they had some courting nights just before the bride wealth for La'ano was accepted and the marriage formalised. She still bore some grudge against La'ano for her not marrying Hoveyau and into the *itehetu* name.

This was potent for starting a World War three in the village, but it never happened until Atuwato split up with the whistler.

It was a standing story in the village that a long time ago the whistler had bespoken for La'ano. La'ano had fought and sought to resist all bride wealth of other suitors and had been waiting for him, wishing the whistler to get his parent and people to act together bride wealth wise.

But when a bride wealth put forth by Hoveyau's parents, her uncle had accepted it. La'ano was getting along and would have turned *sapava* like a fresh new leaf that turns old becoming a *ghetto – an old maid*. Fearing this, her uncle had accepted this bride wealth from Hoveyau's people. Also, the other criteria used was the groom was from an *itehetu* - land owning family.

The whistler had been bitter about his own parents not having come forth with any bride wealth. The whistler trundled along life with a string of failed marriages as La'ano had his heart and he hers.

The marriage had not stopped their frequent meetings and later it tapered off to be an occasional dangerous clandestine liaison where she kept a love triad.

It had been just as unfortunate for Atuwato – the whistler's wife to have carried the brunt of it. He made life difficult for her and she left the marriage. Now another woman took her place.

Nomele was a new wife, a recent happenstance - she could not surely know of their lifelong clandestine love relationship. If somebody tells her, who in the village would do that. Somebody in the village knew - Atuwato might have told them what she knew, and this person might or if it has happened already, must have put a statement about it towards Nomele.

Nomele may have been stalking and watching.

La'ano walked behind the child worried, mentally trying to slowly work through all the myriad of clandestine meetings and hurried lovemaking they did. Were they ever in a place to be seen. She had left some money on a stone for the man in the bush like she always did. If Nomele was watching, she would see him come out from where he was hiding to the creek to pick up that money. He had no reason to be there as she too had heard his whistling just before that, but the man was always whistling away - all types of whistling tunes to mask the special one that he sent out for her.

If Nomele did see him there now, there was going to be a lot of questions for the asking, and begging for answers.

La'ano kept out a watchful eye as they came upon the village. There were virtually no one about but it was hard to tell. An angry Nomele could confront her and derail all she was doing.

Mama Heloiseh was at the neck of the village next to the main road all spruced up and waiting for her.

La'ano looked out over to the track leading to the whistler's side of the gardens.

She was going to be careful with Nomele.

La'ano rued her luck. She was staring down a threat from another woman, but she was missing that x factor of having a man. It was a price to pay if she was caught. She quickly changed into some clean clothes and making sure the door was shut, she got some money from her corner that she had earmarked to spend today. She did a quick count.

It was all there. She picked up her *bilum* and pulled open the door to get out. A shadow breached it. La'ano looked up to see Hoveyau standing before her with a long new bush knife, the sun's ray bouncing off the glistering and recently sharpened cutting edge. He was all threatening.

She exhaled a deep breath of air as tingling sweat of fear ran down her back. All the muscles of her body were at their maximum stress level. Was she found out?

It was the inevitable. She had been playing with this for a long time and though she was expecting it she did not anticipate what was coming from her husband. The man never had reason to have a bush knife in his hands but now he has one shiny one with him and was breaching the door.

She moved back into the house, her hairs on their ends. New sweat was pouring down her back. She carefully watched him and tried to move out of reach of the bush knife, ready to bolt out of the house.

Hoveyau nodded to her and walked in with his lame slow way into the house. The shine of the sharpened edge throwing reflected light onto the blinds of the house.

It was one of the few times she had seen a bush knife in the hands of this man but this morning, she was really scared. She could feel each cold sweat run down the back of her spine. Her heart was *beating a sixty*. She had a fleeting glimpse of imaginary gory thoughts – of mangled limbs and a severed head.

Hoveyau coughed from where he was in front of the entrance. La'ano looked up fleetingly at him working out how she was going to edge quickly past him. She needed to get out of the house.

'*Apo* are you trying to go into town', he asked as he stuck the bush knife into the blind walls. He then turned to sit beside the fireplace.

La'ano breathed a heavy sigh and paused at the door.

The man hardly ever said the word *Apo* and she does not remember the last time he called her out with any endearing sounds with it to her. It sent a tingling sensation up her spine.

'I was trying to go with Mama Heloiseh to get some more supplies', her voice barely audible. The butterflies in the pit of her stomach fluttering wildly.

She held her stomach and ran out of the house. Behind the house she squatted and relieved herself. All the pent-up anxiety for the morning flowed out.

'Phew', she exclaimed to the stars spinning around her head.

Does he know of my clandestine affairs?

'*Apo*, can you get me a bottle of coke, the big one.' He called out to her as she started walking up to the road.

She stood in her tracks.

That was two *Apo*'s in the space of less than ten minutes, something that she had not heard from him in her lifetime living under his roof.

'Is there anything else you want', was all she could ask as her heart tried to find space to settle back into its spot.

The week ended.

Papa Ave and Goi felt comfortable with the bride wealth. The money contributions have surpassed their expectations. Bless the mother, La'ano, if she were not as chirpy and as open handed as she was, these *tolumo gatherings* could have been a bit strained and slow.

It was known that at times like these that families have recounted debts and become very bitter if the debt is not repaid. In some close-knit family units, fisticuff and tussles happen when one contributes less than what was expected.

This gathering of bride wealth did not have anything like that, but it was early days yet.

La'ano's *iye nakavosa* - sticks of pig debts were all spoken for except for four. Seven contributed both in money and made pledges of repaying the pig they owed her.

Tonight, the house was packed very early in the evening. They had come with an expectation of an announcement to the end of the gatherings. Tonight, they will be told the total amount contributed and collected. It was also when plans are laid out for when the *lulu'* - bride wealth is to be taken out for the *walks*.

It was also the night when the groom will be asked if he had girlfriends and if he had no specific girlfriends where his preference for a wife would lie.

There were no child betrothal arrangements for Josiah Mamu. La'ano had no inkling towards this type of arrangement, so none was done. Child betrothal needed a lot of resources and a lot of time and effort to maintain these arrangements. Even then there was no guarantee that the arrangement would work out with the two betrothals actually getting to marry each other. La'ano did not have the stamina to put the work towards its maintenance.

Now that she was considering buying his son a wife, it was now a matter of choice and to *walk* the *lulu'* - bride wealth to find any parent wanting to accept the *lulu'* in exchange for their daughter.

La'ano showed off with her big new kettle giving out instructions not to blacken it. She knew this was a futile direction. Somebody would throw the kettle on an open fire.

In all the hustle and bustle, she found some time to reflect on her marriage and tried to call out the positives in her rather uneventful life.

Josiah was an *itehetu*, a title in name only that had no place in the community unless the owned land was used to benefit the person. At their current rate, his father being only *manbones* and when spades and bush knives would not and will not call him *father*, these traits were already becoming evident in his son.

She made copious amount of coffee for the men and added plenty of sugar adding to her stress worrying unnecessarily if there were going to be enough sugar to last the night.

Papa Ave cleared his throat as soon as Pilipo showed up.

'Pilipo, Goi, Hoveyau, Papa Tota', he addressed his brothers and their one uncle. The rest of those in the house craned their necks and ears to hear him better.

'*Apo*, ya. The money we have contributed had gone beyond our expectations and the pigs too have grown in numbers. Now before all these pigs break ropes and run away or go into people's gardens we must move and *walk* this *lulu*'.'

'Now what is the actual money and the number of pigs pledged live and dead.' Tota asked.

'I'll start with the pigs. There are seventeen pigs called or pledged. Ten of these will accompany the money as live pigs and seven will be used as slaughtered pigs when the bride is delivered to the village.'

'Gosh, I thought the villagers did not care to raise pigs, but seventeen pigs are a huge number of pigs.'

'Six of them are from the family and four a new *dinaus* while the rest are repayments of pigs used by La'ano for people who are now *coming good.*'

'One from the old woman Molowaliso is a free '*paia wara*' gift. She says Josiah Mamu has been taking care for her since he was small, making sure that she had water and fire. She is repaying these '*paia*' - fire woods and '*waras*' - waters that Josh did fetch for her. She now wants her pig to be eaten by the parents of the bride.'

'Gosh, a pig for the bride's parents must be a big pig as we don't want the parents of the bride disparaging our pigs. Does anybody know what the pig looks like?'

'*Ii ii*, Papa! You haven't seen the pig she has been fattening for a long, long time. I have heard her saying for some time that she was caring for the pig in her house that one day she was going to kill and give to Josiah as a thank-you for herself. It is a very big pig with the tusk coming through. But you know, I think she is saying the right thing because since her husband died, Mamu had - sort of adopted the widow. And that all started when Mamu-Josh was still in primary school and that pig would be worth all the effort Mamu put towards her.'

'Oh, so that was good thinking on the part of the young fellow. This is someone with thinking, he wasted his youth building his character and now someone comes out from the blinds and offers him a big pig for his investment in her affairs. I wish all our children would do the same, but we have a lot of lazy children, and we must work our thankless sweat for them.'

'Yeah, he keeps doing the same and he is the waspapa to the *ghetto*s. They too have been coming good for his cause.'

'Give my thanks to Molowaliso, we have now two huge pigs and our new *tambus* will have no reason to fault us. Okay, that is good, now what about the cash money.'

'We got *mulises* that can be counted on *one hand and four fingers on the other hand.*'

Greenie pushed through the door at that moment and was shocked by the announcement.

'*Souu, Mita ghoiha ku pi!!*' He made out a hearty gamakilise to a gaiety accompanying '*Ou-Ous*' a woman yodelled.'

'Greenie, thank you, I have not finished yet, but you have shouted out the *ganine*.'

'Oh, was I premature in the whoop?'

'No, it is okay, stand by to do another one but I will call you this time. I have not yet finished calling out all the groups of people and the money we have collected.'

'Sorry about that but the mention of the huge amount of money pooled has warmed my heart to do the *ganine whoop* without your *toksave*.'

'Okay, this money, La'ano, where are you … thank you, you the mother, you put out *three mulises*, the nuclear family backed you up with *three mulise* for six thousand and the good people, Josiah's uncles and aunties came with *one mulise*. The rest of the village contributed another *two mulise* for good measures.'

'La'ano, *Seghané*, if you had looked upon us to call the *tolumo* gatherings, we would not have got this far. We now have nine *mulises* that is over and beyond the normal amount that is usually put up as *lulu'* - bride wealth money. We however will not tamper and subtract from it. What we have pooled together was for this purpose and it will be for this purpose we will give all of that over.'

'*Big Mama*, La'ano, *Seghané ve,* thank you, you have really blessed the family. We have had a lot of doubts and talks, gossips and bad name calling. We would like to say sorry for that.'

La'ano looked up but her eyes watered as a few tears dropped down her cheeks.

'Now you all will realise that I left out mentioning *one mulise*.' Papa Ave continued. 'That was money that our *ghettos* contributed. On the first night, they brought us a *bilum* and *a half* and we debated whether we should accept it or not. We men were fearing that since it was money from their bodies, we did not want *something to cover our bodies and bring us ill fortune.* However, I said we accept it as money or are people blind. It does not decide who should have it. People must work, and our *ghettos* too worked for their share and since then they have increased their contributions to *a mulise*.'

'Now I would like to thank the *ghettos* and are they here?'

Everyone looked around inside the house. None of the *ghettos* were there and he continued.

'Okay, they are out there making new money for us but let me call out to them that HIV is lurking out there like a monster. Somebody - remind them to always carry the *gumi* and you men, trying to do the same with our neighbouring *ghettos* must always use the *gumi*.'

Laughter broke out in the house.

'I am not funny. We need the *ghettos,* living *ghettos.* Sick and dead *ghettos* will be useless to us. While they are alive well and kicking, they however are needed in the village, and you see here what they did. The few of them put in more than some of you hard working respectable women.'

'Don't try to raise an argument with us mothers of this village.' Mama Heloiseh retorted. 'We, off course value our *ghettos* and respect them, never mind they do these other *gumi-gamy* things. *Ghettos* will bring you good money and one of these days also bring you some good troubles too. Don't go on giving them kudos yet.'

173

What will the *ghettos* do?

Do they get back their tainted contributions?

Continue to read Part Two of A Farmer Brings On a Wife.

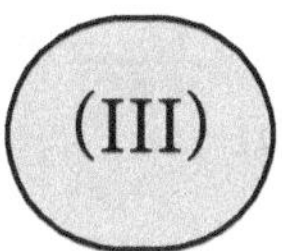

TRADITIONAL TOKANO COUNTING SYSTEM

The Tokano people had a counting system which started with the counting of the fingers on the hands and toes on the feet and it progressed to bigger numbers.

	Primary.	Alternate.
1	*Hamo.*	One.
2	*Seh-ta.*	Two.
3	*Seh-ta ve hamo.*	Three.
4	*Seh-ta seh-ta ve.*	Four.
5	*Ate helaga.*	One hand – all five fingers.
6	*Ate helaga si, ate tolowa hamo ma loti oluto mo lavoko.*	One hand – all five fingers plus one finger from the next hand.

7	*Ate helaga si, ate tolowa seh-ta ma loti oluto mo lavoko.*	One hand – all five fingers plus two fingers from the next hand.
8	*Ate helaga si, ate tolowa seh-ta ve si hamo kisi ma loti oluto mo lavoko.*	One hand – all five fingers plus three fingers from the next hand.
9	*Ate helaga si, ate tolowa seh-ta ve seh-ta ma loti oluto mo lavoko.*	One hand – all five fingers plus four fingers from the next hand.
10	*Ate seh-ta.*	Two hands - all fingers on each hand.
	Ghavosa hamo.	Or alternately one stick.
	Nakavosa hamo.	Or alternately one stick.
11	*Ate seh-ta kisi, gizete lakati tolowa hamo kisi.*	Two hands – and from the foot, one toe.
15	*Ate seh-ta ve gizete hamo.*	Two hands and one foot.
20	*Gizete ate asu ivoko.*	All our hands and feet.

	Ghovasa seta.	Or alternately two sticks.
	Asapu hamo.	Or one wrap.
50	*Holokena.*	A wing - meaning one part of another.
100	*Ghola.*	A mountain top/ also a nose of a person.
200	*Holokena seh-ta.*	Two wings.
200	*Gho hamo/ ghola seh-ta.*	One *bilum* or two mountain tops.
300	*Gho hamo ve ghola-si.*	A *bilum* and a mountain top.
400	*Gho seta.*	Two *bilum*s.
500	*Gho seh-ta kisi, gho-la hamo.*	2 *bilum*s and one mountain top - or two lots of 200 and 1 lot of 100.
	Ghola ate helaga.	5 lots of 100.
	Mulise mi Holokena.	Literally a wing to a pile.

600	*Gho seh-ta ve hamo le.*	
700	*Gho seh-ta ve hamo kisi, amiku ghola hamo kisi.*	
800	*Gho seh-ta ve seh-ta ve.*	
900	*Gho seh-ta ve seh-ta ve kisi, ghola hamo kisi.*	
1000	*Mulise hamo.*	One pile.
2000	*Mulise seh-ta.*	Two piles.

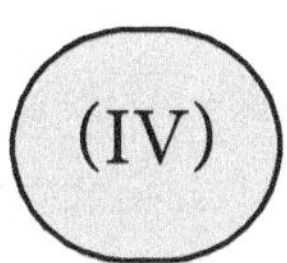

ITEMS OF VALUE THAT IN TRADITIONAL TIMES WERE USED AS BRIDE WEALTH.

Lulu.	Bride wealth/Bride price.
Nakani nakavosa.	A cane from a special cane. This cane is a specie of the canes for making arrows and the cane must be domesticated i.e. Grown as in the wild, they die off quickly.
Lulume.	Any bird of paradise feathers used in head dresses (generic).
Nama Lahone.	Raggiana Bird of Paradise (BOP).
Nama Musso.	Great sickle billed bop.
Waho.	*Bilum* that the men used to carry their *Rasta* hair. It was held in place by a sharpened bamboo stick and that was where each man could put up their *lutume'ne* or a piece of feather.

Nopeya.	Kina shell.
Hitile.	Small shells strung together.
Urackise.	Cowrie shells strung in a loop that is strung in a loop and carried around the shoulder.
Geheko.	A *tapa* cloth with designs that were hung at the back of the body.
Mele – mele.	Small kina shell that is hung on the nose.
Holotane.	Belt around the waist.
Ana.	Arm band around the biceps.
Anama.	Arm band around the forearm.
Hakije.	Band around the calf muscle.
Velasi Iye.	(Live pigs) given over to the bride's people by the groom's people as part of the bride wealth.
Helevi Iye.	(*Dead pigs*) number of pigs slaughtered as part of the exchange of food during the bride price *ceremonies*. Each party is expected to slaughter the same number of pigs.

Iye Nakavosa.   A string of sticks tied together denoting number of pigs slaughtered - the string of sticks is held by the person who killed the pigs as a reminder of the debt.

Note: it is also the name for the club that is used for clobbering the head of the pig before it is slaughtered.

Iye kaka.   Whole cooked pig/pork placed on carriers. *Kaka* is the carrier for transporting the cooked pork, the whole of the pig carcass.

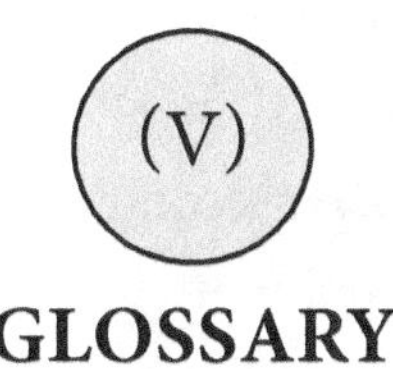

GLOSSARY

Word/s used in book.	Definition/s as it would appear in the book.
A killjoy.	Somebody that tries to stop others having fun by saying something that sours conversations etc.
Aa'hai-ye.	(Tokano) A sneer said out loud as laughter.
Abus.	[Tok Pisin] Any protein that goes with a meal.
Act of giving them the end of the fingernails.	When a person (both male and female) has been involved in adultery, it is deemed that the relationship between and with the family has been dirtied. The dirt around the act would have been said to be snuck into the fingernails. All interactions especially towards and with their children have been dirty and gross. A reparation mumu can be done to fix the relationship with the children. Between the affected partners is another issue.
Adamu.	(Tokano) Adam. Also, Atamu.

Alu iyeyo.	Literally to mean girl-mother and used endearingly to a favourite girl that has gone in marriage.
Alu.	(Tokano) Girl and the female gender. -young girl (small) - Alu koma. -young girl (big) - Alu napa. -Teenager - can court boys - Yaha vena. -Married woman -Vena. -Unmarried girl or a woman who is a divorcee of a widow – Ghetto. -Old woman Elene.
An old leaf	Not useful anymore.
An old maid.	An elderly woman or lady.
Anama.	(Tokano) Anama is the arm band for the forearm. This is different from the armband that goes over the bicep muscles. That is called the 'ana.'
Apo ya.	(Tokano) Used to give credence and recognition to a person during speech in a conversation. This does not have the larger endearment connotation to the expression as it is general made towards any person.
Apo, leva ya.	(Tokano) Same as the above.
Apo.	(Tokano) Apo literally mean namesake, but is also an endearing word for lovers, and now used predominantly as an identity tag for all Eastern Highlanders. There are variations where there is a stress on the relations, 'Apae' is used. There are also more variations and slants to the word Apo depending on the language. Other variables are Ambo, Apa, etc.

Arere.	(Tokano) At the edge.
Aromatic bamboo.	Cooking with bamboo where aromatic leafy vegetables is used.
Asapu.	(Tokano) A wrap or wrapping.
Asaro.	Place name for the people and District adjoining the Goroka District.
Assbeans.	[Tok Pisin] Winged beans.
Atamu ko eva ko.	(Tokano) Adam's and Eve's.
Atamu.	(Tokano) Adam.
Ave-ghama	(Tokano) literally, and you Ave.
Baby money.	[Tok Pisin] Interest on a savings at a bank.
Bai yu kilim bilong ol mahn o long tok tok o long baim meri!	(Tokano) Word for Word Bai (will) yu (you) kilim (kill) bilong (for) ol mahn (people) o (or) long tok tok (for when there is a community social event) o (or) long baim meri!' (To buy a wife). A disparaging set of statements said referring to the owner of the pig and in La'ano's case, about her perceived inability to enable her son to have a wife.
Bamboo bursting speciality.	(Tokano) an act by an oracle reading person who trying to pop a green bamboo to check out the viability of success of this venture to do the walk with the bride wealth.

Beating a sixty.   Running away with haste.

Been jumped over.   (Tokano) a taboo among the people is that a lady or her possessions should not jump over or cause the end of her skirts, or her bag go over or cast a shadow over a man, boy or children. If they are, it will affect their growth and longevity. In certain instances, they may be ill over persistent occurrences of the same incident.

Big bilum.   [Tok Pisin] From the local Tokano adage Gho Napa- A praiseworthy name used figuratively for a person who is usually contributes well both in cash and kind. It can only come from a person who has a big heart and a big bilum.

Big hands.   From the local Tokano adage Ana Napa- A praiseworthy name used figuratively for a person who is usually contributes well both in cash and kind especially garden food. It can only come from a person who has a big hand (impliedly a big hand means a person who works hard in the gardens) and a big bilum.

Big mama.	[Tok Pisin] 1. A praiseworthy name used figuratively for a person who is usually contributes well both in cash and kind. It can only come from a person who has a big heart and a big bilum.
	2. An elderly woman, usual who assumes the role of the matriarch in the family.
Bilas.	[Tok Pisin] 1. Pieces of bush, flowers, animal skin, seashells, bird's feathers, and plumes that are worn as an adornment during singsings and festivities.
	2. Dressing up for an occasion e.g., suits.
Bilum.	[Tok Pisin] A hand woven string bag that is local to Papua New Guinea.
Bridal walks.	Walking the bride wealth.
Brus-smoke.	[Tok Pisin] Dried leaves of the tobacco plant.
Buai.	[Tok Pisin] Betel nut from the Areca plant.
Bulmakau.	[Tok Pisin] A combination of the words bull and cow, the letter m may have crept in for the letter n as then it would have been bulnakau instead of bulmakau.
Coins-coins.	(Tokano) new terminology to describe a situation where a group contribute towards a common cause.

Come good.	Adage – where there is an expectation and if a person can be able to contribute something considerable to the occasion.
Come to loosen and take away these pigs on their leashes.	This is the second part of bride wealth. A week after the cash is accepted, the brides' people will come to groom's village to collect the live pigs that were pledged. Coming to loosen and take away the pigs is the literal meaning of 'iye nalawa wakase.'
Covering our skins.	Adage – if a person deals with wrongs in the village, these actions will come to haunt the person and his or her family and relatives.
Cuscus.	A tree hugging marsupial.
De facto parents.	1. Parents who are living together in marriage and have children. 2. A couple who put themselves out as a parent for a child?
Dead pig pile.	A pile of mumu-ed pigs that were slaughtered before and is used as an item of trade and where connotation of a debt is attached to them.
Dead pigs.	When pigs are slaughtered, they become 'dead pigs' for narration purposes. The people eat pork but deal with dead pigs in their dealings so that, when need be, it can be referred to and differentiated from pork whereas a 'dead pig' will have debt connotation attached to it.

Dinau marit.	[Tok Pisin] Being in a marriage situation when no bride price has been put by the partner. This includes all marriages include a church wedding, registry marriages, customary marriages and includes de facto marriage putting a bride price consolidated the marriages.
Dinau wives.	[Tok Pisin] Similar to dinau marit.
Dinau.	[Tok Pisin] Debt owing.
Don't know what a spade looks like, nor do they know what a bush knife does.	[Expression] This is a reiteration of when a thing says daddy to you. If a person knows what a spade or a bush knife looks like, it implies that the person should know that these items are used for. For a rural village, a person who knows what these tools like, these implies that they will know their uses and put to good use these tools to be more productive and be more attentive to activities in the village.
Dry bush.	(Tokano) used as a pun about a person who does not look too healthy.
Egghe.	(Tokano) A cautionary expression.
Ehe'q.	(Tokano) A warning to say 'be cautious, a watch out word.
Eva.	[Tok Pisin] Eve.

Evako.	(Tokano) And Eve.
Eyes are very heavily closed.	Adage: when the eyes are shut or heavily closed, it is implied that the event or conversation did not go to expectations. If during a long oratory speech, the people deduce that speech may not get the resultant expectation, one can say they sat through the speech and came away with their eyes heavily closed. May also imply a boring event.
Feed our legs.	Mumu done to give energy to the legs to bid them a successful travel.
Fingers and toes, hands and legs and wings and mountains and piles.	The counting system for the Tokano people involves parts of the body.
For the legs.	When travelling to a new place, there is always a feast for the legs so that there is a speedy and safe journey especially when you are leaving behind familiar spirits and going to places where new masalais may look upon you unfavourably.
Frigano.	Place name.
From her 'thing.'	'Her thing' would be the genitals so from 'her thing' would imply that what she is bringing forth is something that were earned from the use of her genitals.

From your skins.
(Tokano adage) using the genitalia for trade and using the proceeds at public gatherings. Has a taboo about doing such things.

Full bilum.
In the Tokano counting system, a bilum is 200, and a full bilum will be exactly 200.

Gamakilise.
(Tokano) These are screams that everyone can make and join in as it just an exhilarating shout out.

Ganine whoop.
(Tokano) Whoops that a person makes to herald the mojos of a particular tribe.

Ganine.
(Tokano) Mojos of a particular tribe to be called by a person who would call out these mojos.

Garanaku.
Place name at Kotiyufa village.

Geheko.
(Tokano) Dress strip made of tapa bark.

ghahali'q.
(Tokano) Sick dog also figuratively to imply that the person has a bad life or is always poor by village standards.

Ghahu tree fibres.
(Tokano) The bark of the Ghahu trees is the traditional tapa cloth.

Ghahu.   (Tokano) Ghahu trees grow in the Wesan area, and the barks are used as tapa cloth. The trunk can be hollowed out as the 'ya motona' or mumu oven where hot stones are transferred into it.

Ghalise knock.   (Tokano) Any knock on the head is called a Ghalise. Ghalise is also the name for louse nits or eggs that would be hanging on the hairs. As mothers preen their children's head for louse and the ghalise eggs, they would bang their fingers to burst out these eggs so any knock to the head becomes a ghalise.

Ghehene tolumo.   (Tokano) Collecting together money.

Ghetolise / Ghetoliso.   (Tokano) Place name for the Bundi people. They are believed to be an ancient lot who practise 'ancient arts.'

Ghetto.   (Tokano) an unmarried girl/woman.

Ghevena viise lo.   (Tokano) Ghevena (people) viise (call) lo (to do) i.e. to make a call out for the people.

Ghewo spirits.   (Tokano) Those who can turn into birds – an ancient art.

Ghilli-ghilli amulet.   (Tokano) An amulet made up of Ghilli-ghilli shells like the ones used in the tabu shells.

Ghilukalu leaves.   (Tokano) A shrub that has variegated leaves. There are two types, one has dark mauve leaves with streaks of brown and the other is light green leaves with yellow streaks in the middle.

Gho.   (Tokano) When spelt it becomes multiple words, when pronounced and depending on the stress applied to the word, this word can be a bilum, or that dawn is breaking or is a counting word to imply one hundred. In this book, it is used mostly as a counting word and a few times as bilum.

Ghohove.   (Tokano) A poor man.

Ghohuno.   (Tokano) a fig family tree whose new leaf shoots are taken as a vegetable known also as Moson lip tree in tok pisin for the little hairy thongs the leaves have. The fruit of this tree is also edible.

Ghola.   (Tokano) The crown or peak or a mountain - is used as a number word holding the value of two hundred.

Ghopoluho.

(Tokano) a small cane like shrub whose young shoots are a delicacy for pigs both raw and cooked. Is used as a covering or borders in a mumu to cook and soften these shoots for pigs to consume. Also bears flowers that flow out and drop like a cat's tail. It is like Fuzzy Cat Tail grass plant but ghopoluho grows like a soft pitpit cane. Comes in green and purple coloured stem and leaves. The green plant can also bear white and purple strand flowers.

G h o t o l o h e y a bilum.

(Tokano) Big old bilum that mothers carry to the garden to bring back all the harvest for the day.

Gia lok.

[Tok Pisin] Gia lok is an expression implying a sterile man. If he is in a relation where no children are born, it is because he is 'gia lok.'

Giaman marit.

[Tok Pisin] Living in a marital relation that is for a short time only.

Giaman.

[Tok Pisin] Falsehood.

Goposalo.

(Tokano) A name of a place where near the village in this book.

Gumi.

(tok Pisin) rubber imputing condom in the story.

Gumi-gamy.

(Tokano) all things gumi or rubber.

Gutpela pik we!

[Tok Pisin] What good pig is this?

Hahn tambu.

[Tok Pisin] A stop work sign that is put up usually a cutting from a fresh pitpit stalk with the leaves knotted.

Hai-e-hi!

A sneering laughter.

Hakije.

(Tokano) Arm band that is made to go onto the calf muscles.

H a l f - m o o n Kina   nopeha breastplate.

Kina shell breast plate that is in the shape of a half-moon crescent.

Hands-upping.

Hands up is made into a continuous verb.

Hanky panky.

Mischievous things usually sexual in nature.

Hap sting yomba diwai long rot.

(Tok Pisin) Literally a rotten piece of yomba tree on the road.

Yomba tree is an iron wood specie that can last a long time and is used as fencing and house time posts.

Hauslain.

[Tok Pisin] The village as all the houses were built in a line.

Hauspik.

[Tok Pisin] This was where individuals-built houses to keep their pigs.

Heavy parts	Adage: when the pork is distributed, the heave parts i.e. the meaty parts are given to preferred relatives. Heavy parts are the rump and shoulders.
Her 'thing.'	Her 'things' refer to her genitals.
Het pei for the children, giving back the backbone, the thighs, and the head.	Bride price is not the end of payment for a bride, there are other obligatory payments made to the maternal uncles and they include, het per for the children and giving back the backbone, the thighs, or the head back to the woman's relative in appreciation for the life of the woman coming as a bride, having children, and dying in the man's village tribe and clan.
Hetuvo.	(Tokano) The leaves used to cover the mumu.
Hii yaga hey one.	Hii yaga hey! is a catchy tune from Manus Province. Instead of calling those from Manus Province, Manusians, they are called the 'hii yaga hey' ones.
Hikise.	(Tokano) Crossbars in the house straddling the yakise centre posts with the door posts. A croft created in a round house by crafting onto the yakise - centre posts and wall runners of the house, three poles on which timber and logs are stored for use on a rainy day or for mumu. Other items too can be stored.

Holey house.

Traditional walls of houses made of woven pitpit can be easily broken into by pigs and dogs. These become a bit difficult to patch up and are left for these pigs and dogs to enter in and out of houses freely.

Holokena.

(Tokano) A wing and in the Tokano counting system a half.

Homasi song.

(Tokano) A worship song that sounded like a dirge.

Homebrew.

Alcoholic drinks that are brewed at home.

Humbins.

Was meant to be human beings. - A zestful play on words.

Ii ii.

[Tokano] an exclamation that carries a negative connotation.

Iimpph.

[Tokano] An exclamation that is sounded through the nose that carries a negative connotation.

Inap ya!

[Tok Pisin] That's enough.

Intestines going small and I will struggle to pass toilet.

An expression to imply some difficulty.

Itehetu.	(Tokano) A person appeared out of the soil - to mean they were first in time to the place or the Adamic family in the village.
Its first walk.	An action that takes place when the bride wealth is taken from village to village looking for prospective brides.
Iufi-Iufa.	Place name Yuhu-yuho Tokano Tok Ples is twelve kilometres west of Goroka town.
Iye kaka.	(Tokano) Stretcher for carrying cooked carcass of pork.
Iye nakavosa.	(Tokano) Stick for indicating pigs and or a club for knocking heads of pigs when they are slaughtered for a mumu.
Iye nalawa wakase.	[Tokano] part of the bride price act where the grooms people tie up live pigs on stakes in the village and the bride's people will then come to release the leash on the stakes and take it back to their village. This act is the second action in laying out the bride wealth in a marriage process.
Iye-numuko.	[Tokano] hauspik or a house away from the main house that is used to house and raise pigs.
Kaka or stretchers.	(Tokano) Kaka-stretcher.

Kandis ples.	(Tok Pisin) A recently introduced word for a place that is determined to be the place for gambling in the village to take place. The circle of gamblers is called the kandis. Note other parts of country will have kandis as the mat or canvas that is rolled out for people to sit on.
Kandis yomba post,	An expression to imply to a person who lazes around the kandis place doing nothing and hoping that someone will share their winnings with them.
Kandis.	[Tok Pisin] A gathering where people are involved in gambling using a pack of cards.
Kapis.	(Tok Pisin) slang for female genitalia.
Kapupu.	(Tok Pisin) fart and farting.
Karuka.	Highland Pandanas nuts.
Kas ol mekim b'long yu oh!	[Tok Pisin] They made the cards for you - a disparaging statement made against another person who spends their days at the kandis place to often.
Kasparr who make kandis all day.	[Tok Pisin] They made the cards for you - a disparaging statement made against another person who spends their days at the kandis place to often.
Kaukau bilum.	Bilum that is used for carting kaukau. It is usually bigger and is stretchable to fill as many crops as a person can carry.

Kaukau.	Root crop.
Kina shell.	Kina shells were used as currency.
Kinas.	Papua New Guinea currency but the shells were traded as a currency in traditional times.
Know what a bush knife looks like.	Adage for someone in the village who doesn't do much physical work that involves a bush knife or a spade.
Kob'le.	[Sinasina - South Simbu language] literally stone but is meant money.
K o n g k o n g cheapies.	Chinese goods that were sold for a cheap price.
Krisimasi.	[Tok Pisin] Christmas.
Kunai	(Tok Pisin) termed cottonwool grass that grows by spreading rhizomes. Kunai grass is used are roof thatching in most areas of PNG.
Kunai eaves.	[Tok Pisin] The end of kunai thatching of a traditional house.
Ladies' skirts.	Adage: if a young man sticks close by to their wives, they are ridiculed as being by their ladies' skirts. They can also be disparaged heavily for it.

Laheko somme.	(Tokano) Somme is goanna in Tokano. Laheko Somme - goanna from Laheko.
Laheko.	(Tokano) Place name for a place at Kotiyufa village.
Lahone.	(Tokano) Raggiana bird of paradise.
Laplap.	[Tok Pisin] A piece of material that is used as a wrap-around cloth.
Lapuluvo.	(Tokano) A wastage.
Leva ya.	[Tok Pisin] Darling.
Live pigs.	In bride price exchanges there are two types of pigs used in the process. Live and dead pigs. A person is expected to take a live pig but in return he is expected to slaughter one to be used in the feasting in the bride price process.
Long piece of evocation.	A long speech about an old act.
Long-long.	[Tok Pisin] Long-long, being mentally unstable.
Lukautim pik bilong raun long garden olgeta taim, skin gras pulap pik ya!	Taking care of pigs that roam into other people's gardens all the time, the pig is even covered with hairs all over.
Lulu ghehene.	(Tokano) bride wealth money.
Lulu.	(Tokano) Bride wealth.

Lulu' tolumo togessa.	(Tokano) Gathering to do the contributions of the bride wealth.
Lupiye-Tapiye.	(Tokano) Spotted one.
Lusowaso.	(Tokano) Doing magic charms.
Lutume'ne.	The one feather that we stick in our head will not have the shake and the bounce.
Make fire' for the young bride.	When a bride is given a crash course in marital life.
Mama ghetto.	[Tok Pisin] An elderly spinster.
Mama lotu.	[Tok Pisin] A gathering of a group of women as a church fellowship group.
Mama money.	[Tok Pisin] The main principal money.
Mamu.	(Tokano) A woven head crown given to boys on an initiation ceremony but is also used as a name and in this book is Josiah's Middle name.
Manbones.	To imply a man's strengths.
Man-lazy	A cultural trait that leaves all the work to women to do.
Mapanuho.	(Tokano) Lemon leaves.
Marit.	(Tok Pisin) marriage.

Marretta season. It is a seasonal plant that yield its fruit annually.

Marretta. A pandanas plant whose fruits produces red cream that is mainly eaten with food.

Marrmarr. [Tok Pisin] An introduced legume tree that is now growing profusely in the highlands.

Marry an empty house. Adage: When a man is absent from the house for long periods. When that happens, the woman may say she is married to an empty house. It can be true too if couples keep separate beds.

Masalais. [Tok Pisin] Spirits usually mischievous ones.

Maski. [Tok Pisin] A term to say, 'Forget it.'

Maunten mahn. [Tok Pisin] Also spelt Mountain man. It places a person in a specific location which becomes an identity tag.

Maus-mahn. [Tok Pisin] A speaker for the group.

Mehe leaves as screen to the door. (Tokano) Leaves that were used as a door.

Mehe. (Tokano) A curtain of banana leaves that were installed over a door and is drawn into place with crisscrossed sticks when the door is shut.

Menehetaka. Place name at the village.

Meri b'long pilai kas tasol ya.	[Tok Pisin] A woman who spends her time playing cards - a disparaging comment assassinating the character.
Meri bilong raun nating-nating long rot ya.	(Tok Pisin) A ridicule about a woman who does nothing but walks the roads forever. It is expected a woman will keep house and garden, if she does not, the ridicule is used against her.
Meri poromahn.	[Tok Pisin] Peer woman, and another woman is shared marriage relationship.
Meri Simbu.	[Tok Pisin] A lady from Simbu.
Meri ting em lukautim pik!	[Tok Pisin] A woman that thinks she is raising pigs -disparaging comment.
Meri.	(tok Pisin) a word to describe the female population i.e. girls, women etc.
Methylated spirit.	Spirit that is used for lighting up a Coleman Lamp.
Miku iye.	(Tokano) A garden going pig.
Mita Ghoiha Ku piii!!!	Mojo for the village.
Mitega ghoi ha kupiii.	(Tokano) Mojo for the village.
Mitega.	Place name for a hill in the village.

Molowaliso.   Common name for a lady in Tokano Tok Ples.

Morobe Waria.   [Tok Pisin] Method of burning sugar. The big scooping spoon was black from the sugar mollusc that she made. It used less sugar, and the tea was sweet.

motona   (Tokano) also ya motona i.e. wooden circular and hollowed out drum oven.

Mounds.   Kaukaus are always planted in mounds as they crop from the end of the cut runners inserted into the soil. There are however exceptions as if the runners are left alone long enough, they can crop from these too.

Mountains.   In Tokano counting system, a mountain is two hundred.

Muho plant.   (Tokano) An herb that grew profusely amongst karuka trees up in the mountains and were introduced to the lowlands where it struggled to grow.

Mulise or pile.   In Tokano counting system, a pile or mulise is a thousand.

Mulise.   (Tokano) [Tokano - counting system] Was a pile of money deemed to be a thousand kina.

Mumu, mumus.   [Tok Pisin] Ground oven.

Mumu-ed.	[Tok Pisin] Ground oven-ed.
Murramurra.	[Tok Pisin] Good magic that is added to a plant to make it grow better including fertilisers and grass that control insect pests.
Musso bird of paradise.	(Tokano) It is a black Sickle Bird of Paradise what has two long plumes as tail plumes.
My intestines going small, and I will struggle to pass toilet.	[Expression] To mean that the speaker does not have the backing to be able to speak with confidence.
Nakani pitpit cane and stick.	(Tokano) A specie of pipit plant that is like those used as arrow shafts. This specie is also a bit heavier and not ideal for use as arrow shafts.
Nakavosa.	(Tokano) Sticks.
Nama loh.	[Tokano] call to sing songs.
Nating-nating.	(Tok Pisin) nothing or do nothing.
Ne'ghe-ne'ghe.	(Tokano) Nagging too much.
Negi nhagii tukai'iq.	[Tokano] Long-long or dumb person.
Negi tukai'iq, long-long.	(Tokano) He was darned crazy; he was not thinking straight and never had.
N i v i - n i v i broomstick grass.	(Tokano) [Tok Pisin] An introduced weed to the highlands that was said to be used as a broom.

N o p e y a breastplate.

Kina shell that is worn as a breast ornament.

Nopeya ghatane.

[Tokano] Kina shell that is worn as a breast ornament.

Nopeya lulu.

[(Tokano) Tokano - bride wealth] kina shell.

Nopeya.

(Tokano) [Tokano - bride wealth] kina shells.

Noses.

A child may be determined by his or her nose as the people are distinct even in the province. Each group of people are distinct and by inference, if the child has nose features that is distinct with a certain group of people, then it is determined that one of parents of that child is from that distinct people.

Ohe! Ohe-ahe!

(Tokano) A yodelling call out to get attention of people.

Oho!

(Tokano) An Exclamations that is negative but has a positive effect.

Oi, oi.

(Tokano) You there.

One hand.

Tokano counting system – five.

Opume.

(Tokano) A specie of kaukau that is usually bears small tubers but when cooked on open fires send outs scintillating aroma. Also name usually given to females.

Ou – ou.	(Tokano) this is an accompanying yodel utterance that the women make to accompany the man shouting out his ganine whoop.
Our blood boil with such gladness.	Adage [Tokano] when all is okay.
Own 'garden'.	Sexually connotation about a female.
Paia wara.	[Tok Pisin] An act of caring for the old by bringing them firewood, fetching water in containers, and generally taking care of them by people who are not family members.
Paia.	(Tok Pisin) fire.
Pamuk meri.	[Tok Pisin] A promiscuous lady.
Pamuk.	[Tok Pisin] A person who engages in sexual activities without a known relationship including marriages.
Pamuking.	[Tok Pisin] Made into a verb in this book.
Peak.	Tokano counting system a ghola is a peak and is two hundred.
Pehe-pehe.	(Tokano) A person standing around upright.
Pehe-peheva ya.	(Tokano) Stress on the noun for a person standing around upright.

Pehe-peheva.	(Tokano) Word made a noun. Stress on the noun for a person standing around upright.
Pekpek.	[Tok Pisin] Excreta.
Penne' banana,	(Tokano) A type of cooking banana.
Pig grass.	Hairs on the pig.
Pig score sticks.	(Tokano) small sticks cobbled together with a string to record pigs used as debts for other people.
Piles.	In the Tokano counting system a pile (Mulise) is a thousand.
Pipia bilong ol pipia ya, yah!	[Tok Pisin] The very bad of the rubbish.
Pipia mahn ya.	[Tok Pisin] A poor man (stressed).
Pipia mahn.	[Tok Pisin] A poor man.
Pipia of your husband.	[Tok Pisin] Make rubbish of your husband.
Pipia woman.	[Tok Pisin] Poor woman.
Pipia.	(Tok Pisin) rubbish
Pipia.	[Tok Pisin] Rubbish.
Pipis.	[Tok Pisin] A child's version of pispis - to urinate.

Pispis.	[Tok Pisin] Urinate.
Pitpit bed.	[Tok Pisin] A bed made of canes.
Pitpit bush.	[Tok Pisin] A cluster of pitpit.
Pitpit sticks.	[Tok Pisin] There are various pitpit specie and depending on the thickness and certain specific uses for each of these different species.
Pitpit.	[Tok Pisin] Cane.
Plastic skin	When a rebuke from a woman bounces of a man's skin and does not hurt the man.
Play-play thing.	[Tok Pisin] A toy or figuratively when a person toys with another.
Poromahn.	[Tok Pisin] Man peers.
Poromeris.	[Tok Pisin] Female peers.
Prized possession.	Usually, a sexual connotation to refer to the genitals.
Puripuri.	[Tok Pisin] Black magic and the arts.
Rabis mahn.	[Tok Pisin] A poor person.
Rabis talks.	[Tok Pisin] Talking poorly.
Rabis.	[Tok Pisin] Rubbish.

Rip top lids from the San Miguel beer.	San Miguel and Swan beers had rip top lids.
Sainamahn.	[Tok Pisin] A Chinese man.
Samting bilong kas ya.	[Tok Pisin] Things for the cards (gambling).
San Miguel beer.	Philippine beer that had a short stint in the Papua New Guinea.
Sanap-sanap long kandis ya, inap ya!	[Tok Pisin] Enough of standing around at the kandis place.
Sanguma.	[Tok Pisin] A belief in the art of black magic.
Sapava.	(Tokano) Like a fresh new leaf that turns old.
Scrooge.	A miser.
See your red and humiliation.	When a person is shown his mistakes and when he is humbled.
See your true colours.	When a person in trouble realises his follies.
Seghané. Seghané ve. Seghané ne ve. Seliné ne.	(Tokano) Thank you in Tokano in singular. The "I" prefixing seliné is a salutation clause but is not compulsory to use.
Seliné ne ve.	Seliné is the plural form, sevalane is thank you singular for person out of view, and Seliné ne ko is plural again for persons out of view.

Selemene bird.	(Tokano) He that does not have a nest of its own but drifts from one old nest to another old nest.
Seme'ne mumu.	(Tokano) Mumu to cook up the concoction made up to break any curses placed on them.
Seme'ne.	(Tokano) A concoction made up to break any curses placed on them.
Sepeku.	(Tokano) That is where he should find his station in life.'
Seveti Nosa.	(Tokano) Small River running besides the SDA college so the replacement of the local river name with that of the Seventh Day Adventist church so the river becomes the Seveti Nosa.
Shee-eeh.	Exclamation in Tokano Tok Ples
Short-hand.	A miser.
Show you the birds.	[Expression] When this is expressed, it means that a person has transgressed badly and shown the birds mean that at the next call of the birds playing the ritual flutes, women and children will be dragged out to see these horrible birds that make these horrible bird songs in the middle of the night.
Shrivelled dry bush.	Adage used as a disparaging comment.

Simbu singsings.	There are plenty of these birds in the forests surrounding their place. Our mountains are full of Lahones.
Sipaki.	(Tokano) Local word for being drunk.
Sipuno orchid.	(Tokano) A local name of an orchid that blooms yellow with red inner spots.
Sisi-vena.	Short cut of Sisipulime.
Skin gras pulap pik ya!	[Tok Pisin] An exclamation to say that the pig raised by the person is not fatty. A well cared for pig will not have many hairs on its skin but a wild and nearly feral pig will have lots of hair. When such are said against you, it implies one does not have the acumen to raise good pigs.
Slekim laplap daun.	A ceremonial mumu event to announce the first pregnancy of a young wife.
Small eyes.	When a person keeps small eyes over you, they mean to be scrutinising you and your activities.
Smoking brus smoke.	[Tok Pisin] Smoking tobacco leaves.
Something bad covering us (and bring us ill fortune).	If something bad or a sacrilege is committed, it will bring curses upon a person and that will create hardship for that person.
Somme.	[Tokano] long tailed earless dragon lizard.

Sopolo.

(Tokano) Bush knife that is always kept on with or near a person's hand.

Sorre, sorre.

apologetic sorry.

Souu, Mita ghoiha ku pi!!

(Tokano) Mojo for Kotiyufa villagers that is yodelled out in a scream.

Spak-brus.

[Tok Pisin] Marijuana.

Spak-wara.

[Tok Pisin] Homebrew alcohol.

Spia money.

[Tok Pisin] Spare money.

Spruiked

A word concocted by the author to mean something superfluously special.

Stakes.

As part of the bride wealth and bride price, there were several live pigs to be given. These were stacked up in the village for the bride's people to come and loosen these pigs on stakes and take them back to their village.

Stick, wrap.

[Tokano - counting system] One wrap one wrap wing two wings top of a mountain a nose is Tok Ples.

Stick-ropes.

A record representing number of pigs a person has reared and slaughtered to people as a debt or in repayment of one they had incurred earlier.

Sticks.	A counting system where one stick represents a ten. Stick was ten-kina.
Stomach-ache grass.	Grass that would be ingested to ward off ailments affecting the internal organs. There are weeds and grass for the pigs and humans can sometimes take it too.
Stomach-pig	(Tokano) Pig slaughtered that will be used as an ornamental pork dressing that will be on a stretcher and presented as a stomach-pig.
Sugar-sugar.	[Tok Pisin] Being soft on a person.
Swan beer.	A Pilipino alcoholic brew that had a short stint in PNG. It was not commercially viable and was deemed inferior to the SP brewed SP lager.
Sweet potato kaukaus.	A root crop starch supplement.
Tambarans.	Family spirits.
Tambu/s.	[Tok Pisin] In laws.
Tanget leaves.	Leaves of the Cordyline plants.
Tanget plants.	Cordyline plants usually planted as border line plants.
Thank you to the relatives	(Tokano) A ceremonious thank you to appease the ancestral spirits.

The end of her fingernails.	A negative statement to imply that the woman is stingy and a miser if she must do anything associated with the end of or under the fingernails.
The nose of the baby.	A child is deemed to wear a copy of either the fathers or mother's nose. Where paternity is in a dispute, it is deferred until the child is born to determine whose nose the child bears. It can work most times but is not one hundred percent true. if it bears the mothers nose, then the question is still left unanswered, if the nose is undetermined.
The soil says daddy.	When a person makes a garden and the soil says daddy, it implies the farmer has a bountiful garden or that the soil responds to his ministration to be high yielding garden.
Their good things.	A sexual connotation to imply their genitals but in a positive comment.
Titivi.	A piglet kept with the family to wean it from its mother.
Togessa mumu.	(Tokano) Mumu for the gathering of bride wealth.
Tóhamo ceremony.	(Tokano) To make them one ceremony.
Tok baksait.	[Tok Pisin] Disparaging talk behind the back.

Tok Pisin.   [Tok Pisin] Creole third national language of
                     Papua New Guinea.

Tok Ples.   [Tok Pisin] A local language.

Tokano Tok Ples.   [Tok Pisin] Tokano language.

Toksave.   [Tok Pisin] Announcement.

Tok-tok.   [Tok Pisin] General talk.

T o l u m o   (Tokano) Pooling together gatherings.
gatherings.
Tolumo mumu.   (Tokano) Mumu that accompanies the pooling
                     together gatherings.

Tolumo togessa.   (Tokano) Pooling together gatherings.

Tolumo.   (Tokano) Pooling together collections.

Tomatutu.   (Tokano) Dragon fly.

Traim   lukautim   [Tok Pisin] Try to care for pigs when you have
pik wantaim gaten!   a garden.
True colours.   [Expression] To present the real picture of a
                     situation.

Tru-tru married.   Mixed Tok Pisin and English with the emphasis
                     on being truly married.

Trying to hook a fish.	[Expression] A rebuke and analogy cited indicating the different cultural practises when bringing on a new bride.
Turned sapava.	(Tokano) Like a fresh new leaf that turns old.
Turuku.	Place name at Kotiyufa village.
Tusking boar.	Humongous male pig that will be growing tusks – used especially as a bride wealth.
Twenty sticks.	[Tokano - counting system] one stick represents 10, twenty sticks will be 200 or one bilum.
Two good asapu - wraps of sticks.	(Tokano) [Tokano - counting system] one wrap is 20 so two wraps will be 40.
Two sticks money.	[Tokano - counting system] one stick is 10 so two sticks will be 20.
Two wings.	[Tokano - counting system] half of each.
U-Lala.	(Expression) General expression to denote surprise.
Use-by-date.	A terminology that is creeping into village life and date stamping things.
Vitriol.	Bad air.
Wan lus.	[Tok Pisin] Loose cigarette sold for one Kina.
Wan marit.	[Tok Pisin] Married into the same family.

Wantrifu.	Place name.
Wan-wan	One each
Wan-wan cherries.	[Tok Pisin] Off season coffee cherries so there will be few berries so the term wan-wan.
Wara	(Tok Pisin) water
Wasa.	[Tok Pisin] One Kina.
Wasa-buai.	[Tok Pisin] One Kina betel nut.
Waspapa and wasmama.	[Tok Pisin] A foster parent's relationship.
Wesan men, our ancestors will show you the birds.	[Tok Pisin] Wesan. Tok Pisin for sands. Place name for people over the mountains in the Ramu Valley where there are lots of sands on the sides of Ramu River.
Whaa, lusim ya.	(/Tok Pisin) an exclamation with the urging to leave it alone.
Whee ii ha-ha.	(Tokano) A stampede jovial nothing shouts.
Whee!	(Tokano) A stampede shouts.
Wheeah!	(Tokano) A stampede shouts.
Wheeah!	(Tokano) An expression of frustration.
Whii.	(Tokano) A stampede shouts.

Wiggi-wiggi.

(Tokano) An expression to show the rotating motion of something mostly associated to rotating propellers of airplanes.

Will size ourselves up.

A statement made by a nuclear family unit to show or determine what they can contribute before going out to the rest of the village. If the family contributions are not good, it will mean the other family units in the village will contribute less and with some disdain. A positive result will bring out a positive ending.

Wing.

[Tokano - counting system] fifty kina.

Worm grass

Grass that was given to pigs to cure their worm ailments.

Wrap.

A bundle of twenty in the Tokano counting system.

Wrappings.

[Tokano - counting system] bundles.

Wraps of stick

Tokano counting system. One stick equals ten, one wrap equals twenty so in a wrap of sticks would equal two hundred.

Y a h a m e t a ghehene.

[Tokano] poisoned money.

Yakise post.

(Tokano) Centre posts in the house.

Yar trees.

[Tok Pisin] Yar - Casuarina trees but is now used a generic term for trees and comes with the specific tree - in this story as 'yar yomba.

Yar yomba.

(Tokano) Yomba Tree. This tree is also called the iron tree as it a very, very hard and does not rot easily. It is used as house and fencing posts. Grows in certain parts of the mountains only.

Yomba fence post.

[Tok Pisin] A fence made from Yomba posts.

Yomba posts.

[Tok Pisin] Posts hewn out to a Yomba tree.

Yomba tree.

[Tok Pisin] Yomba trees are cedar trees that are durable and last a long, long time.

Your body is already outside of this house.

[Expression] To denote a person who rarely sleeps in his or her own house.

Yuhu-yuho.

Place name for the people of Iufi-Iufa, Goroka, Eastern Highlands Province.

OTHER WORKS

Zymur: A *short story* in the Pacific Readers Series published by Oxford University Press which was the author's first attempt in writing and publishing. A further expanded reprint will soon be self-published.

Haffies Are Made, They Are Not Born: An illustrated *novelette* about the dangers of smoking cigarettes that can lead to taking marijuana. Self-published on Amazon KDP.

Curse of the Lamisi: A *novella* which explains why the Lamisi tree grows at Kotiyufa village. Self-published on Amazon KDP.

Man of Calibre: The first *novel* set in the Eastern Highlands of Papua New Guinea about a dispute settlement process after a night of drinking and brawling between two drunken men. Self-published on Amazon KDP.

Winner of 2015 Crocodile Prize's – OK TEDI Book of the year award.

Sweet Garaiina *Apo*; The second *novel* set among the Port Moresby settlements about a mixed-race girl who tries to unravel the mystery of why she is different to her sisters. Self-published on Amazon KDP.

Antics of Alonaa Volume One; The first *anthology* of six short stories about the life of a young boy, Alonaa. Contains lyrics to a popular village ballad in the Tokano language (EHP). Self-published on Amazon KDP.

Musings from Sogopex; A second *anthology*, co-authored with contributions from Emily Bina with various short writings about village life. Self-published on Amazon KDP.

Operesin Kisim Bek Lombo; The third *novel* is a fictitious story set in Port Moresby that tells of a Papua New Guinean Defence Force operation to thwart a Sandline operation that tried to rescue their boss immediately after the Sandline operatives were kicked out of the country. The PNGDF try their hands at using AR 15s laced with *murramurras, puripuris* and a few *'time travellers'* who live in two worlds, this and the nether. Self-published on Amazon KDP.

Tales From Faif: A third *anthology* collated during the 2020 Covid19 pandemic that includes the **Cry Me a River** and **Pineapples** #series. Self-published on Amazon KDP.

RESIS LONG KSSP - This anthology is a collection of 'tukopi' entries to the **COMMONWEALTH SHORT STORY PRIZE** Self-published on Amazon KDP. (2024)

A FARMER BRINGS ON A WIFE: Sigkaut Long Puk'im Moni… **Part One** to a three (3) part trilogy which is a narration detailing the traditional process for bringing on a wife for a son in the Goroka and Asaro Valleys.

Published by First Nations Writers Festival. (2025)

A FARMER BRINGS ON A WIFE: Kali-Kahlim Wokabautim Lulu. Part Two to a three (3) part trilogy which is a narration detailing the traditional process for bringing on a wife for a son in the Goroka and Asaro Valleys.

Published by First Nations Writers Festival. (2025)

A FARMER BRINGS ON A WIFE: Tulaku, Sitaunim Meli Nau. Part Three to a three (3) part trilogy which is a narration detailing the traditional process for bringing on a wife for a son in the Goroka and Asaro Valleys.

Published by First Nations Writers Festival. (2025)

Of course he has other titles being prepared.

(VIII)

END NOTES

The traditional way of getting a wife for a son.

There were various ways marriages were arranged in the Goroka Valley of the Eastern Highlands.

Firstly, there were child betrothals where two children were marked out from an early age and food was exchanged between the families to maintain their respective interest. The children grew up and, when the time was right, bride price was exchanged, and the bride would be delivered to the groom's village.

Secondly, if there was no such arrangement, bride wealth (money, pigs, shells, feathers, and other things of value) was collected and, when there was enough, it was taken to villages where a prospective bride resided.

The brothers and uncles of the girl can reject the bride wealth for any reason, including the inadequacy of the bride wealth and/or if the young girl is not ready to be married. Or the people may not be ready to meet the demands of the exchange. The person who wants to *'eat of the bride wealth'* must have his own supply of pigs that may be required of him to *'kill pigs and send off'* the bride in marriage.

When the bride wealth is accepted, then it shows that her people are prepared to complete the process.

This contrasts with new people living together in *'dinau marit'* for lack of the bride price.

The story narrates the process without it being an anthropological study.

As it were, there is a running saga that threatens to derail the process. These sagas throw village romances amongst married people to the front and centre. Occasionally these incidents, once a fidelity is caught and brought out into the open, it revealed may reveal long-kept secrets.

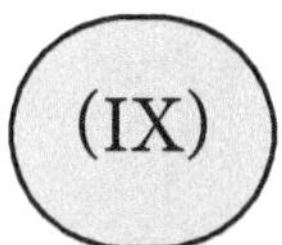

ABOUT THE AUTHOR

A customary practise can only be learned if a person lives in places where this particular practises happen. Bringing on a Wife can be best understood if one can immense themselves into the village life. This 3 part book tries to do that – to get the reader to live a Goroka village life.

Baka Bina narrates this tale of bringing of a wife for a son through relating each and every small event as it occurs in the village in that short window of time of 90 days. There are village politics that can derail the whole process, The mausmahn has a hard job trying to keep everyone focused on the one task.

Other spicier events happen that augments the village and gives it meaning to be a villager. Adultery and out of wedlock pregnancies makes everyone jittery and they still have no bride yet.

Baka Bina attended Iufi-Iufa Primary, Goroka High, Asaroka Lutheran High and Sogeri National High Schools. He attended Goroka Teachers College and taught at Kainantu High School. Later he attended the University of Papua New Guinea and the Legal Training Institute.

He works at the Waigani National Court Registry in Port Moresby.

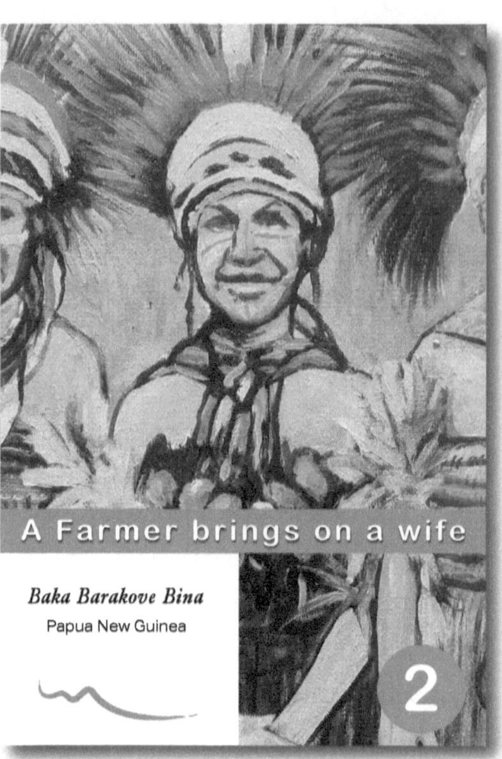

A Farmer brings on a wife
Baka Barakove Bina
Papua New Guinea
2

A Farmer brings on a wife
Baka Barakove Bina
Papua New Guinea
3